Strongholds

Also by Vanessa Davis Griggs

"The George Landris/Johnnie Mae Taylor" Series

The Rose of Jericho

Promises Beyond Jordan

Wings of Grace

Blessed Trinity Trilogy

Blessed Trinity

Strongholds

If Memory Serves

Strongholds

VANESSA DAVIS GRIGGS

Kensington Publishing Corp.
http://www.kensingtonbooks.com

This book is dedicated to God.
You woke me at 4 A.M. one morning in July 2004
and told me to write a book and to call it Strongholds.
My heart and prayer is that this book is all You desired
it to be.

Acknowledgments

When God told me to write this book, I was instructed not to deal with it from a sin standpoint but from a stronghold standpoint. I wrote the first chapter that same day and put it away not knowing what God's plans would be in delivering this to the people. I fasted and prayed and listened to the voice of God as I proceeded to write it. My prayer now is that it will be a blessing to millions.

I have acknowledged people in previous books, and truthfully, I wasn't sure whether I would do the same in this one. But I must send my eternal love to my mother, Mrs. Josephine Davis, who has faithfully been in my corner, praying for me, believing God's best for my life from the time I was in her womb until this day. Thank you, Mama. To my father, Mr. James Davis Jr., who continues to teach me what perseverance really is about. He is a man who refuses to let obstacles or setbacks (namely a stroke in 2000 that left him with limited use of his left side) stand in his way of doing what he sets his mind to.

Editor Rakia A. Clark: You came onboard at Kensington/ Dafina as my editor well after I had turned in this book. I want to thank you for your attitude and the work you have done, having inherited an author (me) that you honestly didn't choose. Rakia, you made this process one I could feel good about, and I thank you so much for that.

To my family and friends: husband, Jeffery; children Jeffery Marques, Jeremy Dewayne, and Johnathan LeDavis Griggs; grandchildren Asia and Ashlynn; sisters, Danette Dial and Arlinda Davis; sister-in-law, Cameron; brothers Terence Davis and Emmanuel Davis; cousin Mark Davis; and friends Rosetta Moore, Vanessa L. Rice, Zelda Oliver-Miles, Linda H. Jones, Marilyn Davis, Stephanie Perry Moore, Bonita Chaney, Pamela Hardy; and the members of The WBRT Society book club in Gadsden, Alabama, please know that I love and appreciate all of you more than words can ever relay.

To those of you who are blessing me by choosing *Strongholds*, I offer you a heartfelt thank you. I've said this before and I'll continue to say it: Without you there to receive it, what I do as a writer really doesn't matter much at all. As always, I do love hearing from you, and I appreciate your continuing to spread the word about my books. May you walk in God's exceedingly, abundantly, above-all-you-can-ever-ask-or-think blessings!

Vanessa Davis Griggs

www.VanessaDavisGriggs.com

Chapter 1

Hear the voice of my supplications, when I cry unto thee, when I lift up my hands toward thy holy oracle.

—Psalms 28:2

Fatima

There comes a time in your life when you just get tired of pretending. Get tired of wearing a mask. You know the mask I'm talking about. The one you put on to make people think you're fine when you're not. The mask that helps to cover parts of the real you—the you that you don't want anyone else to even know exists.

Fatima Adams is my name. But I have a feeling I could easily substitute your name for mine and you'd know the story. That's if you'd be honest and fess up. Now tell me this doesn't sound familiar to you: you live your life hoping no one discovers the real you, because if they did, you figure, they might surely not care to know you. Or worse: you're afraid someone is going to find out you're a fraud . . . a fake. That you've been acting out a script (oh, we all have individual scripts created just for our character) that no one forced upon you, except you.

Sure, you want to tell me right now that that's not you. You've always had it together. Or better yet: the way you are is actually someone else's fault. Now if you are one of those rare folks who happens to be perfect and always has been, then far be it from me, this imperfect being, to say anything to you. But as I stand here at the altar on this sunny Sunday morning in March (although it's not a true altar like in biblical days), I see at least four other people I personally know who had the guts to come forward when the pastor called for those who wanted to break the strongholds of their lives.

"Take off your mask today, won't you?" forty-five-year-old Pastor George Landris pleaded. "God already knows the true you. Don't be so caught up in what other people think that you miss your opportunity to be set free. For whom the Son sets free, is free indeed."

I knew he was talking to me. As I glanced at the crowd surrounding me, it became quite apparent that I was not the only one he was speaking to either. Who would know that I-got-it-all-together Fatima Adams—a thirty-one-year-old Christian woman with a knock-out body; perfect hairdo *every* single time I step out of my three-story, brick house; designer labels gracing me from head to toe; incredible-paying job that affords me the kind of money where I don't *even* need a man to take care of me—who would know that I am deeply and hopelessly in love with a married man.

"You don't have to tell me or anyone else what you've done or are doing right now that has caused you to come up here," Pastor Landris said as he bounced on the balls of his feet. "God already knows whatever it is. But this . . . this is about you getting things right between you and God."

Yes, Pastor Landris is right. God already knows. And He knows that I'm not just in love from a distance with a married man; I'm committing consistent fornication while my Mr. Right is committing adultery. Look at him sitting there with his wife as though that's where he belongs instead of up here alongside me trying to get himself right with God!

"What's wrong with us being together?" Darius had asked when guilt hit me after the first time we were intimate. "I can't help that I fell in love with you. Neither one of us sought this out. And God knows that. Besides, I'm planning to make things right with you someday. Soon. I just need a little time."

Yeah, and "soon" was some three years ago. I've tried to walk away. I've prayed so hard to God to help me. I even managed to break it off with Darius Connors—the true classic of a tall, dark, and *handsome*, oh Lord, handsome specimen of a man. He seemed crushed but claimed he understood my convictions and admired me even more for them.

"Fatima, I'll respect your wishes if you really want me to leave you alone," Darius said seven months ago. "God knows I wouldn't ever want to do anything to hurt you. Not ever."

For three weeks, like a champ, I pushed through the withdrawals of being without him, marking off my mental calendar the number of days behind me as each one passed. But I couldn't wrestle thoughts of him out of my mind, nor could I manage to uproot him from my heart. And on the third day of the fourth week, there at my front door, he stood.

"Please leave. Please," I begged him. "I can't do this anymore with you."

"Fatima, I will be happy to leave." He looked at me with those eyes that always made me feel like I was instantly melting. "Truthfully," he said, "I didn't come for you."

My heart fell to the ground with those words. I'm just being honest. It's okay he was honoring my wishes to leave me alone. But couldn't he at least pretend like I meant something special to him, make me believe this was as hard for him as it was for me?

After what seemed to be a long pause, he said it.

"Fatima, I didn't come here for you. I only came here today, to get back my heart. That's it. I just need to get back my heart."

Those words—I probably don't have to confess—caused me to fall right back into his arms again.

Literally and figuratively—I fell.

But today . . . today, Pastor Landris spoke about strongholds and being truly set free. I'm tired of sitting by the phone waiting to hear Darius's voice, practically willing the phone to ring only for days to pass (sometimes weeks) before he could finally "break away" to be able to call me. I'm tired of not being able to go out in public or to popular events with him because "word might get out" and "ruin things for us both." Translation: mostly ruin things for him.

I'm tired of spending days upon weeks alone when I could have someone who loves me, someone willing to pledge himself to me and only me. I do deserve to be number one in someone else's life. Not the spare tucked conveniently away inside some old, dark trunk. But out front—chromed in, with, and surrounded by the good things of life.

God, please . . . please, God—You have to help me. Please. You just have to!

Desiree

Personally, I don't think I am totally responsible for my present condition. I have determined—although for the life of me I can't get a doctor to confirm this or agree with me—that I have a serious allergy and my problem stems merely from an allergic reaction.

I'm allergic to meat, starches, and sweets. Whenever I eat any of these things, my body begins to blow up like a balloon. And since my alternatives for food consumption are vastly limited, my body has no alternative but to continue to manifest this reaction.

My dilemma originated with my smoking. Now I'm a constant eater instead. My stronghold seems to be that I must have something in my mouth at all times to be content. The pattern has held: when I smoke, I don't eat much; when I eat, I don't feel the need to smoke.

You should have seen me when I was a chain smoker. I was top model thin, but of course, that was way back when. Then I started seriously considering what cigarettes were doing to my body, and I said, "Desiree Houston, if you don't love yourself enough to put an end to this, then who will?"

Boy, did I sound just like my mother when I heard those words come out of my mouth. I'd seen this woman I'd known growing up, all hooked up to a tank she had to carry around with her everywhere she went because she'd smoked. I realized if I continued to smoke, that might be my fate. It hit me like a ton of bricks how cigarettes were actually killing me, and I had somehow become an unsuspecting accomplice to the plotting of my own murder. Yeah, I could blame tobacco companies for adding addictive additives in order to keep me as a profitable customer (for as long as I lived, that is), but that was too much of a cop-out even for me to go out like that.

So I turned my attention to food, and not just any kind of food either. Maybe it's just me, but I happen to like the kind that tastes good. Why is it the foods that taste the best also happen to be, most times, the ones containing megacalories?

Yes, I know all about calorie counting, glycemic loads, fat intake, carbohydrates, and the benefits of fiber. If there is a diet out there, you can believe we've probably met. Let's see, there was the Cabbage Soup Diet (yeah, that one makes you want to run right out and sign up for membership), the Lazy Zone Diet, the Atkins, Scarsdale, Weight Watchers, Jenny Craig, Hilton Head, South Beach (which was a lot like Atkins only this diet says to lay off the bad fats as opposed to piling them on), the Two-Day Diet, the 3-Day Diet, the 7-Day All You Can Eat Diet (now you know I tried this one!), the

3-hour Diet, the One Good Meal Diet, the Chicken Soup Diet (sure, you can eat whatever you want for breakfast but it's chicken soup, their recipe of course, for the rest of the day), the Metabolism Diet, the Russian Air Force Diet, the Grapefruit or Fruit Juice Diet, the Amputation Diet (don't ask, I wasn't even interested enough to look into that one further, although I do believe in stripping down to the bare essentials before stepping up on anyone's scale), the low-fat, no-fat, low-carb, no-carb diet, and my all-time favorite—the Chocolate Diet.

Did you know on the Chocolate Diet you can have pasta and popcorn in addition to eating chocolate? Breakfast is always fresh fruit and fruit salad (sounded like the same thing to me, but I worked with it), shredded wheat with nonfat milk and strawberries. Morning snack is popcorn and fruit. Lunch is salad, pasta salad (low-calorie dressing, which goes without saying), and spaghetti. Afternoon snack is popcorn, vegetables (they suggest cutting them into sticks—don't even ask me why), and a fruit smoothie made from blending one half a frozen banana, a half cup of frozen peaches or whatever fruit you like with one cup of nonfat skim milk. Dinner is fettuccini with garlic tomato sauce (I'm getting hungry just thinking about it), whole wheat pasta primavera, salad, and steamed vegetables. The evening snack consists of popcorn and (here's the best part) up to one ounce of chocolate. And on all the diets, I can have all the water I can (and can't) stand to drink.

So here I stand in front of this preacher with dreadlocks feeling drawn to bring my true burdens to the Lord and leave them. That's one of the reasons I grabbed my husband, Edwin's, hand and dragged him to the altar along with me. Cause and effect.

My husband (the cause) actually drives me to smoke or overeat (the effect).

I know you think I'm playing the blame game here, but it was Edwin's actions that caused me to start smoking in the first place. Okay. See, he's an obsessive gambler, bets on everything from the office pool to the lottery (there's no lottery in Alabama but that doesn't stop him and a slew of others from crossing the state lines to get tickets).

We've been married for twelve years, and of those twelve years, he's left me almost every night, including our honeymoon night on the cruise, for some kind of gambling event. No, I am not exaggerating: every night. Mondays through Thursdays, he goes to the dog track; then on Friday nights, he catches a bus down to Mississippi to the bright lights casino and stays until Sunday afternoon. Most of the weekend, you can find him at either the blackjack table or pulling on some lady luck's steel black arm trying to get three things to come up a match so he can win some money—big or small.

"You don't have to pull an arm on a machine anymore, Baby-cakes," Edwin said one day when we were discussing this. "Now you can push a button on the front of the machine and it does the same thing."

"Whatever, Edwin! Pull, push, it's still gambling, and it's still a sin," I said.

"That's commandment number what?" he said, folding his arms across his chest as he smiled. "Show me chapter and verse where it says gambling is a sin. Show me."

I stood with both hands on my hips and just stared at him. He knew he had me; we had been around this mountain several times before. I'd searched the Bible and even posed the question to several preachers for some biblical assistance, to no avail. There was one preacher who took a scripture out of context and tried to make it work for gambling. That dog wouldn't hunt in my sight, and I was an easy mark. Another preacher talked about how the Roman soldiers gambled (cast lots) for Jesus's robe. That was his feeble attempt to make it fit the bill. And yet another preacher pointed to a scripture, making the claim that we're not supposed to receive something for practically nothing.

O-k-a-ay.

"You can't, can you? You can't show me anywhere in the Bible where it specifically states that gambling is a sin," Edwin said as he smirked. "Now, smoking on the other hand, which literally destroys the temple—your body—and gluttony of food, again which can destroy the temple—your body—are different matters. I can prove those."

"I've quit smoking and you know that," I said, letting my hands hang limp by my side, a clear admission of defeat.

"Yeah, and when you finally did stop, you seemed determined to eat us out of house and home, as if—no matter how hard—it would be the last thing you'd do."

"Edwin, don't you dare harp on my weight! I declare, I'm not in the mood today."

"So I guess that means you've either started another grand diet or just finished one?" He opened the refrigerator door. "What's the name of this one, Baby-cakes?"

"Edwin, don't try to change the subject. We were talking about your gambling problem." I watched him as he took out the strawberry cheesecake I'd pushed all the way to the back of the refrigerator so I wouldn't be tempted. He took it out and practically whizzed it around the room like it was his dancing partner, making sure he passed my way twice before he did a dip with it. "Besides," I said, "you drive me to do what I do."

"Oh, so now it's my fault?" He sliced the cheesecake and placed it in a saucer. When he placed it in his mouth, he made a moaning sound. "Baby-cakes, you know you can outdo yourself. This has got to be the best strawberry cheesecake you've ever made."

"And you have the nerve to ask how it's your fault?" I walked over to the refrigerator, opened it, took out some prepackaged carrots and broccoli florets, and proceeded to chomp unenthusiastically on them.

"Yes, how is it my fault? I don't force you to smoke or to overeat. You just need a little willpower, that's all. You can't blame me because you don't have any."

"Willpower, huh? You mean like you don't have the willpower to stop gambling?" I said. "That's how you force me to smoke and eat. You're gone practically every night, Edwin, and most of the weekend. I'm here all alone with nothing to do but watch television and think. My nerves are practically shot from worrying about bills that keep piling up and seemingly getting further and further behind."

He placed another fork full of cheesecake in his mouth and closed his eyes as he shook his head and smiled. "Well, I bet you I can stop gambling anytime I choose to. I just have never chosen to."

"Yeah, well, I can stop smoking and bingeing whenever I choose to, but I-I-I . . ."

"I what, Desiree?" He looked up at me and grinned.

"I guess, I guess . . ." I felt a tear stinging my eyes. "I guess—you know what, Edwin? I don't care anymore! Keep gambling! Forget the fact that you're taking money out of our home and losing it or that you're leaving me home all alone. You don't care? Fine, I'm through talking to you about it! You've never won any great amount of money, yet you keep thinking and believing you're going to hit that 'big one' because you were 'so close' the last time. But you never do! Okay, fine. Have it your way!" I looked at the remaining carrots and broccoli, threw them in the garbage can, and stormed out of the kitchen.

So here at the altar, Edwin and I now stand, holding hands like everything is peachy-keen between us. Suddenly, I realize his hand is clammy, and it's at this precise moment that he gently squeezes my hand with three gentle pumps. And I, understanding this unspoken message, can't help but smile.

Edwin

Desiree grabbed my hand and started for the front of the church before I could protest. I might have put up a better fight, but she caught me totally off guard. Although in truth, I was already debating whether or not I should go up there. Normally, I wouldn't have even been at church, but my money was acting funny for the bus trip down to Mississippi this weekend. I hung around Birmingham and went to the dog track instead of my usual three-hour ride to the bright lights of the casino.

Don't get me wrong; I don't have anything against the dog track. In fact, I'm pretty much a regular Monday through Thursday. But I love being able to feel like I have more control over whether I win or not. Holding those cards and making the decision to stay with what I have or letting the dealer hit me again can be such a rush. Or being able to wrap my hand around that black stick on the slot machine and pull it just right, or push the button with precision as I wait for those blessed three symbols to stop one at a time; that's pure skill with just a tad of luck. That's me being the captain of my destiny.

With the dogs and the horses, I'm left trying to figure out which animal is going to do its job on that day or other factors I have no control over. Like that time that one crazy dog broadsided that other dog. Now, who could have predicted something like that in advance? And I had that trifecta straight, too: 2–5–7. Right up to the finish line, almost, it was 2–5–7. Then five seconds before they crossed, that crazy number four dog came out of nowhere and clipped the seven dog. Well, seven flipped and rolled, hitting the number five dog. Yeah, you guessed it: the number two dog stumbled, although I have to give him his props; he did try to recover. The trifecta came 4–1–2. Paid $8,267.

I almost had that one also. My ticket said two with one and four, which meant the number two had to come first with the one and four coming in second or third (any order) after the two dog. For four more dollars, I could have boxed those numbers and they could have come in any order and I would have won. But I was so doggone sure about the two.

That's what I was trying to tell Desiree. I do this for us. Imagine how happy she would have been had I won that money. A few of our financial troubles could have been taken care of with that. She acts like she has major problems with my gambling, but when I hit it big—and I *know* it's coming—she's going to see all of these years have been worth it.

Now, don't get this twisted. I'm not stupid. I have won money, but it's a known fact that you have to invest back into any business if you want it to grow. I win, but when I do, I take my winnings and go for an even bigger payout.

Baby-cakes (I started calling Desiree that back when she used to be sweet—*used* to be) complains that I'm sinning when I gamble. When I ask her to show that to me in the Bible, she can't. Here's what I fail to understand: Monday through Friday, I take a chance that I'll make it to work safely. But that's okay. I can take money and buy some stock or invest it in real estate. And that's acceptable. Yet it's still gambling, if you ask me. I'm putting my money on something I believe will increase my return. I don't know for sure; I'm merely "taking a chance." I personally know plenty of folks who "invested"—all right, gambled, let's just call a spade a spade—in the stock market and lost everything including their homes. Ever hear of E-toys? At least my antics haven't caused us to lose our house—yet. Although, unbeknownst to Desiree, we've come close . . . *mighty* close.

Okay, it was like this: a sure deal. All the experts had followed this one horse and felt pretty confident he would win. I don't play the horses as much as I do the dogs, but this horse was a guaranteed favorite. Top breed, couldn't lose. One other reason I don't play the horses much is because you have to put up a lot of money in order to win a lot when it's a favorite like that. Plus, you have two more unstable variables to factor in: the horse *and* the jockey. So I needed $1,000 to put on that horse to win if I wanted to walk away with a measly $3,000 when he won the race. Like I said, it was a sure deal, the way IBM stock used to be once upon a time. I figured I'd use the house money, replace it after I won, and spawn a cool $2,000 profit for all my troubles. Again . . . a sure deal.

Well, that sure deal turned into an Enron investment real quick. That sorry horse didn't even show (that means to finish fourth). Didn't even show! I lost all my money.

"Edwin, why is the mortgage company saying they haven't gotten our last month's payment yet?" Desiree asked a month after it was due.

"Baby-cakes, I don't have a clue. You know how these businesses are. I'll call them and get it straightened out. You know they're probably going to blame it on a computer error like most of them usually do."

Desiree looked at me like she didn't know whether to believe me or not. I had to replace the money fast, so I took some more from our account and went to Mississippi hoping to hit it big. I did okay. I won about $1,500 but lost all of it back except $200. It took me a while, but after two months, I had us back on track with our house notes. I learned one important lesson from this: if I'm going to use money from our household, make it the grocery money. All that requires is my convincing Desiree she's gained a lot of weight the past few weeks. I then suggest we skip buying groceries altogether for the next three to four weeks to help her lose some of her excess weight, and I pocket that money.

Trust me when I say Desiree *will* find a way to buy groceries. Especially when she thinks she's sneaking behind my back to do it. So in the end, it usually works out.

But she and I got into a big argument Friday afternoon. I needed money to go to Mississippi and she wasn't falling for the redirected-grocery-money-diet-plan this time around. She had started attending this new church a few months back and had been insisting that I visit with her. This was the first time I've been home on a Sunday in years, so there was no getting out of going, especially if I wanted any *semblance* of peace today. I figured I'd go to church for those couple of hours just so I could enjoy the rest of my day without having to hear a sermon from her on why I was "going to hell in a hand basket."

Frankly, I'd gotten fed up with going to church.

Watching those good-old-holier-than-thou church folks treating collection time like they were playing a slot machine that was hot and on a roll. Then there were the admitted church-bingo-playing-for-money folks who called themselves trying to look down their holy noses at me, with their hypocritical selves. Yeah, I said it: hypocritical selves. A bunch of sanctimonious hypocrites!

"Edwin, how can you possibly compare church folks to you and your gambling?" Desiree asked when we were heavy into this discussion some years back, before I ceased going to anybody's church altogether.

"Have you seen them when it comes to putting their money in the plate?" I cocked my head to the side and opened my eyes wide after she looked at me like she didn't have a clue where I could possibly be going with this. "Before they drop their money in the plate, it's like some of them are doing the same thing I do before I plop my money down. I put my funds in, pull the handle or push the button, or place it down and say, 'Come on, Jesus!' Well, few people, Christians included, are actually putting their money in church because they love God and desire to give out of love. A good many, not all of them, put money in the collection plate expecting to hit the 'windows of heaven' jackpot. Seven, seven, seven. B-ten—Bingo! They drop their money in and pray for an even larger return. It's like they're saying, 'Come on, Jesus! Rain me down a blessing! Here's my ten, double or nothing!'"

Desiree shook her head. "Edwin, I just don't know about you sometimes."

"You know I'm right. How many people, in truth, pay their tithes and offerings only hoping to get that back plus some more? 'Return unto me and I will return unto you.' 'I'm believing for a hundredfold return.' 'Open up the windows of heaven, God, and pour me out a blessing. Pour me out a blessing!' Well, that's no different from what I do. I put my money in the machine, or lay it on the table, or give it to the clerk at the window, and pray for a blessed return."

The past few weeks, Desiree has been going on about this fancy-talking Pastor Landris and how he was teaching around the offering about giving out of love for God.

And that was precisely what he said today as I sat there. I mean, that man broke it down where even a fool could understand it.

"Don't give out of obligation or manipulation. Nor out of necessity, but give because the Lord loves a cheerful giver," Pastor Landris said. "Give because you love God. You see, it's easy to give and not love; but it's impossible to love and not give."

So I gave. Today, I actually gave. And all I thought about during that time was how much God loves me in spite of my shortcomings, and how much I truly love God just for who He is. For the first time in my life, I gave not because I wanted anything back from God, but just because I loved Him. Period. I felt so free for the first time in a long time.

Then Pastor Landris spoke about strongholds in our lives. I was really feeling what he was saying. This man was actually speaking a Word into my life. And when he finished and asked for people to come to the altar for prayer, I felt my body being lifted from my seat even before Desiree grabbed hold of my hand and finished yanking me up all the way.

Standing there with Desiree's hand in mine, I felt a stirring in my heart. Looking up at the minister as he was talking, I began to realize how much trouble I'd gotten myself in with my problem. And I'm not sure if even God can get me out.

Trinity

"You're so blessed, Trinity." That's what everybody keeps telling me, that I'm blessed. I suppose I'd have to agree with them. All these years I've lived with my various internal personalities only to almost totally lose my true self to a personality who calls herself Faith. But thank God, God didn't let it be so.

My name is Charity Alexandria Morrell, but most people at church knew me first or better as either Hope or Faith. Then I completely lost it while taking care of Johnnie Mae Taylor Landris's mother, Countess Gates, and the truth emerged. Faith, Hope, and Charity could be best summed up as Trinity— three distinct separate persons in one.

Oh, how I do miss Mrs. Gates. Of course I can no longer take care of her. I have to first get well myself. Some folks call me Trinity because of my three manifest personalities. This way Hope, and especially Faith, aren't being excluded when I'm being addressed now. And in truth, one can never know for sure which one of us is present.

The doctors have diagnosed me with Dissociative Identity Disorder (DID). People used to call it split personalities, with Sybil (remember that movie?) being the poster child. I wanted to stick exclusively with my therapist, Sapphire Drummond, a true Christian therapist, as my psychologist, but my personality called Faith doesn't like Sapphire very much. She refuses to cooperate if she's present when Sapphire is asking questions. So Sapphire hooked us up with another colleague, a Dr. Holden, and Faith—according to what they tell me—seems fine with him. In fact, Dr. Holden is standing with all of us who came forward because of our strongholds; although for the life of me, I can't imagine what he could possibly be dealing with.

Dr. Holden and Sapphire have explained Dissociative Identity Disorder more clearly to me. They're helping me better understand what may have happened to cause Faith and Hope to show up in the first place, as well as when it may have likely occurred.

I understand now how Dissociative Identity Disorder is the most chronic and harsh expression of dissociation. Dr. Holden believes it had to have been brought on by a severe trauma, but for the life of me, I can't make myself remember it.

"Along with this disorder, distinct, coherent identities can exist within one individual and can manage to assume control of the primary person's behavior and thoughts," Dr. Holden said. "In DID, a patient can experience amnesia about personal experiences, which can include the identities and activities of alternate personalities."

Sapphire had already explained to me how people with DID may experience depression, mood swings, become anxious, have a hard time maintaining their attention span, and even become psychotic. She said a lot of folks try to self-medicate with alcohol or drugs, but I thank God that was never a problem for me.

"People are frequently misdiagnosed as being solely bipolar or severely depressed," Dr. Holden said. "It's not an uncommon thing for years to pass before a correct assessment of DID is properly made in order for a patient to be treated appropriately."

For years, especially in my church upbringing, people were frowned upon if they had to seek out a head doctor.

"All you need to do is pray about it," people at church would say. "God can work it out. He will heal you. You just need enough faith."

And I agree that God can work it out and that He can heal me. That's why I'm standing here at the altar and being up-front about my stronghold. But I'm also aware that God can send various people to help us through our healing process. That's where Sapphire and Dr. Holden come in. Sapphire stresses to all of her patients the importance of seeking the Lord and praying, and she prays and asks God to help her bless His people with the knowledge and skills He has endowed her with.

My faith in God is strong, which is ironic because my personality named Faith is also strong. She knows her time is short as an independent persona. She's also aware that we don't want her to leave until I face what happened to split my personality in the first place. I think I was around seven or eight, but it's important that I remember the details clearly so I can heal.

Faith remembers. But she's not talking.

I don't know. Maybe it's just as well that I don't remember. Maybe the best thing for me to do is to get this dissociative stronghold out of my life and move on, whether I know what happened or not. That's why Faith won't tell us anything. She knows once I recall everything, I'll get better. She'll have to go, or what the doctors say, "assimilate," no, "integrate" with me. Hope knows something, but only Faith knows everything—the whole truth. I am getting stronger mostly because I'm learning to stand in the power and might of God Almighty. And yes, I believe I'm delivered now. Now.

" 'For the weapons of our warfare are not carnal,' " Pastor Landris said as he continued his sermon on strongholds, quoting Second Corinthians 10:4–5. "'. . . but mighty through God to the pulling down of strongholds. Casting down imaginations, and every high thing that exalteth itself against the knowledge of God, and bringing into captivity every thought to the obedience of Christ.' "

I've got to do this. I must cast down images and every high thing that exalts itself against what I know of God. I must bring my thoughts into captivity.

"Captivity has the Greek word conqueror with the word sword attached to it," Pastor Landris said We have the Sword of the Spirit—the Word of God. Use your sword to conquer your stronghold. Use your sword to bring down wrong images and every high thing that exalts itself against the knowledge of God. God knows, but we must look our stronghold in the eye and let it know that I believe what the Word of God says, and the Word of God says . . . then you speak the Word that applies to your situation. Speak the Word that you're standing on. Whose report are you going to believe? You have to take a stand and let the devil know you're going to believe the report . . . the Word of the Lord. Say it like Jesus said: 'It is written . . .'"

So I stand here at this altar on this Sunday in March, believing that God is a mind regulator. That Jesus has given me His peace, perfect peace . . . a peace that surpasses all understanding.

I believe it today and I speak it: I have the mind of Christ.

Bentley

When you have a last name like Strong and a first name like Bentley, you know you're being set up for some great things in your life. Of course children made fun of me. Most of them had heard of a car called Bentley, so that just made their teasing that much easier. Now that I'm twenty-five and doing *very* well, those same people who picked on me years ago are flocking to wherever I happen to be, asking for financial handouts.

It turns out that being a computer geek at the age of eight (even though we were dirt poor and didn't even get a computer in our home until I was eleven) was an additional blessing unto itself. But my mother always told me as long as I owned a library card, I had the whole world—along with some of the most brilliant minds and teachers ever to live—forever at my fingertips.

"Just reach out and take hold of all you can get," she said.

My mother was the brilliant one. The library was full of books and access to computers. The librarians were so impressed with my diligence; they allowed me more time on the computer back then than they were supposed to. I, in turn, taught them some things they didn't know how to do. When it was time to upgrade to newer, more powerful models, the main librarian, Ms. Kemp, did something that ended up literally changing the course of my life.

"Bentley, you're a bright young man," Ms. Kemp said one cloudy afternoon. "I've arranged for you to have something, if you would like it." She led me to a storage room. "We were required to wipe all of the information off the hard drive other than DOS, but if you can get someone to come pick this up for you"—she pointed at the lifeless, monstrosity of a machine, an IBM computer— "then it's all yours." She then handed me a bag filled with various types of software.

"For real, Ms. Kemp! I can have it? Flat out own it and take it home with me?"

She smiled. "Yes, flat out own it and take it home with you."

My mother came and got the computer. She couldn't thank Ms. Kemp enough. Some five years and a brand new computer later, I learned how Ms. Kemp had actually purchased the old and the new computer for me with money from her own pocket.

What most folks in my neighborhood and school didn't know was that I could take a computer apart and put it back together again. And there wasn't software out there I couldn't master. My mother was right: at the library I found all the answers at my fingertips. Books upon books contained answers to any questions I even *thought* about having.

True: books can be a blessing. However, I also discovered, some things in print can be dangerous. My uncle on my mother's side came to live in our home shortly after I turned eleven. If my mother hadn't taken him in, I believe he'd still be homeless today. For certain, none of the other family members wanted to put up with his drinking and womanizing ways. But my mother didn't have the heart to turn anyone away, especially someone with nowhere else to go. And particularly not her own blood. He didn't like the fact that I had my head inside of a book 24/7 or that I was forever on the computer.

Uncle Tank had been a promising musician. From what the family says, there wasn't an instrument Uncle Tank couldn't play. The way they talk, the artist originally known, then formerly known, now known again, as Prince, had nothing on him. I'm told Uncle Tank learned to play instruments by ear, and he started playing the piano for the church. They say he could practically raise any roof off any building with a saxophone. But they claim he had a little *too* much sass laced in his playing for a church or gospel career.

"There wasn't much money to be made in gospel music back when I came along, Bentley," he

said during one of our little talks. "For some reason, church folks don't seem to believe in paying
folks like the world will. 'Course now, things done
changed a whole lot since folks like that Kirk
Franklin fella and the rest of 'em done come on
the scene. I guess I was just born ahead of my time.
You know that song he sang called 'Stomp'?"

"Yeah."

"Well, do you know he took the music track of a
classic from back in the day by the Parliament-
Funkadelics and put Christian words to it? Made it
into a Christian song. See, that's something I would
have done if the church folk had'a left *me* alone."

I looked at Uncle Tank with a deliberate smirk
to let him know I knew he wasn't telling the truth.
Saying something like that had to be the result of
those spirits everybody said he carried around in
his pocket and sipped regularly.

"Don't believe me? All right then. Give me a day
or two to get my hands on my album collection. I
see right now I'ma just have to prove it to you,
young blood."

And that's what he did. When I heard the original song, I couldn't believe my ears. That was so
tight! Soon afterward, Uncle Tank and I became
good buddies.

That's when he told me he thought I was a bit
out of balance, reading all those "smart books" all
the time and "living on the computer." He believed
every young boy needed other "book-learning," especially in my case, not having my father around to
teach me men stuff. I needed to expand my "reading repertoire" was the way he put it.

That's when he pulled out a magazine, flipped the pages so I could see it was chock full of pictures, and gently laid it down before me like it was a mint condition Michael Jordan rookie card or something.

My first reaction was that I was too old for a picture book and that he really didn't understand boys my age *at all.*

"Uncle Tank, I don't know if you realize this, but I am thirteen now. For sure, I'm too old to be reading picture books."

"See what I mean, boy? Most boys your age would have picked up on just seeing the cover that this is no children's book. That there is a pure, double-D, Grade-A, certified woman right there on that cover. I guarantee you won't find these here pictures in no children's book." He turned several pages and began to grin. "Here." He handed it to me. "Take this and try studying somethin' other than all that boring stuff you done got brainwashed to. And if you find you like what you see, I've got plenty more where this one come from stashed away. Plenty. You just let your good ole Uncle Tank know, and Uncle Tank will take care of you. You can believe that."

"I don't know about this," I said.

"Boy, do you want to grow up and *be* a real man, or do you want to grow up and be *with* a man? This book is like a test. If you're straight, we'll find out by how you react. Consider this my gift to you. Just don't let your mama know or see it. Women don't seem to understand or share our appreciation for God's human art in full, living color."

And that was how it all began, where the seed was planted and my addiction to pornography took root. And like most addictions, it has only progressed over the years.

Now here I am married to Marcella, a wonderful, smart, beautiful woman, with a baby girl on the way, and I still find myself sneaking—late at night after my real, live, can-actually-be-touched wife is asleep—to look at porn. That's crazy. I have my own stash of magazines, videos, and DVDs galore, conveniently squirreled away. And the very thing Uncle Tank claimed a huge waste of my time—the computer—as it turns out, actually gives me the greatest access (via the Internet) to unlimited sites. There is categorically no shortage of porn lurking in cyberspace.

The thing that disturbs me is the amount of deceptive e-mail sent to people who really aren't interested in viewing pornographic sites, a good many of them being sent to innocent children. Children who, like me, could later become hooked. After all, it wasn't that long ago when I myself had only been a naive boy, minding my own business.

Now look at me. As a grown man, I can't seem to stop myself from practically gawking at naked women whose certain sexual acts I have no place or business looking upon. Marcella deserves better from me. Our new baby, due in about five months, deserves better. Although honestly, some of the books Marcella and her friends have been reading lately (called erotic fiction) seem to simply be just a more acceptable version of my own stronghold. Much of it is, from what I've seen and heard, clearly porn in words—sexual pictures created through the power of language.

And as Pastor Landris just said in a recent sermon, "Imagination is imagination. All images—real or imagined—are equally real when it comes to your brain."

True, Pastor. They're all images. And some of them just need to be pulled down.

Dr. Xavier Holden

I can't believe I actually stood and walked up to the front like this. I'm the one who is usually helping others to get *their* lives together. I'm the one people look to for answers, although in truth, I merely pose the questions that help draw out the answers.

"Dr. Holden, I desperately need your help." "Dr. Holden, it's urgent that I talk to you today. Please, can't you just work me in?" Who would think a psychologist would be on call the way I appear to be? I've even had to go to various emergency rooms to see about a few of my patients in the middle of the night.

When I began my practice, Avis and I had just gotten engaged. Avis is my sweetheart. I remember the day I first knew I liked her. We were in the school yard.

"Ouch!" Avis yelled as she turned around and glared at me. "Boy, why did you pull my hair?"

"Who you calling a boy?"

"If you pull my hair again, I'm going to do more than call you a boy," she said.

"Oh, so I'm supposed to be scared of you?" I asked.

"You'd better be."

"And who are you supposed to be?"

She put one hand on her hip, which truthfully already had some nice curves going on, cocked her head to one side, and turned up her nose at me. "Avis Denise Miller!"

I smiled. "Avis? What kind of a name is Avis?"

"You pull my hair again, and you're gonna find out what kind of a name is Avis. 'Cause I'm gonna run you down and roll right over you." She turned and walked away.

I didn't know it at the time, but I fell in love at the age of ten, right then and there next to the seesaw. It took Avis another five years (she was thirteen by then, two years younger than me) to come to her senses and realize she hopelessly loved me, too. Some folks claim I merely "wore the poor girl down." The truth is, she felt the electricity the day I yanked that luscious, long, black, springy plait of hers.

I know what it's like to grow up doing without. So does Avis. We both knew education was the golden key to our escaping the great state of poverty. I always knew I wanted to be some type of doctor, but the thought of being on call 24/7 didn't appeal to me. I realized I had a knack for talking to people, but an even greater gift when it came to listening, analyzing, and giving direction to folks regardless of their age, race, religious background, or gender.

People think they're helping by trying to tell

others what they should do. But I learned early in life, if you give people time to talk and to listen to what's inside of them already, they will, for the most part, discover the answers they seek. The problem I find with us black folk is: we consider it a sign of weakness to go talk to a professional when it comes to psychological things, like being depressed. Church folks in particular considered it weak faith if a person had to seek help from a "head doctor" or a "shrink" as they were called back in my day. It's changing some, but we still have a long way to go.

I look at what I do as being an extension of ministry. Some people can talk to their pastors about everything. Some people are fortunate enough to have a really good friend they feel comfortable enough sharing intimate details about their lives with in order for them to heal. Lately, however, it seems my practice has exploded *because* of the mega churches that are springing up. Folks are finding it increasingly more difficult to get an appointment to talk with their pastors without a three- to six-month wait.

"Look, Dr. Holden," one of my patients—a tall, heavyset woman with short, cropped hair—said. "First off, I don't really believe in head doctors or shrinks."

"We're not head doctors or shrinks."

"You know what I mean. You people do like to mill around in folks' heads trying to fix problems, real or imagined."

"Okay. So you don't believe in head doctors or shrinks."

"Anyhow, I didn't really want to come, but I

called my pastor's office so I could talk with him about an urgent matter, and he's booked up for the next five months. They have others on staff you can talk to, but I don't want one of his clones; I want my pastor. Especially with the kind of money I put in church every year. There was a time, before the church grew so large, when I could pick up the phone, call the church, and he would be the only one there to even answer the phone. Now, I almost have to schedule an appointment just to shake his hand after service to tell him I enjoyed his sermon."

"So, is this what you came in to talk to me about?" I asked. "It bothers you that you can't talk with your pastor whenever you want?"

"No, that's not what I want to talk about! And I guess as much as it's costing me an hour to talk to you, I should get to my problem and my point." She started laughing. "Maybe that's why black folks don't believe in shrinks. It costs too much, especially when it used to be something we could do for free. But a friend of mine did highly recommend you. So here I am. Hurry up and fix me; I'm on a fixed income."

People have discovered through word of mouth that I'm really good at what I do. My practice grew after the first five years to more than I could handle in the time I had originally allotted to work. For this reason, I had to extend my Monday through Friday hours to 7 P.M. and a half day on Saturdays. The problem is, I rarely leave the office before 8 P.M., and the half day Saturday somehow doesn't end until after 3 P.M.

That's partly why in late 2003 a therapist named

Sapphire Drummond and I decided to hook up. She had moved to Birmingham from Atlanta back in 2002. I'd heard talk on the circuit about how good she was, and I was hoping the two of us partnering would relieve some of my workload. What appears to have actually happened is our reputation as a team grew, and we both were working longer days and nights.

Avis is completely fed up with all of this. I've been working these crazy hours for over ten years now. We have four children, two girls and two boys. When I first began my practice, some fifteen years ago, I couldn't make enough money to even pay half our bills. Avis and I both worked, but we had student loans. It was hard as a young married couple starting out. Add to that, Avis got pregnant two months after our wedding. Birth control failure—definitely not part of our well laid-out plan.

That first pregnancy was hard on her. She was often sick and missed a lot of work she didn't get paid for because she didn't have enough time built up for sick pay. Add to that, we didn't have company-paid insurance at the time because my practice was my own business and she hadn't worked long enough to qualify for health insurance yet where she worked. We could have paid the premiums after she started working until she qualified, but the payment was around $450 a month for family coverage. Today I pay $780, but of course, I can afford that now with no problem. Back then, we were struggling just to pay our rent and utilities—forget finding enough money to pay for health insurance. Creditors started harassing us about late bills. It was extremely stressful.

I secured a full-time job working in a plant from 11 P.M. to 7 A.M. Then I would go into my office to see the handful of patients I'd managed to acquire already from 8 A.M. to 5 P.M. Some days it wasn't but three people, but their appointments were spread out, so I had to be there all day regardless. If there was enough time in between appointments, I would take a nap. Most of the time that would provide me with only about an hour of sleep, although every little bit certainly did help.

After Avis had the baby, we had a huge hospital bill to contend with. She had to have a C-section, which is considered surgery. It was necessary for me to keep up that intense work schedule just to maintain our new bills. Gradually, I got used to working all the time. Even after things got better for us and we had a nice cushion of money in the bank, I continued to work long and hard. I just didn't want my family to want for anything.

Eventually I said, "Avis, why don't you stop working completely and stay home with the children?" Three years after our first child, we had a second. Four months after the second, while she was still on a leave of absence from work, we learned we were expecting our third. Yes, we did know about birth control, but the pill was not a viable option for Avis for medical reasons. Some other methods we didn't care to use because of side effects like migraines, weight gain, excessive bleeding, and allergic reactions; future health concerns; or being controlled by a calendar, which wasn't always convenient and tended to conflict with our schedules while alienating spontaneity.

"Xavier, you're already overworking yourself,"

was Avis's response to me asking her to stop working and letting me take on all the bills.

"It's all good now. My practice is growing well. In fact, I'm planning to put in my two-week's notice down at the plant," I said.

And I fully intended to quit that job in two weeks, except it occurred to me that I was one year away from being vested with their pension plan. And besides, it made sense to work until the new baby came. That would just be more money for the household.

With three young children, Avis did decide to leave her company and stay home. I quit my job at the plant four months after our little girl, Jasmine Monet, was born. It looked like I was slowing down, but I soon discovered I didn't know how to have that much downtime. So when I found myself with all this "free" time, I revved up my efforts to acquire more clients. When some of my colleagues wanted someone to cover for them while they were out of town or vacationing, I was the go-to guy. Then Dr. Preston had a stroke, and I was asked to maintain his client base until he recovered and returned. He never recovered, and I ended up inheriting ninety percent of his lucrative clientele.

"Xavier, when are you going to slow down and spend time with us?" Avis asked again three years ago, right after our fourth child, Brandon Skylar, made his entrance into the world. "We don't go on vacation. You're hardly ever home. When you do make it home, it's close to most of the children's bedtime. You fell asleep while eating supper the other day. For goodness sake, you fell asleep while you were putting Brandon to sleep."

"It's not going to be like this always, Avis. I do this for us. You know this. We have this huge home with luxury vehicles parked in all four of our garages because of my hard work. Our children don't want for anything. Everybody has the latest gizmo—"

"But we don't have you," Avis said. "You and I don't even go out anymore."

"That's not true."

She looked at me like I had grown another head. "When was the last time you took me out?"

I thought for a few minutes. She gave me time.

"Okay," she said. "If you don't remember when, where did we go? And church doesn't count."

I admit she had me with that one, too. It had been so long, I couldn't recall the last place she and I had gone anywhere together other than church. Not even on one of our past anniversaries, although I did give her beautiful diamonds each year and a car for one.

"I promise, Avis. I'm going to cut back. You can't just do something like that all at once."

"That's what you keep saying, but you never do it. What's the point of having a family if you're not ever around to enjoy us?"

"I'm just trying to ensure our security, Avis. I want you and the children to have the best. I know it may be out-of-date thinking, but I'm supposed to provide for you."

She walked up to me and grabbed my hand. "Money-wise, you provide plenty, Dr. Holden. Where we seem to be deficient is me having a husband around, and the children are desperately in need of a father. I don't know, Xavier. There's always a trade-off in whatever decisions we make. I just pray you don't find yourself losing your family while in the pursuit of the almighty dollar that no one is forcing you to chase except you."

When I came home yesterday from the office, my family was gone. There was a note from Avis.

> Xavier,
>   When you decide you really want to be part of a family, let me know.
> I love you,
> Avis

I called Avis on her cell phone and promised her I would cut back starting first thing next week. She wasn't hearing it anymore. If I was serious, I would have to prove it.

So today I went to church, albeit alone, seeking God's guidance. And as Pastor Landris was preaching, he pointed out, once again, that strongholds aren't always the obvious things we think of as strongholds.

"Strongholds aren't always sins. Some people are people-pleasers," Pastor Landris said. "That's not a sin, but it can be a stronghold. Food. Various drugs. Some people might be habitual liars. It's not one of the Ten Commandments, though it is addressed in the Bible. It's a major character flaw, and can be a stronghold. Believe it or not, even things we think of as being good things can be strongholds. How many of you work so much you neglect to spend time with your family? As great and noble a virtue as honest, hard work is, if you're not careful, work *can* be a stronghold. Being married to a person who beats on you—abusing you physically and mentally—and staying in that marriage because you vowed 'until death do us part,' which may very well happen sooner than you think, can be a stronghold. Anything with a hold on you, anything that controls you instead of you controlling it, is a stronghold."

So today, I've made the decision I *will* take back my life. Satan has deceived me in the most clever of ways for long enough. I'm a workaholic. Today, I'm breaking my stronghold. I'm going into the enemy's camp, and I'm getting my family back!

Arletha

This was my first visit to this church, Followers of Jesus Faith Worship Center. When I saw that preacher stand up with that long hair, I started to get up right then and there and walk out. There are just certain things I believe and don't believe in, seeing as I was practically raised in the church. If anybody should know . . . I should. One thing I know: women ain't supposed to be wearing pants in church. I don't care what folks say. And for sure, men ain't got no business with hair that's longer than mine, looking like some woman.

I've been running for Jesus a long time, and all these newfangled philosophies people are trying to introduce into the Lord's house just ain't gonna fly with me. I don't believe you can be saved just by confessing your sins and believing in Jesus. Now don't go get all confused about what I just said. I do believe in Jesus, Lord knows I believe in Jesus. But the notion that all you have to do to get into heaven is to just confess you're a sinner, then accept Jesus as your savior and that's it—you're now guaranteed a place in heaven without proving you're worthy—is a bunch of hogwash! Excuse my French. But frankly, I'm tired of people telling and buying into that lie.

The Bible clearly tells us we must work while it's day because when night comes, no man can work. I joined the church sixty years ago, after I'd just turned six. It didn't take me long to make the decision, like it seemed to have taken many of the others. I knew back then that God had a call on my life, and I've been working in His vineyard ever since. Why do I work, you ask? 'Cause I want to get into heaven. I only pray I will have done enough to make it in. I want to hear my Lord say to me on that great day, "Well done, thy good and faithful servant. Come on up a little higher." For sure I don't want to hear, "Depart from me; I know you not."

That's why I'm in church every time the door opens. Trying to be good enough to make it into heaven. Trying to ensure the Lord remembers me. I believe He's keeping a record of our attendance, and everything we do and don't do.

I attend Sunday school every Sunday. I'm secretary of the Missionary Society, a faithful doorkeeper, president of the senior usher board. In fact, I'm so diligent on my usher job, nary does a gum chewer get past Ms. Arletha Brown. I run the floors of the church with an iron fist.

"Ms. Arletha, do you *ever* smile?" one of those little fast teenagers, Sister Penny's oldest daughter, asked me a few weeks back.

Who's got time to be smiling? "I'll have plenty of time to smile once I get to heaven," I said. "Ain't a thing to smile about down here. The devil is busy and he wants nothing more than for me to miss getting into heaven. I'm on my job, little girl, and I expect Jesus will smile when He sees me coming. Now, y'all go on somewhere and *set* down," I said as I gave her and her little friends my best frown, "like I done told you to. And don't be over there talking during service, 'cause I will escort you out if I have to."

Them children started laughing like something was funny. Ain't a thing funny about going to hell. A lot of folks are gonna miss heaven and bust hell wide open! Just watch and see. And them same folks who think I'm some kind of a religious fanatic gonna be the main ones begging me to dip my finger in water and cool their parching tongues. Well, they can forget about that. 'Cause I'm working too hard now, trying to make it into heaven myself while they're laughing and carrying on like tomorrow is promised. If folks want to stroll past those pearly gates and walk on streets paved with gold, they best be trying to follow in my footsteps.

Six days a week, you'll find me working the church door, manning the aisles, or sitting reverently on a pew with my Bible in tow every one of those days. On the seventh day, I rest, just like God did. I only hope I'll have done enough to make it in.

Folks around here be treating their salvation like it's a game or something. Well, my eternal life ain't no plaything.

I don't smoke. I don't drink. I ain't never done or even tried to do drugs. In fact I'm so committed, I won't even take aspirins for my headaches. I don't cuss. I ain't never gambled a day in my life. I don't lie; I tell folks the truth and I don't care whether it hurts their feelings or not. I don't overeat. In fact, I do some type of fasting at least once a month. Most times I do a three-day, no food fast. But I have done the Daniel Fast (ten days in a row) where you eat fruits, vegetables, and nuts; no meat, sugar, or caffeine.

When I pray, I get down on both my knees, and I pray for at least an hour. My head does not hit the pillow until I have read my Bible a minimum of one hour, every single night. I give money to the poor. I pay my tithes. I give offerings. Well, at least I did pay tithes and offerings up until a few weeks ago when I decided to leave where my church membership has been for the past forty-six years in search of a new church home.

I confess: I don't agree with my soon to be ex-pastor and his decision to start allowing them young people to be doing that dancing and junk in the Lord's house like all these other churches have begun to do here lately. I tried talking to Pastor Rainey and the deacons, but they seem bent on following the popular, worldly ways of late—trying to get more people to come to church and fill up some of those empty pews. Just selling out.

I figure if folks don't want to come . . . too bad. We shouldn't change the type of songs we sing just because the attendance has fallen off and folks are flocking to all these other churches. Contemporary gospel, hip-hop gospel, gospel rap, praise dancing: whoever heard of such nonsense! When will folks get it? Church is supposed to be dull and boring. I figure that's how the Lord can tell who's sincere and who's not. People want to start changing everything, liven things up. Cutting out testimony service. Talking about folks holding too long just because they want to get out of church earlier. Wake up, people! These are the last days.

I contend if it was good enough for my mother, good enough for my father, then it's good enough for me. The only person I can do anything about is me. And I'm just trying to make sure if nobody else does, I'm gonna make it to heaven. I ain't got time for folks who don't care about their own soul. Folks reading all kinds of filthy magazines and books, sleeping with any and everybody, smoking, doping, lying, cheating—sinning like there's no tomorrow. You can't hardly walk into a store these days without half-naked men and women jumping out at you off the covers of stuff. And the TV, Lord, you talk about an idle mind being the devil's work-shop. I have to protect my eye and ear gates.

Then I heard it. This Pastor Landris fellow said it, while the devil (I know it was him) tried—for a minute there anyway—to tell me this long-haired, ungodly man was talking to me.

"And some of you sitting here today are plagued by a stronghold of religion. You think you're going to make it into heaven based on what you do here. You think you can live right enough and good enough to get in," Pastor Landris said. "Well, let me tell you something. *You* cannot live good enough to make it into heaven. You don't get into heaven based upon your works. Church, none of us are good enough. That's why Jesus had to come. We are saved by grace. When you brag about what you're doing that's going to get you into heaven, it's equivalent to saying: 'What Jesus did on the cross, and God raising Him from the dead, was of no effect. I'm good enough to make it in on what I do and not what Jesus has already done.' That just doesn't line up with scripture."

I watched Pastor Landris as he seemed, for one minute, almost to peer into my very soul. Then he said, "Break the stronghold of religion, legalism, and tradition. Just because you've always done something one way or believed in something all your life, doesn't make you right. There's a big difference in religious dogma and a relationship with Jesus the Christ. If religion has a stronghold on you, it's highly likely you don't truly know Jesus. And if you know *about* Jesus and don't know *Him*— if you haven't truthfully accepted Him as Lord and Savior—then you're no better off than a sinner who has never accepted Jesus. Don't deceive yourself. Ultimately, every knee will bow, and every tongue will confess that Jesus is Lord." He nodded his head several times.

"When you get to heaven, you won't be asked:

What's your religion?" Pastor Landris continued. "Don't be deceived. You don't want to be standing there trying to say what you did in God's name, and have Him tell you He never knew you merely because you failed to confess your sins, accept Jesus and all He did on the cross, and believe that God raised Him from the dead." Pastor Landris's voice began to wind down. He scanned the sanctuary. "Joining a 'church' is not equivalent to being saved. And that's what some of you unknowingly did at the time—you joined a group, but not the body of Christ."

Blasphemy! That's what I thought of Pastor Landris and his sermon. *Blasphemy!* Oh yes, I rebuked that. And I fully intended, after I got out of this place, to never darken this church's doors again. But then Pastor Landris said words I've heard myself say to so many people over the past years of my life.

"If you died today, do you know—with certainty—where you'll spend eternity? Because you are going to die, if you're not caught up during the rapture; and you will spend an eternity somewhere. If you died today, do you know—with assurance—where you'll spend *your* eternity? Salvation is not based on works, lest any man or woman should boast. If you've been living under the strongholds of merely a religious disguise, don't gamble with your eternal life. Come . . . sign up for Abundant Life Assurance and make sure you're not just covered against fire, but that you receive all you're entitled to. full life coverage that includes among its many benefits theft protection with complete and full restoration.

People, this is too important." He held out his arms. "Won't you come now? If you're not sure, you can change things today. Let's pull down some strongholds today."

Before I knew anything, I found myself standing with a crowd of people who I'm sure, have boo-coo problems. I then heard a voice deep inside of me whisper, "Get the plank out of your own eye, before you worry about removing the splinter from someone else's."

I can't help but wonder: Who was *that* message for? *God, who here do You want me to relay that message to? Who can it be?* This has to be the reason I was drawn to come up here. It must be to help someone already up here.

Has to be.

Elaine

I didn't want to come to church, but the woman I've been staying with is something of a church fanatic. In fact, one of the reasons I chose to move in with her as opposed to getting my own place was because I believed she'd be a great cover.

I've been sort of in hiding for the past four years, just laying low until people quit looking for me. The only reason I came with her today is because Arletha is upset with the church where she has been a member for about a half a century (boring!), and she didn't want to visit this new church by herself.

"I hear it's rather a large church," she said with what I'm learning to be her signature whine as she stood in my rented room in her house. "They say white people go there, so you wouldn't feel out of place." I didn't bother to tell her once again that although I look white, I'm not white. "I just don't know," she said. "You have to be careful with some of these so-called churches."

If I could have put her off, I certainly wouldn't be here. But I can't afford to get on her wrong side and get kicked out of her home. Not yet anyway.

Just last month, someone came knocking on the door where I was staying in St. Louis. The person who answered the door managed to turn him away, but still. For the life of me, I can't figure out why, at seventy years old, I'm still such a high priority for anyone to want to find so badly after all these years. Every time I think they've left me alone, there's another knock on the door or ringing of the telephone. "Yes, I'm looking for Memory Elaine Patterson Robertson," they always say, before using the name I may be using in that place at the time.

Of course, I don't always use my real name when I move to a place. But somehow, this private detective or whatever he is, has a way of figuring out just where I am. I barely had time to get out of St. Louis a month ago. I decided to come down deeper south this go 'round. Who will think to look for me here in Alabama, especially with Ms. Super-religious Arletha Brown answering the door? For sure, if anybody's going to get into heaven, it *has* to be this straight-and-narrow woman. She can be as mean and ornery as a rattlesnake, yet she forever brags about what all *she's* doing *for* the Lord.

I figured out early, this woman doesn't have a clue. And quite honestly, I think she needs to buy another vowel. Her "I this . . ." and "I that . . ." has gotten on my last nerve, and I've only been with her for this short time. Somebody please give her a *u* or an *o*; anything else! But like I said, she is a great cover and her home is the perfect place for me to hide until I decide on my next move. Few people seem to want to be around her; that's a plus for me. I don't even think Jesus has come to her house in years, if he's ever been here at all. There's no room for Him, especially since she seems to believe she's saving herself, all by herself, with all of her goodie-good works.

I *am* getting tired of running though. This moving around . . . being in constant hiding in more ways than I can say, takes a toll on you. I know Lena and Theresa are still upset with me about that Alexandrite necklace. No matter what I try to tell them, they're not going to believe me. That's the problem when you lie and deceive people (although I wouldn't totally say I did either): people won't believe anything you say after that.

To begin with, that necklace *was* mine. I don't care how anybody might try to spin, dice, or explain it away. In my heart that necklace has always belonged to me. I asked Lena if she knew where the contents of that wooden box were a long time ago, and she said she didn't, which, as it turns out, she obviously did. What else was there left for me to do other than what I was forced to?

Clearly, I couldn't just walk up to Theresa's door, ring the doorbell, and say, "Hi, my name is Memory Patterson. Theresa, I'm your grandmother, and Lena is my daughter. I'm not really here trying to get to know either one of you better. In fact, I really only came to get a necklace I am convinced Lena has in her possession. If one of you could go and get it and give it back to me, you could save all of us a lot of trouble and heartache, and I can be on my merry little way and out of your hair for good."

Had Theresa protested, I could have told her what a horrible, self-centered person I was, and how much they all would be better off having me out of their lives sooner rather than later. Nope, that would never have worked.

But I did make one, ultimate miscalculation. I didn't count on them treating me like family. Nor did I know being with my own flesh and blood like that would cause me to start changing. I admit: I got a little soft.

Whoever is looking for me, though, I hope it's worth their while. I would have given up after all these years myself. So cither Lena or Theresa called the police on me and filed a report that has caused the police to try and find me (which I seriously doubt the police would be looking this hard for somebody like me), or someone else I've wronged somewhere through the years has hired someone to stay hot on my trail.

Nobody, which includes Lena and Theresa, can prove I took anything. And even if they could prove anything, they have no evidence. I figure little Miss-High-and-Mighty Theresa is the likely culprit behind this man who has been following me from town to town. She's probably more upset about me having left her back in 2001 the way I did when she was in labor than anything. And there was the 9/11 World Trade Center and all those other tragedies happening that day, alongside the joy of her baby being born. . . .

The baby. I hear it was a little girl just like I told them it would be. The 9/11 thing had me a little worried for a while as I did wonder about what may have happened to Lena. But then I'd already done what I did, and it was too late to turn back. Gosh, who had a way of knowing? I did eventually learn Lena was okay. I also heard something about Beatrice dying; I'm sure that had to have sent Theresa completely over the edge.

Theresa seems to be vindictive enough; she would pay money for someone to hunt me down just for the principle of the thing. And I'll give it to whomever it is searching; they are attempting to be quite clever about sniffing me out. Like when they had that detective tell folks I'm possibly heir to some huge fortune in, of all places, Asheville, North Carolina, and that it's imperative my family locate me. Like I would really fall for that one. As soon as I took that bait, they would be reeling me into the nearest jailhouse and threatening to throw away the key or who knows what else.

Lately, I have considered making things right with my family. Just go on and allow that man to catch me and face the consequences. Frankly, I'm just tired of running. I'm too old to continue living this kind of lifestyle. Moving constantly, looking over my shoulders, hustling for my next "pay" day by any means necessary.

This minister was preaching about strongholds and being released from them.

"God can release you from the strongholds of your past," Pastor Landris said. "Some of you may have done things you think you can never be forgiven of. There's not a sin out there that you can't bring before the Lord and ask Him to forgive you of that He won't forgive. And God won't bring up your past to you again. But now Satan will take your past and try to keep you in bondage. He'll tell you how horrible you are. He'll tell you that God could never forgive someone like you. But Satan is a liar, and the truth is not in him. Come, won't you? Come, and let God release the shackles from around your ankles today. Let Him break the chains that have you bound." He pulled his fist in different directions to show a chain being broken.

"If you're tired of carrying around heavy weights that are holding you down," Pastor Landris said, "then come. Let's pray to have your stronghold released. If you want to be free, get up out of your seat and walk up here right now. Don't wait for tomorrow. Today is your appointed time. Don't worry about what the person sitting next to you will think. This is about you. Get up and come forward now. Right now. Today. Today is your day to be set free. For whom the Son sets free, is free indeed."

I stood up, and the next thing I knew, I was standing at the altar with tears streaming down my face. I already knew the Lord; I'd given Him my heart when I was a young girl. True: I didn't know what all that meant at the time. And I had turned away from Him and all that I knew to be right. But now it appears that in the midst of all my running away, I may be finding my way back to Him. It's as though today, I am running into the arms of my Lord, who has been standing there waiting for me all this time.

"Take me back," I found myself singing quietly as I walked to the front. "Take me back, dear Lord. To the place where I first received You."

Chapter 2

Providing for honest things, not only in the sight of the Lord, but also in the sight of men.
—2 Corinthians 8:21

Pastor Landris stood at the front of the conference room. "Many of you came forward today when I extended the call for those who were dealing with various strongholds. I prayed for you at the altar, and as much as all of us would love for your deliverance from your stronghold to have been instantaneous, that's not always the case. It's not as if prayer alone will always cause everything to suddenly be all right," Pastor Landris said as he took a few steps forward. "I believe in the power of prayer, but I also believe there are times where some work, strides, and efforts must be made on our part for a change to completely take hold and become effective."

A woman raised her hand.

"Yes," Pastor Landris said, acknowledging her.

"So coming forward today didn't automatically break me from my stronghold?"

Pastor Landris smiled. "Sometimes some people

experience an immediate manifestation of deliverance. Sometimes there is work that has to be done as the process is taking place. I've known people who have come up and asked me to pray for them to be released from, say, overwhelming debt. Now, I know everybody would love to just walk up to the front, have a minister slap them upside their head, and everything is set straight, right then and there. But God doesn't always work that way. I'm not saying that He can't do it that way; it's just many times things are done in progression. First the blade, then the ear, then the full corn in the ear."

A man raised his hand. "So you're saying some of us may be released from our strongholds already?"

"Yes. And some of you may have to work it while you believe God for your full manifestation. I believe God did a work in each of you when you stood up, took that step of faith, and came forward. It might have been just the blade for some of you; for others, the full ear." Pastor Landris looked toward the back as another hand went up. "Yes?"

"Then what you're saying is that prayer alone doesn't work?"

"I'm not saying prayer alone doesn't work. But I feel people have misconceptions about prayer. Prayer is not designed to be a magic cure-all. Prayer is a way to bring a request before God. Look at prayer as being an usher who escorts you and your request front and center. That's why I wanted all of you to come in here so we could talk more in-depth. My desire is to equip you with every tool needed to win your individual battles. God's desire, as is mine in having done all these sessions on strongholds, is to set captives free. Think of my giving you information as bringing you before a locked door. Prayer delivers the key designed to unlock that door for you. If you have a key and don't use it, what good does it do you? If you use the key—faith—but you refuse to walk through the unlocked door, it still profits you nothing. You must fully act on your faith to overcome your strongholds. But you also need a powerful weapon to fight with. This"—Pastor Landris picked up his Bible and held it up—"two-edged sword, the Word of God, applied consistently in daily living, *will* set captives free."

Dr. Holden raised his hand.

"Yes?"

"How long does this process *generally* take? And is there any way we can accelerate the processing time . . . get to the full ear? I'm sort of in a hurry."

A few people laughed while others looked intensely toward Pastor Landris for the answer.

"Much of where you go and how fast you get there from here will depend upon you. God has already done it. It's finished in His eyes. But as the Bible says, without faith, it is impossible to please God; and faith without works is dead. You can believe you've been healed, delivered, your stronghold has been placed under your feet and that you're free. But unless you act on that belief, in the end it doesn't really matter what you believe. That's why faith—action—is so important." Another hand went up. "Yes?"

"So what's next for us?"

Pastor Landris smiled and clapped his hands one time. "Glad you asked. What I'd like to do is to have our Deliverance Support Ministry meet with any of you who are interested in a specially created Bible study on this subject. This is a brand new ministry we've started here. This Wednesday will be the first time for this group to meet. The first two or three weeks will be used to disseminate information and tools with which you'll learn how to cast down imaginations and every high thing that exalts itself against the knowledge of God, and to bring into captivity every thought to the obedience of Christ. But to get you started, and for those who are not interested in this Bible study, I do have a handout for you to take with you so you can begin to make changes in your life today."

Pastor Landris nodded to Sherry and her team to distribute the handouts. "For some of you, this handout may be enough to help usher you into the full manifestation of your deliverance. If that's the case, then that's great. If you desire to come to the Deliverance support group, we welcome you and believe it will bless you. Again, if you feel you don't need it, that's fine. After the first few weeks' study, you can still come together to continue the support as well as pray and receive teaching for as long as you need it."

Pastor Landris noticed Sherry had finished passing out the reading material. "I would like to ask anyone interested in this Wednesday night session to please sign up here on your way out." He held up a notebook. "That way we'll have an idea of how many to expect and prepare for."

"If we sign up and change our minds later about coming, is that okay?" someone asked.

"Yes, that's fine," Pastor Landris said.

"What about if we don't sign up now? Can we

come anyway if we see we need to?" another person asked.

"Yes. We're not here to make things difficult for anyone," Pastor Landris said. "Our goal is to be a blessing and not a burden on God's people in the process. If you need to come, then come. If you sign up thinking you need to and you find you don't need it because you are totally delivered, that's wonderful. God bless you."

"We just need a general count today so we'll have some idea of the size room to secure, at least to begin," Sherry said. "We're also posting this class on the Web site."

An elderly, Caucasian-looking woman in the back raised her hand. "Should we decide to sign up, what information will we have to disclose?"

"Just your name, address, and phone number."

"Will we have to openly disclose our problem at any time?" a young man asked.

"No, you don't have to tell what your specific problem is unless you desire to tell it or unless you feel you need to reveal something in order for us to help you."

"One more question, Pastor," a man said. "What if we need individual counseling? Can we come and talk with you privately?"

Pastor Landris looked around the room of about sixty people. "Well, as you can see just from here, it would be taxing to try to counsel everyone individually. That's why we're doing this form of corporate counseling by way of this special Bible study. After the initial weeks, we will likely break the group down into more specific smaller groups."

"Will you be the one in charge of this ministry?"

"No, actually, we have some wonderful ministers who'll be leading this support group effort," Pastor Landris said. He then looked around the room. "Any more questions?" He scanned the room once more. "All right then. I thank you for your time, and please sign up if you're interested in joining this Deliverance support group as you leave."

Pastor Landris watched as the older woman who sat in the back and seemed to hang on his every word got up and walked out of the room without signing up.

Memory looked back after she walked out the door. "That prayer he prayed when I was up there had best be enough to break my stronghold," she mumbled to herself. "There's no way I'm coming here weekly for some meeting." She walked to the car and found Arletha waiting inside, drumming her fingers with a frown and tight, buttoned lips.

"Sorry," Memory said. "You know how it is: when you got to go, you got to go." Truthfully, that really wasn't a lie. She did have to go; she just didn't say go where.

Chapter 3

For if they do these things in a green tree, what shall be done in the dry?
—Luke 23:31

Darius rang the doorbell twice. Fatima sat on her couch trying her best to ignore it. She already knew it was Darius. He had called and said he was on his way over.

"Darius, don't come here. I'm not playing; we're through," Fatima said.

"Well, if we're really through, then you can at least have the decency to tell me to my face."

"I don't have to tell you anything to your face. Look, you're the one who's married here. This is wrong . . . for both of us. I hate this. Do you understand? I hate this!"

"Is that why you went sashaying up to the altar yesterday at church?"

"That's none of your business," Fatima said.

"Oh, it is my business. Especially if you told what you went up there for."

"You don't know why I went up there. That's between me and God."

"Well, I know you. And knowing you, you were up there because of us. I just want to know if you happened to tell anybody why you came forward."

"Darius, look. If you're worried about your sweet reputation and word getting out that you have—oh, I stand corrected—*had* a woman on the side, you don't have to sweat about that. This is about me. It's about me doing what's right for me."

"So what are you saying? That I'm not right for you?"

"Look, I don't want to talk about this with you, okay? You and I are history. Finished. Through. It's over. You can just go on with your wife and try to work things out with her. That's what you should have been doing all along anyway. She's the one you chose and decided to spend your life with—"

"But she doesn't make me happy," Darius said.

"Well, that's not my problem."

"I'm coming over there."

"Don't come here."

"I'll be there in ten minutes."

"Darius, I'm not playing. Don't you come over here!"

"Just don't have me standing outside making a fool of myself. Because if I come and you don't let me in, I will cause a scene if I have to."

"Yeah, right. Mr. Darius Discretion. I bet you will."

"I'll see you in ten minutes."

"Darius—" Fatima stood there as a dial tone hummed in her ear. "Okay, God. What do I do now?" Fatima could only think to recite a Biblical passage. "The weapon of my warfare is not carnal, but mighty through God to the pulling down of strongholds. My weapon is not carnal, but mighty through God."

Nine minutes later, Darius, as promised, was ringing her doorbell. She refused to answer it. He rang it again and again. She stood praying to God for strength not to give in and open the door, which was what she really wanted to do. Darius began to bang on the door. She continued to pray.

"Fatima, I know you're in there!" Darius yelled. "Open up and stop playing games!"

Fatima continued to pray.

"Fatima, open this door!"

"Thank you, Lord, for strength," Fatima prayed. "I am mighty through you, God. I can do all things through Christ Jesus who strengthens me. I can do this. I can."

There were a few more pounds on the door, then finally . . . silence.

Fatima listened as she heard the car crank and tires squeal as Darius drove away. Tears streamed down her face. "God, I do love him so. Please, take away these feelings I have for him. Please. Take away these feelings. Oh, Father God, this hurts so much!"

Chapter 4

*For we wrestle not against flesh and blood,
but against principalities, against powers,
against the rulers of the darkness of this
world, against spiritual wickedness in high
places.*

—Ephesians 6:12

Desiree and Edwin had walked up to the altar hand in hand. While standing there, he squeezed her hand three times. Her mind had wandered back to the time when she and Edwin first fell in love, back when she believed he was everything she wanted in a man.

"Desiree," Edwin had said after the first time he ever told her he loved her, "I'm not real good with words. In fact, saying 'I love you' was a major accomplishment for me just now. I wasn't raised to show affection in that way. So I'm going to devise my own special signal specifically for us. On those days when I can't get the words out, I'm going to squeeze your hand three times. That way you'll know that I love you, no matter what's going on or if I haven't said it verbally." He squeezed her hand three times. "I love you, Baby-cakes," he said, and squeezed her hand three more times.

"Baby-cakes?" Desiree had said with a smile,

then a slight blush. *My very own pet name.* "I love you too, Edwin."

Desiree knew as they stood at the altar that Edwin was saying he loved her. It had been such a long time since he'd said it or used their special signal. It had been two days since they'd discussed their own strongholds. Edwin seemed to be struggling big time.

"You know my stronghold is gambling, don't you?" Edwin had said on their way back home from church. "But I felt something on the inside of me caused me to get up."

"I thought it was me pulling you up," Desiree said.

"No, there was this feeling down deep that was gently nudging me to get up and go forward. You know I haven't been to church in a good while. And when I have gone, I rarely ever went to the altar, even for general prayer. I especially wouldn't have ever gone while visiting a church I'd never been to before."

"What did you think of Pastor Landris?"

"He's definitely different. I don't know. I can't help but wonder what kind of a scam he's running, though. You know how I feel about preachers these days. Still, that prayer he prayed was pretty powerful. I felt something similar to electricity surge through my body when he touched my head with his hand."

Desiree looked at Edwin. "I suppose we'll have to see if anything happens for either of us," she said.

It was now Tuesday night and Edwin hadn't gone to the race track yet. That was a miracle in itself. Desiree had no way of telling whether he was changing or just forcing himself to stay away from the track. Either way, she was thankful. Yet, she could see he was definitely struggling with being at home instead of out gambling.

Edwin's mind did wander every now and then to the track. The handout Pastor Landris had given all of them said to cast down imaginations. Whenever a wrong thought or an image came to his mind, he would divert his attention elsewhere. The past two days had truly been a wrestling match for him. And he now knew for sure that gambling had a stronghold on him. Pastor Landris had emphasized how God gave them dominion over everything and it was not the other way around. He had to be strong. However, he understood it was not through his own might, but through God's might that he would be victorious.

"Baby-cakes, where's the Bible?" Edwin asked around eight o'clock that night. He and Desiree had both signed up for the Deliverance support group. They would be meeting for the first time tomorrow night. He just needed to make it through one more night. On Wednesday, he could look forward to getting some reinforcement from the Bible study to cope with these strong feelings he was having.

Desiree went and got her Bible. "You're going to read the Bible?" she asked. A sound of shock, although she seemed to be trying to mask it, laced her voice.

"Yeah. I'm working on that 'bringing every thought into captivity' part. Our handout said that God has thoughts in the Bible I can direct my mind to instead of what I usually think about. I figure the worse case scenario will be that while I'm reading, I end up falling asleep. Either way works for me."

Desiree laughed. "You know you need to stop."

"Desiree, now you know reading the Bible can put you to sleep, so don't even try fronting with me. I've come home late many a night and found your Bible resting on your chest and you knocked out and calling hogs," Edwin said with a grin as he referred to her snoring. "Let's see now. How should I do this? Open the Bible to a page and see what page decides to speak to me, or be more methodical about it?"

He closed his eyes and said a quick prayer, then turned the Bible to Proverbs, the first chapter. "Thirty-one chapters, one chapter a night, and according to the handout, it takes twenty-one days to break a habit. I figure by the time I finish reading the book of Proverbs, I should be done with my gambling problem. My only real concern will be figuring out how to make it through the long weekends. Work manages to keep my mind occupied during the day through the week, but the weekends—that's a whole lot of hours to fill with something other than my usual activity."

"Don't you worry about your weekends," Desiree said with a mischievous grin. "I'll make sure we find *something* to keep you occupied." She stood up straight. "While you read the Bible, I think I'll go get on the treadmill and work out for about forty-five minutes. Maybe you and I can start walking together after you get home from work?"

Edwin smiled. "Sounds good to me."

Desiree leaned over and kissed him on his lips. "Thank you."

"For what?"

"I know this is hard for you."

"No harder than yours is for you. You haven't smoked. You're watching what you eat. You're exercising. We're going to lick these strongholds, Desiree—together. It's me and you against the world."

"Correction: Me, you, and God against the world," Desiree said. "And Jesus has already overcome the world."

"Right." *Because I definitely won't be able to do* this *on my own. I bet you my numbers hit tonight. I just know it. This is probably the night my regularly played numbers will come in as a straight trifecta. I just know it.*

He began to read to himself. "Proverbs, chapter one, verse one: 'The Proverbs of Solomon the son of David, king of Israel.' Verse two: 'To know wisdom and instruction; to perceive the words of understanding.' "

Oh yeah, this is going to be a long twenty-one days. A looong twenty-one days.

Chapter 5

And certain women, which had been healed of evil spirits and infirmities, Mary called Magdalene, out of whom went seven devils. . . .
—Luke 8:2

"Faith, can you hear me?" Sapphire said as Charity lay on the couch in the therapist's modestly furnished office. Charity was getting better, but they still hadn't gotten to the root of her problem and her two other personalities were very much still intact.

"Faith, this is Sapphire. I need to speak with you. Will you please come out and talk with me? Faith. Come on. I know you can hear me."

It had been almost an hour now, and Sapphire was becoming frustrated. "Hope, can you hear me? I need to speak with one of you. Come on, somebody talk to me."

Trinity began to make a whimpering sound.

"Hope, is that you?"

"Yes, this is Hope."

"Hope, this is Sapphire. I need to talk with you about Charity."

"What do you need?"

"First, can you tell me why Faith refuses to talk to me?"

"Faith doesn't trust you. She thinks what you're trying to do is ultimately going to destroy Charity. And we both are aware that *should* you succeed, we will no longer be this powerful trinity we have become. Yet Faith, especially, does appreciate when you refer to us as Trinity. It makes her feel like we're not being completely ignored or disrespected," Hope said.

"Okay, Hope. I appreciate you for being willing to help. I've asked this before. Something happened when Charity was a young girl. Do you know what happened?"

Hope released a sigh. "I know the first part, but only Faith knows everything."

"Can you tell me the part you know?"

Hope began to twist and turn. "No, no, no. Stop it! Stop it!"

"Hope, what's wrong?"

"He's there talking to Mother, and he's hurting her again. Charity sees him and she's telling him to stop. But Mother yells at Charity for her to go to her room and close the door. Instead, Charity goes outside to get Motherphelia. When Motherphelia comes inside, he's being nice to Mother and Mother is playing it off like Charity got it all wrong. But Charity didn't get it wrong."

"Okay, Hope. You're doing very well. Hope, do you know who this man is?"

Hope began to twist again. "Stop it, Faith! Stop it. Let me tell her what I know."

"Faith, Faith? This is Sapphire. Can you hear

me, Faith? I'm trying to help. I'm trying to help all of you. This is going to help Charity heal. I'm only trying to help."

"No, you're not. You're trying to destroy our very existence," Faith said.

"Faith, I'm not trying to destroy anyone," Sapphire said. "Charity deserves to be healed, and she can't do it without facing her demons—the demons of what happened that caused this—and coming to terms with it all."

"Charity can't handle it. I know she can't. And I believe I know her better than you, and what's best for her, better than you."

"What makes you think she can't handle it? Charity is a strong woman. Look at all she has accomplished so far, without anyone's assistance."

"Charity was standing up there Sunday at the altar. Did you see her? I guess she thinks Hope and I are her strongholds. She wants to get rid of us, and much of this is your doing. We were all doing fine before all of you Jesus freaks started poking your noses in our business."

"Faith, all of you were not doing fine. Charity's mind was and still is being tormented."

"Oh, I guess you blame me for that? I didn't create myself. Charity needed me. Don't you get it? She allowed this blessed trinity to develop in order to cope."

"She has the Trinity: God the Father, God the Son, and God the Holy Spirit. This is the true, blessed Trinity. This trinity can help Charity if only you'd let go and allow them in completely to heal her. Help me instead of fighting against me," Sapphire said. "Work with me, Faith."

"Where's Dr. Holden? I'll talk to Dr. Holden and tell him."

"Dr. Holden is taking time off for the next few weeks."

"I'll speak with Dr. Holden, and only him. I don't trust you, Sapphire. You know this. If you want me to tell what I know, you get Dr. Holden for me and I'll tell him."

Sapphire sat back in her chair. "Right." She and Dr. Holden had had a long talk earlier on Monday when she came in to work. Sapphire had no idea something was going on in his life. She knew he was a hard worker, but he confessed to her how he'd become a workaholic to the point his wife had left him and taken their four children with her. To prove to his wife that he was a changed man who had seen the errors of his ways, he was taking off the next three weeks to spend time with his own family. There was no way Sapphire was going to call him in. And even if she did, according to him, he wasn't going to allow anything or anyone to interfere with proving to his wife he meant what he'd promised so many times before but hadn't followed through on. He only came in to work on Monday to clear up his calendar.

"Faith, Dr. Holden won't be back for another three weeks. There's no reason for you to be this way. You and I can work this out; you know I care about you."

"You don't care about me!" Faith said. "You only care about Charity and maybe Hope a little, although you're still willing to sacrifice Hope's existence in order to save our sweet little Charity. So don't be using that psychology junk on me. I'm the ultimate professional when it comes to mind games."

"Is that how you convinced Charity she needed you?" Sapphire stood up. "Using mind games? You do know there are other ways I may be able to help Charity without your cooperation, don't you?"

"Yeah, probably. But can you be certain Charity will truly remember? And you really need to ask yourself whether or not she truly needs the information I hold in order to be made whole. See, the way I calculate things: if you're wrong and I'm gone for good, what I know will be lost forever. Once I'm gone, I'm not coming back, even if you both beg me to. So the question you must ask yourself is: Is what I know about what happened so important that Charity not ever knowing it could end up ultimately destroying her completely? What if what I know sends her to a place of no return?"

"I think you may be underestimating Charity. What if she decides to integrate without you telling me anything, and then what you remember becomes part of her memory again without you? I believe it would be better for all concerned if you were to just tell me what you know since you seem to have handled this information so well all of these years. Personally, I believe in Charity. And believe it or not, I truly do believe in the power of you three becoming one again."

"Get Dr. Holden for me, and I will tell him everything I know," Faith said. "Everything. Get him and we can proceed from there."

And then she was gone.

Charity came out of it and slowly sat up. "What happened?" she asked Sapphire.

"Well, I got Faith to talk to me this time around."

"Did she tell you—?"

"No. She refuses to tell me anything, but she did say she would tell Dr. Holden."

"That's good, isn't it? Or do you think she's stringing you along again like she did the time before?"

Sapphire smiled and shook her head. "I don't know what she's up to. But I did tell her I feel you may be able to remember on your own. And it's possible, Charity. If you were to reconnect . . . to integrate your personalities back into just you, you would remember everything without Faith's cooperation."

"Yet the question remains: Can I handle knowing it? Can I handle it, Sapphire? To be honest with you, I'm just not so sure that I can."

Chapter 6

But every man is tempted, when he is drawn away of his own lust, and enticed.
                                    —James 1:14

Bentley Strong was glad he had signed up for the Deliverance support group. He was still having major problems even though he had been prayed for. After he'd gone to the altar about his stronghold, he went home and, later that night, gathered up all his magazines, books, tapes, and DVDs with pornography. Around 3 a.m., he drove them to a Dumpster near an apartment complex away from his upscale neighborhood. It was difficult to throw away so many years of collecting. It took him four trips carrying large boxes to his car to get everything out of his house. But he refused to take a chance on Marcella catching him and learning about his problem. She just could never know.

That's what made him go up front on Sunday. That and what Pastor Landris said.

"You don't have to tell anybody what you've done or what you're doing right now. That's between you and God," Pastor Landris had said. "Just come and bring it with you to the altar. Take that first step, why don't you?"

Pastor Landris had also told them while in the conference room that everybody's manifestation may not be immediate. He advised them it might take some work on their part. But that was okay. "Just trust in the Holy Spirit as you do your part. God will work out the rest," Pastor Landris said.

Bentley was definitely struggling. Even with everything out of his house, he found his television still had the Playboy channel (with a special access code to unlock it, of course). He had called to have that channel taken off, but naturally it hadn't been done immediately—just a ploy of the devil. Two days later, he found himself unlocking the channel for a mere few minutes of a glance that turned into two hours of intense gawking.

Before Wednesday, he had thought about not going to the Deliverance support Bible study; he didn't want anyone knowing he possibly had a problem he couldn't beat. But he knew if he didn't go, he would be right back where he had started from, if not worse.

"If any of you are dealing with any type of an addiction," Minister Jackson said during Wednesday night's Bible study, "you must rid your house and your immediate access of all forms of that temptation. Don't give the devil any room to enter in. All it takes is a crack to get a toe in the door. And that's all Satan needs, to get his toe in the door. If you're serious about getting rid of a stronghold, you can't be playing around. If you're subject to smoking, then place cigarettes out of your reach.

Don't keep one around for emergencies. If you drink, remove all forms of alcohol from your house. Don't even keep wine in the kitchen cabinet for cooking. If you're prone to gossip, stay off the telephone, especially when it's someone you know you're going to start up with. If pornography is your problem, you need to turn your eye gates and ear gates away. Don't try to sneak a little look. There's no such thing as a little look. When you're feeling tempted in an area, take out your Bible and start reading it. Beat your stronghold with the Word." He held up his oversized Bible.

People began to snicker and giggle quietly.

"I'm serious. That's a great way to consciously break yourself of anything. Put your attention on something else. As soon as your mind goes to the wrong thing, go get your Bible, sit down, and start reading as long as the other thing is trying to rear its iron head inside your mind. If you're really being pulled in an area, you could end up a Bible scholar in no time flat using this strategy. I know it sounds like I'm trying to make a joke, but reading the Bible will take your mind off what's trying to get your attention. If it's not appropriate to read the Bible, then quote scriptures you have memorized. You'll be replacing negative thoughts with what God says. It doesn't get any better than that."

So that's what Bentley tried doing over the next few days. And he found himself reading his Bible *a lot*.

Then it happened,

He was on the Internet, and those e-mails kept coming and coming with subjects that couldn't help but draw his attention. He fought and fought, but before he knew anything, he had clicked open an e-mail, and there it was—a photo inside the e-mail. He mulled over how underhanded this was, especially with the number of children online daily. The thought began to disgust him. He had a child of his own on the way.

Sitting there staring at the photo that some sicko had e-mailed him trying to entice his patronage to see more (at a cost, of course) by clicking on a link, he realized how little these people really cared about anybody other than themselves. And if he continued on this path, he was part of the problem and not part of the solution. If there was not a market for it, and a lucrative one at that, then these scumbags wouldn't go to such lengths to get e-mails into people's in-boxes who didn't even request it to begin with as they seek out old and new blood to contaminate.

He logged off the Internet and went downstairs to find his wife. "Marcella, I need to talk to you about something," he said.

Marcella was chopping bell peppers. She stopped and looked up.

"I don't know quite how to begin. I have a serious problem, and I need help."

Marcella put down the knife, rinsed off her hands, and walked over to her husband as she dried her hands. "What is it?" She had a look of fear on her face as she waited.

He looked hard into her brown eyes. "I have an addiction."

"An addiction? To what? Drugs?"

"No." He looked down at his hand, then back up again. "Porn."

"What?" She flopped down in a chair at the kitchen table. "Porn?" Her voice shrieked. "Porn? When did this happen?"

"I've had this problem for a while now. It started back when I was a teenager."

"But I don't understand. You were a deacon at the other church we just left. You're on track to work in the ministry now that we're members of Followers of Jesus Faith Worship Center. And you're telling me you're addicted to porn? Pornography? So what are you saying? I wasn't enough woman for you that you had to go elsewhere?"

"Come on, Marcella. It's not like I actually cheated on you."

"Yes, it is! It's exactly like you cheated on me. You're telling me you have a need . . . a desire to look at other people . . . other naked people . . . naked women other than me, your own wife, in order for you to be satisfied? My God, that is so sick, Bentley!"

Bentley squatted down and tried to hold her hands. She jerked away.

"Marcella, please listen to me. Just give me a chance to try and explain."

Marcella looked him in the eyes as she wiped away tears that now flowed from her own. "Go ahead. Explain. Tell me how inadequate I must be as a wife. Tell me how unattractive I must be that it would cause you, even after we married, to sneak behind my back so you could be with other women."

"I'm not with other women. They're just pictures and movies. Not real flesh. Entertainment, just like those books you've been reading lately. You know the ones."

"Oh, don't you dare. Don't you dare! There's no comparison!"

"No comparison? You read books that go into detail about sexual encounters. Remember you've read passages to me and to some of your girl-friends over the phone to show how 'juicy' the story was. Those books described certain acts and body parts so vividly, who needs photos! But that's okay. I don't suppose you see that as a problem: the fact that you get turned on by books without pictures because they're only words. Well, images are pictures. And words create images. You love to read your little romance novels and to watch your little soap operas, too. What do you think those seemingly innocent type things are doing for you?"

Marcella looked at him. With teeth clenched, she spoke. "Don't you even try it! Don't you dare try and turn this on me. We're talking about you looking at naked pictures of women and men per-forming sexual acts. You know how I feel about men who look at porn. So don't you dare use me as a scapegoat or try to justify what you do!"

"I wasn't," Bentley said as he stood up, reached down to grab her and pull her close to him. "I didn't mean to say all of that. All I came in here to do was to confess to you that I have a problem. Two Sun-days ago, you asked why I went to the altar. Well, I went up there for prayer hoping that would solve everything. But it didn't. And I have tried, Marcella. I am trying. Every pornographic thing I had here in the house, I threw it away. But all I can think about lately is getting some more. I need help! I'm at-tending the Deliverance support Bible study, but I need your help, too. I don't want to do anything to lose you; I need you in my life."

Marcella cried as she allowed him to hold her.

"We're going to fix this," he said in between her sobs. "Together. You and I. I promise I'm going to find a way to make things right. You mean too much to me. Our family means too much. I'm confessing my sins to you just like the Bible says to do. And I am going to beat this! Just please, stick with me. I need you."

Chapter 7

For he hath made him to be sin for us, who knew no sin; that we might be made the righteousness of God in him.
                              —2 Corinthians 5:21

"I don't know what I could have been thinking," Arletha Brown said as soon as she and Memory started out of the church's parking lot following the service. "Before I thought about it good, there I was standing up there at the altar with that preacher, sporting—what do they call them? Dreadlocks? Yeah . . . dreadlocks to be prayed for. Me, standing up there with all those sinners who, God only knows, are committing all kinds of un-Godlike acts against my Father in heaven. I must have just gotten caught up in the wave or something."

"Well, you weren't the only one. I went up there as well," Memory said.

"You probably went because you saw me. I'm sure your respect for my walk with the Lord caused you to examine your own life in that moment and compare it to mine. Of course you would come up there when you saw me. You figured if I was up there, it was the right thing to do. I'm so sorry,

Elaine. I'm usually careful about what I do in my life. I don't know what happened with me today. Maybe they really are a cult. And maybe that Pastor Landris did some kind of mind control stuff that caused us not to think straight."

"I don't think they're a cult," Memory said. "He's a powerful preacher." She saw the disapproving look Arletha threw her way. "In my opinion. I'm just trying to figure out why his name is familiar to me. But a lot of what he said made so much sense. It's practical, everyday-living type teaching."

"A lot of what he said made sense for those who are practicing sin. I just can't believe I got suckered into going up there. I don't have any sin in my life. I usually am at church six days a week except here recently. I've been in church all of my natural-born life, really. I treat folks right. I mean, look at you." Arletha glanced over at Memory as she got on the freeway. "You needed somewhere to stay, and what did I do? I took you in just like the Bible says for us to do. I'm not charging you much to stay with me. I just allowed you, a stranger, in my home like the Good Book says is the right thing to do."

"You did, and I appreciate that more than you'll know, too."

"I know you do. But I did it because the Lord speaks about those types of things in His Word. They're important to Him. You came to Birmingham with nowhere to go. You couldn't get into an apartment on your own. And then to hear how your own flesh and blood—your daughter and granddaughter—turned their backs on you the way they did. Especially after all you did for them. Your husband dying, leaving you to be a single mother whose own mother ended up dying while you were still rather young. You having to fend for yourself without any support system at such a tender age."

Arletha continued, shaking her head slowly as she spoke. "Your daughter having been burned in a fire like she was . . . I can't even imagine what all you've endured. And then for your family to leave you out on the street with no place to turn like they did, that's just a sin and a disgrace. Taking you to the bus stop and dropping you off, leaving you there all alone. But the devil is a lie! 'Cause God has provided for you through me. And I've got a feeling," she began to sing the words, "everything's gonna be all right!"

"Yes. And I thank you for allowing me to come live in your home." Memory looked out the window. It was strange. Since she had gone forward to be prayed for, something different was going on inside her. When she first met with Arletha on that day, she didn't exactly tell her the whole truth. Everything she told her, other than that her name was Elaine Robertson, was a variation of a lie. And she almost totally lied about her name, which would have backfired on her since Arletha ended up asking for some form of identification before she would allow her to step foot into her home. Memory had something that still had Elaine Robertson on it. She didn't tell Arletha that her first name was Memory or that her daughter, Lena Patterson, lived in Atlanta, just two hours away.

"You can never be too careful," Arletha had said. "I may be a child of God, but Satan would like nothing more than to put a soldier like me completely out of service. Well, God gave me good sense and a gift of discernment. And my senses tell me even though you appear to be a nice person, I need to make sure you're who you say you are."

"I understand," Memory had said, while handing her an old ID card with that name clearly printed on it. "I don't drive so I don't have a license. This is all I have. I hope it will do," she said. Arletha looked at it and nodded her approval.

But Memory stood ready to flee at a moment's notice, just in case. Her bags remained virtually packed at all times. She'd originally only needed a place to lay low until she could figure out what her next move should be. Arletha's place turned out to be a blessing in disguise. No one would ever think to look for her there. No paper trails. Things were working out perfectly, better than anything she could have planned herself.

That was, until today. As she sat there in church listening to this man pour his heart out to the people, a heart that clearly loved God and loved God's people, Memory suddenly realized who she really was in Christ. There was nothing she had done in her past that was so bad that she couldn't come back to the Lord and ask Him for forgiveness. She had wronged so many people, so many over these past decades.

Starting with her own mother, who had done nothing but try to show her love and protect her all of those years. She had wronged Lena, oh, how wrong she had treated her own child. How could she have come back home after her mother died and taken everything away from Lena, her own flesh and blood like she'd done?

She'd left her sixteen-year-old daughter to practically fend for herself with nothing. She'd taken everything her mother left for Lena and sold it. She had—in actuality—bullied her own child and stolen her inheritance. And for what? Just so she could do what she wanted to do. Today for the first time in her life, walking up to that altar, she'd openly acknowledged she hadn't really cared about anyone other than herself.

Memory thought about the necklace . . . the famous Alexandrite necklace. The only thing Lena had left from the past. And what had Memory done? She came looking for Lena, not because she cared about her. Not because she was family. Not to ask for her forgiveness. She came because there was a million-dollar reward on a necklace she believed Lena still held in her possession. Memory had come for the necklace, pure and simple. And nothing or no one else had mattered. But she had also learned the hard way: you really do reap what you sow.

Whatever had occurred to her when she went to the altar, she knew she had to shake it off. It didn't pay to be nice. Lena was living proof of that fact. Look at what being nice and doing the right thing had gotten her: mistreated, stepped on, used, and abused by the very people she tried to love and help. The last thing Memory needed was to go soft, especially now. And whoever was looking for her might be out there trying to find her still. She had to shake off this feeling of wanting to tell the truth. She had to shake off this desire to want to confess all she'd done and this feeling of wanting to talk with someone about it.

She sat on the couch in the den next to Arletha and listened to her as she went on about how righteous she was because of her works. Memory may not have been as religious as Arletha, but she knew that we are made righteous because of what Jesus did. It was crystal clear to Memory that Arletha was neck deep in religious traditions. Arletha believed what she was told by others as being gospel without question or without ever searching scriptures and seeking the true interpretation from the Holy Spirit for herself.

Memory smiled as she thought about the story of the prodigal son. How most folks focused on the son who did the outward sins. As she listened to Arletha going on and on, even after they arrived at the house, about how perfect she was, how right she was, how wrong everybody who contradicts her was, Memory couldn't help but see the other son in the story—the supposedly good son.

The son who became upset when his brother returned home after finding himself in the pig pen . . . the son who—because he was only focused on himself—couldn't celebrate a lost soul coming back to his father. A father who had watched and waited for his son to one day return back to him; a father who put a ring on his was-dead-but-now-he's-alive son; a father who told his servants to kill the fatted calf so they could make a joyful noise in celebration of his son's return home. Memory's thoughts were directed toward the other son, who appeared perfect on the outside, but inside, he had what could only be described as sins of the heart, and he didn't even know it.

It was obvious to Memory that Arletha was representative of the good son, the son who stayed home and didn't do anything wrong. The son who believed himself righteous because of all *he* had done, not realizing he was righteous because of what his father had done for him.

"But by the grace of God, go I," Memory said.

Arletha turned to Memory. "What?"

Memory didn't realize she'd just spoken those words out loud. She turned and smiled at Arletha. "I was just thinking about how well some people have it and how they think it's because of who they are and what they do. But you know, I realize if it wasn't for the grace of God, where would any of us be?"

"What?" Arletha said again as she frowned at Memory. "Sister Elaine, what are you babbling like a brook about?"

Memory smiled. "Oh, nothing. I was just thanking God for His grace and mercy."

"See what I mean? I'm talking about that cult-leading preacher over there brainwashing those unsuspecting folks into believing his lies, and you're mumbling about grace. We will be saved after we are judged by how well we live down here on earth. God is going to see who lived right and who was living wrong. He's going to judge us based on those criteria, and I don't want to hear no mumbo-jumbo from some woman-haired-looking man talking about just accepting Jesus as your savior makes one saved."

She sucked her teeth and lifted her nose higher into the air. "But by grace? Yes, accepting Jesus gets you started. But you've got to live right and perfect. That's why I don't have time to be trying to lead folks to Christ. I'm too busy trying to get into heaven my own self. I'm gonna get mine; the rest of them had better be trying to get their own the best way they can. You included. And if they don't make it in, it won't be any different than in Noah's day when he built that ark." She patted her face with her handkerchief as she got up off the couch and beckoned for Memory to follow her as she headed for the kitchen.

"Noah told them folks it was going to rain," she said as she glanced at Memory. "But did they listen? No. When it started raining, they were beating down the door trying to get in. But it was too late then. That's the way it's going to be for a lot of these folks living today. Well, I'm planning on being in heaven to sport my long, white robe and wear my golden crown with all my jewels encrusted in it. Oh, Miss America won't have a thing on me! Praise the Lord. It's just good to be on the Lord's side."

Memory looked at Arletha and smiled. *Yes, this was definitely a great hiding place.* No one ever seemed to care to come around dear Sister Arletha Brown. And the more Memory sat and listened to her talk, the more she came to understand just why.

Chapter 8

*Submit yourselves therefore to God. Resist
the devil, and he will flee from you.*
—James 4:7

Darius was determined to talk with Fatima.
Every day, for three weeks, he called and left a
message on her home answering machine.

"Look, Fatima. I'm not giving up on us. I love
you too much, girl, just to let you walk out of my
life like this. You're going to have to talk to me
eventually. You can't turn me away forever."

"Fatima, this is Darius. Listen, I really need to
talk. Things aren't going well with me and my wife
these days. I just need a friend. Somebody to talk
to, that's all. Do you remember when you told me
no matter what, we'd always be friends? Well, I
don't have anybody who understands me like you
do. Come on now, if you're there, pick up. I just
need to talk. I love you, Boo."

"Look, girl. Now this has gone on long enough.
I don't deserve to be treated like this. I've been
straight up with you from the beginning. You knew
I was married, so don't be acting like I did you

wrong. You can't just shut a man down like this. I thought you were different from the other women out there. I'd expect something like this from somebody trifling, but not from you. All I'm asking you to do is talk to me. That's all. Talk."

"Now see, Fatima. A real woman would have at least cut things off to a man's face. You know you're wrong. But that's okay. That's o-kay. You of all people know: God does not like ugly. What goes around comes around. You're gonna reap what you sow. Whatever you put out there is going to come back to you one of these days."

"Okay, okay. Listen. I was wrong for what I said the last time. I'm just so messed up right now, I don't know what to do. You won't talk to me. I'm losing my mind over here. Is that what you want? Me to lose my mind? To go crazy? You know I'm crazy in love with you. I didn't realize how much you meant to me until now. They say you don't miss your water until your well runs dry. Well, girl, I miss you. My pure, sweet water. What do you want from me? You want me to leave my wife? Is that what this is about?"

Fatima had listened to each message, sometimes more than once. She was even tempted to save a few of them, but in her spirit she heard, "Delete it. Don't even go there."

"God, this is so hard!" she said as she lay on her back across her bed. "You know I love him. And you know how much I love him. I'm trying to do the right thing here, but these feelings just won't go away. What am I supposed to do with these feelings I have for him? Tell me, God. What am I supposed to do with my love? I love him. I don't have a clue how to turn off these thoughts that keep popping up in my mind. I can't seem to turn off my heart from loving him either. Do you have any idea how hard it is to see his number come across my caller ID and not pick up, or to hear his voice and resist literally snatching up the phone? Do you know how much I want to be inside his arms right this minute so I can forget about the miserable days I've had without him for what feels like forever? Do you have any idea just how much I really, really miss him?! I'm trying to do what's right, but this hold is so strong."

Fatima's phone rang. It was Darius again. She listened as he left yet another message.

"Okay, Fatima. Have it your way. You want me to leave you alone. Fine. I'll leave you alone," Darius said with a defeated voice. "I'm going to work on my marriage. I'm going to put more attention toward my wife and children. Are you happy now? Is this what you want? Well, you got it. I'm leaving you alone. Alone. Are you listening to this message? If you ever change your mind about us, give me a call. Hopefully, I'll treat you better than you're treating me right now. I didn't deserve to be dumped this way and you know it. My only crime was falling in love with you. That was all. I suppose that's why we men are the way we are. It seems we just can't show our sensitive side. Women like you just end up taking our hearts and stomping on them when we do. I suppose had I been a dog, like you and your friends say most men are, then things would be different between us now, huh? Just got to have a rough neck. A good man can't show a woman how much he loves her. I see that now. That's what I've taken away from this experience, Fatima. Never let a woman know you truly love her. 'Cause if you do, she'll treat you like a bug. She'll turn on the light to watch you scamper around; she'll laugh when she sees you're trying to find your way to a safe place; she may even play with you to make you believe she thinks you're cute; and then splat!—she'll squash you when you least expect it to happen. Well, Fatima. I get your message loud and clear. I see how you really feel about what I believed we had together." He laughed. "I guess the joke really is on me."

She replayed it. "End of messages," the prerecorded woman's voice on the machine said after the message finished.

Fatima began to cry.

The Word of God is your answer.

She pressed play on the machine, skipping messages until she came to the one Darius had just left her, then listened to it again. She began to cry harder.

The Word of God is your answer, she heard again in her spirit.

She picked up her Bible off the nightstand, sat back on the bed, opened the Bible, and began to randomly flip through the pages. She stopped; her eyes looked down upon Ephesians the fifth chapter, verse three: "But fornication, and all uncleanness, or covetousness, let it not be once named among you, as becometh saints."

"That's great, Lord. Great! Is that all You have for me? I hope You know that wasn't especially comforting for me. I was hoping for something that would make me feel better. Look, God, I'm trying. I really am trying. Can you help a sister out down here? Please, just make it stop. I beg You; please, make the hurt stop."

She lay down, buried her face into her brand-new, baby-blue bedspread, and cried herself to sleep.

Chapter 9

And if thy right eye offend thee, pluck it out,
and cast it from thee: for it is profitable for
thee that one of thy members should perish,
and not that thy whole body should be cast
into hell.

—Matthew 5:29

"Bentley, we need to go and talk with the pastor," Marcella said to her husband as she held the remote control to the television in her right hand.

He looked up at her as she stood over him. "What? Why?"

"You and I need to make an appointment to go talk to Pastor Landris."

"Talk about what?"

"About your problem." She tossed the remote control onto his lap. "For starters, why the Playboy channel is available on our television downstairs in the den."

Bentley moved his foot off the coffee table and set the remote on it. He had been asleep watching the TV upstairs, but quickly stood to his feet. "Look, I called them last week, Monday of last week to be exact, to take it off. I guess they haven't gotten around to doing it just yet. I'll call them again. Right now in fact." He walked toward the phone.

"Oh, and I guess you just couldn't resist watching it while you were waiting, huh? I suppose there was always a lock on that channel. All this time, you've had this. I suppose you must have forgotten to lock it back when you finished watching it late last night or early this morning."

"What are you talking about?"

"Don't 'what are you talking about' me. I suppose you were so into the program, you forgot to lock the channel back after you finished. That's what I'm talking about. When I turned on the TV just now, guess what came up and guess who got an eyeful?"

He came over to her. "Baby, look. I'm sorry. This won't ever happen again. I promise you that. Look, I'm going to call them right now and *demand* that they take that channel off our cable today."

"Yeah. And call the church while you're at it and make us an appointment," Marcella said.

"Look now. It's bad enough that I had to tell you I have this problem. There's no way I plan to tell a man of God—my pastor at that—I'm having problems with pornography, of all things."

Marcella frowned. "I don't believe what you're standing here saying. You have a problem, Bentley. *Pluck* it out. You need help, *Bentley. Pluck it out.* You've got to get rid of it." She pressed her lips together. "And I know you're not telling me because of some foolish pride on your part, you don't want to go and talk to the man God has placed in our lives as our overseer to help us in cases such as this very thing? I know that's not what I'm hearing here."

Bentley grabbed Marcella by both shoulders and squared his body with hers. "Do you have any idea how he's going to look at me if he hears about this? I will look weak to him. Do you honestly believe he'll want to let me work in any ministry at the church, let alone place me in charge of one, if he learns what I've been doing? I can answer that. No. Listen, Marcella. Baby, you and I can handle this. I told you. I shared my weakness with you and God. You and God are all I need to overcome this. Look at how God has already used you to help me just today. You're keeping me straight."

Marcella wriggled out of his grip. "Yeah, you've had me all this time, and a lot of good that seems to have done you. No, Bentley. This is spiritual warfare, and we need some machine-gun-powered Holy Ghost help for you, I see. Pastor Landris is not here to judge you or anybody else. He's here to help. He preached on strongholds because he knew people were dealing with these very type of things in their everyday life. Some are maybe dealing with stronger holds than others, that's all. But we're all dealing with something or other. The Bible says pride goes before destruction. If you're too proud to let a man of God know what you're dealing with so he can help you, then you're likely going to be destroyed by this."

"See, I've just never had to face reality before like I do now. I know what I'm up against. I can beat this. We just need to pray and trust God. We don't need to spread our business all over the place. How do you know Pastor Landris won't judge me? How do you even know if he'll keep something like this just between us? I don't know him that well. He could be just like some of these other preachers we've dealt with who divulge folks' personal business, in their own little sneaky way. That's how a lot of folks' business gets to circulating in the church. That's how some folks find out other people are having problems in their household—church folks spreading it among church folks."

"You're referring to that incident with Pastor Rudd at the church we left, aren't you? When he got up and told the congregation that time that we all needed to pray mightily for Brother Wayne because he was having some serious marital issues."

"Precisely," Bentley said. "Who even had a clue that Brother Wayne and his wife were having problems? But after Pastor Rudd said that from the pulpit, it seemed like everybody and their brother made it their business to try and find out what exactly was going on with them. I don't want something like that happening to us. Nobody has a clue what goes on in our house, and I'd like to keep it that way."

"I don't believe Pastor Landris is like that at all. He's so down-to-earth. And have you seen how excited he is about his wife being pregnant? He's just like you and me. I believe we need to see about getting an appointment to have him counsel us with what you're going through now," Marcella said. "He's a man; I'm sure he understands."

"What if we can't see him anytime soon? What if we have to speak with one of the other ministers?" Bentley shook his head. "I don't see myself talking with anybody else about this. If I have to confide in anyone besides you, it would have to be Pastor Landris. That's it."

"All I know is that we need help. Pastor Landris seems to really care. And I'm going to be honest with you, Bentley. I don't know if I can take knowing what you've been doing and finding you're sneaking around still doing it."

"I know. If I can just shut down my thoughts, I would be all right. It's just hard to explain to anybody why I feel I have to keep doing this in the first place."

Marcella bit down on her lip. "Especially since you have all this at home," she said as she did a slight shimmy. "So are you going to call and make an appointment, or do you want me to do it? Because somebody's calling today. Not tomorrow, today."

Bentley took both his hands and slowly slid them down his face. "It's my stronghold; I guess I need to be the one to make the call."

"Yeah, and you need to get that junk off our TV while you're at it. Or we really may be plucking out something for real. I'm not going to stand for this, Bentley. I'm just not."

He reached over and pulled Marcella into his arms. "I'm so sorry. You don't deserve this. You really don't."

Chapter 10

For where your treasure is, there will your heart be also.

—Luke 12:34

"Xavier," Avis said when she came to the glass storm door and saw her husband standing there. She cracked open the door. "What are you doing here?"

"I came to see you. I brought you these." Dr. Holden held up a bouquet of roses.

Avis looked at the flowers. "So I see."

Dr. Holden smiled as he lowered the roses down by his side. "So are you going to let me in or what?"

"It depends."

"On what?"

"On how long you're planning to stay. Five minutes? Ten? Maybe an hour or two since you came all the way from Birmingham to Jacksonville, Florida."

"Avis, I love you. You know that."

"I guess that means a whole day. Whether you love me or not has never been the question." She opened the door wider. "I suppose the question is: is love enough to survive two relationships?"

Dr. Holden stepped inside. "Two relationships?"

"Yeah, two."

He shook his head. "I don't understand. There's no one else other than you."

"Me," she said as she walked toward the sofa and sat down, "and your work."

"I work for you and our children. All of this has been for our family." He came over, placed the flowers on the table in front of her, and sat down next to her. The house was quiet; he knew the children had to be gone. "It's always been about us . . . our family."

She scooted over so their bodies wouldn't touch. "It may have started out that way. But somewhere down the line, it seems you fell more in love with your work than with us. Me and you . . . you and the children . . . us." She shrugged. "I just don't know about *us* anymore, Xavier. But I do know that, as for me, I'm tired of being alone."

"But you're not alone. I come home every night to *you*. I bring my money home to *you*. We've built a family together. Me and you. I thought things were fine."

"See, that's my point. Things aren't fine. When you're not around because you're working nights and practically every day of the week, what exactly do you think I'm doing? Then when you do get home, you're too exhausted to do anything except fall asleep wherever you happen to land at the time."

He looked into her eyes. "I know. I get it."

"You get it? What do you mean, you get it?"

"I get what it feels like for me when you're not around, and I get what it must feel like for you when

I'm not there. It doesn't matter that I think I'm doing something noble by working hard for my family in order for us to have more things . . . life's finer things—"

"Yeah, things," Avis said. "Xavier, here's a news flash for you. We don't care about things. I've *never* really cared about *things*. I care about you. I care that our children really need you in their lives. We want you, not more things."

"I know. I told you. I get it. I've always heard the scripture, 'What does it profit a man to gain the whole world, yet lose his own soul,' and I always applied it to the spiritual side of life. What I get now is: I can work day-in and day-out for the rest of my life to acquire more things, but without having someone to share those things with, it doesn't mean a thing."

Avis looked into his eyes. "That's what I've been trying to get you to see. We have a nice big house, but you're hardly ever there. We drive around in nice cars to nice places, but you can't go because you're always working. The children miss you so much. You're really a wonderful guy, but when you don't spend time with them, how will they ever know? I miss my friend; I miss *doing* things with my friend. I miss laughing about nothing. I miss fixing a meal the way we used to back when we were praying just to be able to pull something together in order for us to have something to eat. I miss *you*."

Dr. Holden took the palm of his hand and placed it softly on Avis's cheek. "I love you."

"I told you, Xavier; I already know you love me." She leaned her face more into his hand as she closed her eyes. "That has never been the question." She sat up straight, then gently moved his hand to his side. "So, how long until you have to go back? I'm sure there must be some crisis needing your immediate attention and you just flew in to quiet this one. I wouldn't doubt if you don't have the plane standing by—even as we speak."

Dr. Holden stood up without saying a word, leaned down and kissed her hard, then headed toward the door. He turned around and looked back with a real sadness on his face.

Avis reluctantly looked up at him. "Precisely what I thought," she whispered.

"Avis, I really do love you. I do."

Avis looked away from his loving gaze. And without another word, Dr. Holden walked out the door. As Avis sat wiping away the tears that had begun to fall, she heard the door as it softly closed.

Five minutes later, there was a banging at the door. "Excuse me, Sweet Woman," Dr. Holden yelled. "But would you be so kind as to open the door for me. I sort of have my hands full."

Avis got up and walked to the door. "Xavier?" she said with a puzzled look on her face. "But I thought . . ." She wiped the tears off her face.

"What? That I'd left. Oh, you don't understand. I'm planning to spend time with my family, uninterrupted time, in fact, for the next three weeks." Dr. Holden walked through the now fully opened door carrying one large suitcase, a duffle bag on his shoulder, and a garment bag. "Whatever my family wants to do, I'm here for them."

"I don't understand. What about your patients? Your practice? All the folks who need and depend upon you? Those 'can't-do-without-you-Dr.-Holden' patients?"

Dr. Holden set the suitcase and the duffle bag on the floor, then took the garment bag and laid it across the arm of the sofa. He walked back to Avis, lifted her face up by her chin, and said, "Well, I suppose they're just going to have to learn how to cope without me, because the next few weeks are reserved exclusively for me and mine."

His eyes began to dance as she blushed. "I told you, Sweet Woman; I get it. I . . . get . . . it. I'm not about to lose the best thing that's ever happened to me, other than accepting Jesus into my life, of course. Dear Sweet Woman, you mean more to me than all the money, all the houses, all the fine cars, and all the fine name-brand clothing. . . ."

Avis smiled. "Well, let's not get *too* carried away. I like my name-brands now."

Dr. Holden leaned down and gently placed a kiss on her lips. "I'm all yours, Mrs. Holden. So there. Now what are you going to do about that?"

Avis smiled as she looked deep into his eyes. "Oh, I believe I have a few ideas, Dr. Holden. After all, you are a real doctor, you know. So we wouldn't have to play doctor." She let out a slight laugh. "I still can't believe you actually came all the way down to my mother's to see me. Do you know how long it's been since you've been anywhere that wasn't work related?"

He kissed her hard again and hugged her like he never wanted to let go. "I know. But this is *just* the beginning."

Avis hugged him just as tightly back. *Dear God: I pray, let him really mean it this time. Let him really mean it.*

Chapter 11

Can a man take fire in his bosom, and his clothes not be burned?

—Proverbs 6:27

"I'll be back in a little while," Edwin yelled as he walked out the door.

Desiree came out of the kitchen just as the front door closed. She had been here before. In the past when Edwin went to the race track, he never told her that's where he was headed. It was always "I'll be back in a little while," which he never was.

Edwin had been doing so well. Desiree was praying after a month of him not gambling that he wasn't slipping back to his old ways.

She was asleep when he came home. Edwin tried to be really quiet so he wouldn't wake her, but Desiree was a light sleeper and she heard him when he went into the bathroom. She opened her eyes and glanced at the clock: 1:17 A.M. Edwin had been gone since a little after seven o'clock, over six hours ago. There was no question now in her mind where he had been: at the race track.

The next morning she awoke and was getting

ready for work. Edwin got up, walked up behind her while she was in the bathroom, and placed a kiss on her neck.

"Good morning, Baby-cakes," Edwin said in his most pleasant voice.

Desiree couldn't understand how he could wake up acting as though last night never happened. "Where were you last night?"

He stopped and looked at her. "No good morning back?"

Desiree turned around completely and stared at him to let him know she was not in the mood to play. "Edwin, where were you last night?"

He smiled. "See, you just can't help but ruin my surprise. Okay, since you just have to." He pulled a wad of money out of his bathrobe pocket and placed it in her hand. "This, my dear, is for you."

Desiree looked at the money he'd just given her. "What is this?"

"Wow, it's been that long since you've seen the real thing, huh? I suppose that's what happens when everybody goes electronic. Direct deposit, debit cards, charge cards, checks, online bill paying. That, Baby-cakes, is what is called cash."

Desiree cocked her head to the side without cracking a smile. "I know this is cash. Where did it come from?"

"It came from me to you. I want you to take it. That's three hundred dollars you hold there. Buy yourself something really nice. You've worked so hard and lost quite a lot of weight in the last month. I think that deserves some kind of a reward," Edwin said.

"Once more. Where did you get this from, Edwin?"

He huffed and walked into the bedroom. "What difference does it make where I got it from? The point is I'm giving it to you."

She followed him. "The point is you're not supposed to be gambling anymore. And this is a lot of money, which I'm sure if you're giving me this much it means you have even more than this. Which means, you probably went to the dog track last night."

"Do you want to know what your problem is? You've become such a nag, you don't even know when to turn it off. Okay, so I went to the track last night. It's been over a month, and I haven't gone anywhere near a track or anywhere else where I could gamble. But yesterday, I kept running into the same numbers: six, one, eight. Everywhere I turned those numbers were popping up in my face. I took it as a sign. And you know what, last night I won! And I won big, too. I played those numbers and ended up hitting a trifecta."

"So why was it after one this morning before you got home?"

"Because, as it turned out, I had to play almost every race in order to hit it. But I didn't use a lot of money. And the only thing I played was those three numbers. I boxed them and played them straight. It cost me six dollars a race to box them and two dollars to play them straight: eight dollars all total. But I promised myself I was not going to veer from my plan. I also made a deal with God that if those numbers didn't come in, I was through with gambling forever." He grabbed Desiree's hand and took the money he'd just given her out of it. Holding the bills up to her face, he said, "But I won!

Can't you see? And the only person I was thinking about was you and how great you've been even through your own problems. You stuck to your guns. You haven't smoked, that I know of anyway, and just look at you . . . slimming all down. What did you tell me? Two whole dress sizes?"

Desiree walked away.

"Woman, what is your problem? You've worked so hard to stop smoking and overeating. Look at yourself, Baby-cakes. Just look at you. We've walked together almost every day. I've seen how hard it's been for you to resist things that aren't good for you. I wanted to win this money for you. I wanted you to know how proud I am of you and just how much I love you."

Desiree stopped and turned around. "You didn't do that for me, Edwin. So don't try and make yourself feel better about having taken your first official slide back, possibly to your old, destructive ways."

"Look, I went one time. It's been over a month. Going to the track one time doesn't mean I have a problem. Can't you just give me credit for all I've accomplished, like I've done with you? Do you have any idea how hard staying away from the track and the casinos has been for me these past weeks?"

"Which only proves my point, Edwin. Anytime something is that hard, it means it's a stronghold. Sure, I'll give you credit. I'll be the first one to give you your due. You went a whole month without gambling. It was hard, but you did it. And I was so proud of you. But the fact remains: you couldn't resist going last night. What's going to keep you from going again tonight or tomorrow night or the night after that and the night after that?"

"It was for fun! It doesn't mean I'm going back into any trap. If God had wanted me out of it for good, He could have ensured I lost. But I won with numbers that came to me as though they were from God. I won!"

"Edwin, don't put God in this. You had some numbers. You went to the track. You won with those numbers. Think about it: if I were your enemy trying to pull you back into something that will hurt you later down the road, what would be the best way to do that?"

"What are you talking about?"

"I'm saying if I were Satan and I wanted to get you back into the same trap I knew you'd prayed about getting out of, I'd do just what happened last night. I would put thoughts in your mind. Convince you to take a step to see if it would work. I'd ensure you won that time, because one leads to two." She walked back over to him and took the money he'd given her. "Edwin, why don't you just keep this money. Because I have a feeling if you continue on the path you're on now, you're going to need this a lot more than I will. And just for the record: I'll be handling the bills from here on out. So if you get yourself in too deep, you won't end up taking us both down with you this time around." She crammed the money into his hand and walked out of the room.

"You are a trip!" Edwin said. "A trip! I don't have a problem, Desiree. I go to the track one time in a month and you blow everything all out of proportion. You don't want the money? Fine! I'll keep it then." He shoved the money back into his bathrobe pocket. "I don't have a problem. Do you hear me?" he yelled at her as he watched her disappear down the stairs. "I might have had one earlier, but I have things under control now."

He walked back into the bedroom. "Women!"

Chapter 12

And I will come down and talk with thee there: and I will take of the spirit which is upon thee, and will put it upon them; and they shall bear the burden of the people with thee, that thou bear it not thyself alone.
—Numbers 11:17

Pastor Landris was tired. He'd been working a bit longer because of the increase in appointments the congregation had been scheduling since he finished the series on strongholds. There were others, ministers and trained laypeople, on staff who were also available to counsel. But for some reason, most people still preferred to talk to him. No matter how the staff told those who called that there were others just as good, capable, and competent as Pastor Landris in this area (if not better), there was just something about them being able to talk with "their pastor" that permeated throughout the congregation. Pastor Landris was allowing appointments later in the evening and nights as well as half of Saturdays, just to accommodate the increased demand.

"Landris, you know you can't keep this up," forty-four-year-old Johnnie Mae said when she watched him practically fall asleep while eating supper one night.

"This won't last forever. What else can I do?"

"Well, let's evaluate this objectively. I'm pregnant, and you're missing out on a good part of that because you're staying later at the church to handle everything you're being required to do. You're too tired to spend time with, let alone enjoy, your own family—which have I mentioned lately?—is about to grow to one more person come this August." She gently patted her four-and-a-half-month pregnant stomach. "I'm not trying to tell you what to do, but Landris, if you're not careful, you're going to end up a byproduct of your own sermon."

"Meaning?"

"Okay, you were teaching on strongholds. I'd say you could possibly be embarking on one if not two of those you emphasized during your teaching: the workaholic who neglects himself and his family and religious tradition."

"What?"

"You're neglecting your health by not getting enough rest because you're extending your time at the church. That's fine, but is that wisdom? You're neglecting your family because of the time you're taking away from us so you can extend your time to work at the church. I'm not complaining, but I am reminded of the scripture where Moses's father-in-law, Jethro, in Exodus eighteen-fourteen asked him; 'What is this thing you're doing to the people? why sittest thou thyself alone, and all the people stand by you from morning unto evening?' Moses thought he should be the one listening to everyone's problems and concerns and giving counsel, but the line was always huge and the people waited so long just to be able to talk to him. Moses's father-in-law suggested he choose others for the people to go to, so as to take some responsibility off Moses, and that wouldn't cause the people to go through such hardship just to get the help they so desperately needed."

"We already have others on staff who counsel, but for some reason, people still insist they would rather speak to their pastor, in this case me. For some reason, they don't want to make appointments with the others available to them, some of whom they could see that same day if not the very next," Pastor Landris said.

"That leads me to the second of the two strongholds: religious traditions. You and seemingly all of these members believe that the pastor should be available to all the people of the congregation at all times. That's fine when it's a small group, but have you checked the count of the membership recently? Since we moved into the new building, the place is practically full both services. There is no way one man—meaning you—can keep up a tradition of being everywhere; attending every thing; performing every wedding, funeral, baby, house, and car dedication; going to see every person who's sick or has lost loved ones; teach, preach, and counsel every member of this church. No way is this humanly possible. At least, not that I see. Is that fair to the people? Is it fair to you?"

"And more importantly, is it fair to my own family?" Pastor Landris said.

"It's about balance. You just need to be sure

there's balance in your life. You're human, Landris, not God. As for your family, I believe we'll be okay, but that's not the point I'm trying to make here. I don't want to lose you to a heart attack or stroke either."

"No, even though I'm the pastor, if I'm not careful and if I continue on this track, I'm going to find myself having to make an appointment to get some counseling myself. Even preachers—I clearly see now—have to be alert to what's really going on."

"So, what are you planning to do?"

Pastor Landris looked toward the window. "I suppose I need to address this with the congregation. I believe when we take the time to teach and explain things better, people understand it better. I'll just have to have a heart-to-heart talk with them about what's really going on and see if I can't get them to understand that we do have people in place to meet their needs. And that my not being able to counsel every single member personally doesn't mean I don't love them any less. In fact, because of my love for them, I want them to get assistance and have their needs met as quickly as humanly possible. It's not fair for them to have to wait for months to be able to talk with me when they could speak with someone in a few days and resolve what's going on in their lives that much quicker. I need to persuade them to agree to speak with those we have prayerfully appointed and anointed into these positions."

"You do understand the problems this will likely cause though. If you counsel some and not others, people will accuse you of favoritism. So, I think you need to consider how you approach this and try to alleviate those types of accusations in advance."

"In the past, my decision was: whatever I did for one, I should do for all or not do for anybody at all. But it wouldn't be fair for me to not see anyone because I can't see everyone. I'll really have to pray about how to implement this," Pastor Landris said.

"I spoke with Sarah Fleming today. Just briefly. I feel so bad for her. Three and a half years and she still hasn't been able to catch up with her daughter. She turns ninety this year. I just don't know how much longer she has—" Johnnie Mae placed her hand on her stomach.

"What is it?" Pastor Landris asked, seeing his wife had stopped talking in midsentence.

Johnnie Mae reached down and took his hand. She placed it firmly on her stomach and waited. "There. Did you feel it?" she said with a smile.

Pastor Landris bucked his eyes and started laughing. "That was the baby? The baby kicked? Oh, my goodness, I felt our baby kick!"

Johnnie Mae laughed. "Yeah. The baby kicked last night and I wanted you to feel it, but you were still at church. That's what I mean. I suppose if you're not careful, even being a man of God, you may miss out on some true blessings from the Lord."

Pastor Landris continued to hold his hand on her stomach, hoping to feel another kick. "I get it. I think people believe because we preach something it means we have mastered it and that we have all the answers. Even we ministers need to lis-

ten to the sermons and practice what we preach."
He smiled. "Oh, wow! I felt it again! Man, this is so
awesome!" He leaned down close to her stomach.
"Hey there! Can you hear me in there? This is your
father speaking. Daddy's going to have to do a little better out here. I can't wait to meet you. Keep
on kicking, little one. Keep on kicking."

"Oh yeah. That's easy for Daddy to say," Johnnie
Mae said as she looked down and smiled. "Daddy
doesn't have a clue how big you're going to get inside there before you make your grand debut."
She took Pastor Landris's hand and held it as she
looked into his hazelnut-colored eyes. "But don't you
worry," she said to the baby, although her eyes remained on Pastor Landris, "you'll have plenty of
opportunities to jump on Daddy."

Pastor Landris smiled, then leaned over and
kissed her. "Plenty." He grinned even more.

Chapter 13

*Again, the kingdom of heaven is like unto a
merchant man, seeking goodly pearls.*
                                    —Matthew 13:45

"Hi, Xavier. It's Sapphire."

"Sapphire. To what do I owe the pleasure?"
Dr. Holden said.

"Just checking on you and seeing how things are
going."

"A week and a half and I'm actually learning
how to spend time with my family. It's amazing
how hard it can be to kick back, relax, and just
have some fun. I've been conditioned all of my
adult life to work. I had to learn how to sit still and
enjoy myself. It's like I convinced myself to believe
that I had to forever be doing something in order
to prove my worth to the world. I've learned these
past few weeks, there are other things in life besides work, and I'm worth it because I am."

"Physician, heal thyself," Sapphire said. "I'm sure
this has been quite an adjustment for you."

"And I'm sure you didn't merely call just to

check on me. So—how's everything back in good old B-ham?"

"Things are going pretty well here. A lot of your patients weren't too happy when they learned you really were taking off this time and that you were serious about other people filling in for you. A few of them threatened to track you down and drag you back. But when I counseled them on how crazy that actually sounded, they decided I was right and changed their tune."

He laughed. "Leave it to you."

"So are you still planning to stay the entire three weeks like you said?"

"Absolutely. This is one of many promises I've made to my wife that I'm definitely going to keep. It has been such a joy spending time with my family. I don't know what I was thinking about before. When I consider all the time and experiences I've missed out on with my family while chasing the almighty dollar . . . now that's what's really crazy. I think it's true what people say about when we reach the end of our lives. We're not going to regret not having spent more time at the office; we're going to wish we'd spent more time with the ones we loved. I don't want that regret hanging over my head. In fact, I think I'm going to see what I can do to redeem some of the time I've already lost. I just may take off another week or two. The kids are all homeschooled, so hey."

"I hear you, Xavier. Listen though, if and when you do decide to return to work, I need to be placed pretty high up on your 'got to get with as soon as possible' list."

"What's up?"

"Charity, Faith, however not too much Hope."

He laughed. "The blessed Trinity. It sounds so funny the way you said it, though. 'Charity, Faith, however not too much Hope.' Like you're being prophetic or something."

"You know what I'm dealing with. Anyway, I don't intend to make you break your no-work-while-you're-vacationing-and-spending-time-with-your-family rule. This will keep until your return. Meanwhile, Faith is insisting she'll talk to you and only you. She maintains she'll tell you what transpired with Charity. I told her it would be a while before you came back, but she declared she's more than willing to wait on your imminent return."

"Still doesn't like you, huh?"

Sapphire laughed. "That's putting it mildly. It's funny. Charity adores me. Hope likes me just fine. But Faith can't stand to be in the same room with me. I have such an interesting job. Listen, I'm going to get off the phone and let you get back to your family. Tell Avis and the children I said hello. You guys have lots of fun for all of us overworked stiffs who have no idea when we'll get some time off."

"Will do. But you really need to try this rest and relaxation thing. It is so cool! Oh, and thanks, Sapphire, for checking in on me and for making life so much easier for me, knowing that my patients are at least in loving, capable hands even sans me."

"Sans—you mean without you? Au contraire. Like anyone could ever fully replace you,

Dr. Xavier Holden. I'll see you when you get back. That's providing you ever do decide to come back."

He laughed. "Oh, I'll be back. In spite of what my family says about *me* being enough for them, just wait until the money starts to get low or run out. You'll see just how much they wanted me around when they start pushing me out the door to get back to work and bring home some more moola."

"Have fun. I'll see you when you get back to the office. Whenever." She laughed.

Chapter 14

*And now she is planted in the wilderness, in
a dry and thirsty ground.*

—Ezekiel 19:13

Arletha vowed she would never set foot back in
Followers of Jesus Faith Worship Center ever
again. At first Memory was fine about that since
she hadn't been keen on going to anyone's church
anyway. And she'd only succumbed to Arletha's
whining. Yet, it had been three weeks since their
last visit, and there was now a gnawing in Memory's spirit, whispering to her to go again. She
couldn't shake it. She'd tried, but she hadn't been
able to shake it.

"Arletha, I know you said you didn't want to
ever go back to that church with that Pastor Landris again," Memory said after she entered the
kitchen where Arletha stood.

Arletha was preparing spaghetti for the second
time in a week. "That's right."

Memory sat down. "Have you found a church
you like yet?"

"Nope. If you ask me, all of these preachers

have gone loco . . . literally lost their cotton-picking minds. Every one of them. I just don't understand how the devil has wormed his way into the Lord's house like he has. It's a shame and a disgrace."

"Well, I was wondering if you might consider dropping me off at Pastor Landris's church on your way to whichever church you plan to attend on Sunday."

Arletha stopped and looked at Memory. "Please do not tell me you were sucked into that brainwashing jive like all the rest of them going there?"

"I don't look at what I experienced that day as a brainwashing. Something happened to me when I went there. I tried to play it off myself, but I feel like I'm supposed to be at that church. It's as though I'm being summoned there for some reason I don't have a clue about," Memory said. "I don't know what it is; I can't explain it, but I can't seem to shake this desire to go again."

"What you need is to get your Bible and study for yourself while I find a decent place to attend. There's nothing for you at that church. Nothing. Believe you me, if I thought there was a true anointing even visiting let alone residing there, I'd be making my way there myself. That man believes in and teaches things that go against almost everything I grew up being taught was right."

"So does that make it wrong?"

Arletha looked at Memory hard. "Does that make *what* wrong? His beliefs and teachings? Him? Yes, it does. Look, if you won't stand for what you believe and you allow every Tom, Dick, and Harry to come along with all their newfangled doctrine and change your belief, you're going to find yourself in a whole world of trouble. Women weren't allowed to wear pants in church when I came along. Now, almost every church you walk in, the women are sporting them like they have a God-given right to. Well, they don't!" Arletha reached up and took down the noodles in the tall, plastic container from the cabinet.

"Women had their assigned places in church," she said. "But now you find them all up in the pulpits preaching and such. It's blasphemy! And it's not right. I'm not going to participate in this deception. People allowing hip-hop rap, talking about if it's spreading the gospel it's okay. It's not okay in my book. We've brought too much of the world into the church and folks are just sitting around almost welcoming these ungodly things as they're taking over. One preacher even had the nerve to attack one of my all-time favorite songs. Talking about, 'Why do you want to sing for the Lord not to move your mountain when the Bible tells you to speak to the mountain and to tell it to be thy removed and be thy cast into the sea?' I love that song, and I believe if there's a mountain in your way, then you just ought to climb it, ask the Lord to give you the strength to do what you got to do, and keep your mouth shut about it being there as you climb it."

"So you'd rather climb a mountain than to speak to it and have it just move?" Memory asked, confused by her statement.

"Tell me: Do you *really* believe you can speak to a mountain and tell it to move and it's going to move? I mean, really now?"

"Well, you say you believe what the Bible says,

and the Bible does state that if you have enough faith you can speak to the mountain and tell it to move and it should move."

"Is that right? And when did you become such a Bible scholar, Mother Robertson?"

Memory suddenly found herself offended, but she knew she had to be careful. Yes, she was the elder of the two, but Arletha was nothing if she wasn't judgmental. Memory knew from having been around her, Arletha somehow felt it her duty to execute judgment on others as she saw fit . . . almost as though she were God himself.

"I didn't mean to imply I was a scholar, by any stretch of the imagination," Memory said with a sincere smile. "I'm well aware nobody knows the things of God like you, dearie." Her tongue poked the inside of her cheek. "It's almost as if you know every thought God has."

Arletha cut her eyes over at Memory. "Well, personally, I don't like that Pastor Landris or his church. And frankly, I believe you should keep as far away from there as you possibly can. No telling what evil will come to you being there. You mark my words, there is no good to come to you if you find your way to that place again." She started breaking the spaghetti noodles in half and slid them into the pot of rolling, boiling water. "Regardless, I'll not be the one to ever take you over there unless I happen to be dropping you off for good. I don't want any misguided vibes coming up in my house. Now you can defy me and go on your own if you want, but I believe you will regret it if you do. I just don't permit wrong spirits to have access to my home. And evil spirits do have a way of attaching themselves to people, especially when it helps them gain a right of entry to God's chosen ones such as myself."

Memory smiled, then nodded. She knew what all that meant. If she went to the church and Arletha found out, she'd likely have to find herself another place to live.

Fortunately for Memory, she wasn't as bad off as she'd led Arletha to believe. If she ever had to leave, she would do just that. One thing she did feel: God was doing something in her life. Maybe it was just her age kicking in. Maybe the time was getting closer for her to leave this world, and that's why she was feeling so differently about her life. Maybe she really was just tired. Whatever was going on, she felt herself being drawn in another direction from her usual self. And in truth, she really did want to know what this was all about.

"We'll be eating in about twenty minutes," Arletha said. "The sauce is simmering in the cast iron skillet here, and the noodles are almost done. If you want to go and get washed up so you can set the table, that would be great."

Memory smiled again as she got up. "Of course."

That was another thing she hated about Arletha: she enjoyed bossing other folks around. It was always her way or the highway. Probably why she never married. Who could stand to be around her for too long? *One day though,* Memory thought, *somebody is going to set that woman straight.*

"Well, don't just stand there looking at me like a Chesh cat. You know how I hate eating late. I have to take my meds and I have to take them at a certain time. Besides, God expects us to do everything decent and in order. That includes our daily living. It's decent to sit down at the table and eat. I don't know about you, but I'm eternally grateful to God just for having a roof over my head and someplace to lay it and food to put on the table. Not everybody can say that." She looked at Memory through her oversized, pink-rimmed glasses that magnified the size of her eyes five times larger than their normal size.

"Amen," Memory said as she walked casually away. "A-men to that!" *Yep, one day somebody is going to set her good and straight! About a lot of things, too!*

Chapter 15

Drink waters out of thine own cistern, and running waters out of thine own well.
—Proverbs 5:15

"Well, hello there. Fatima Adams, isn't it?" a male voice said behind her.

Fatima stopped. It couldn't be. She turned around. She was on her way inside the sanctuary, and yes, trailing behind her was Darius Connors along with his wife.

"Good morning," Fatima said in a deliberately dry tone.

"And how are you this fine, blessed Sunday morning?" Darius was particularly upbeat and cheery, different from the way he usually interacted with Fatima.

"Fine," Fatima said, continuing on and trying not to look at either of them.

"Honey, have you met Fatima Adams?" Darius said. "She's been a member here for what? About a year now?"

"Nine months," Fatima said, trying her best to sound polite instead of irritated.

"No," Darius's wife said, "I don't believe I have." She walked up and offered her hand to Fatima. "I'm Tiffany Connors, Darius's wife. Pleased to meet you."

Fatima shook her hand. "Nice to meet you." She then quickly turned back around and started walking even faster, hoping to put enough distance between them to ensure she wouldn't end up having to sit anywhere near them.

The ushers were directing everybody to the seats they wanted to fill up first, as always. Fatima attempted to go over to the other side, but they motioned for her to sit in the row on the side where she had entered. She sat down, and just as she figured would happen, Darius sat right next to her with his wife next to him. She wanted to get up and go to another area, but that would have been too suspicious and too obvious.

You can do this, Fatima, you can do this. Just keep your mind on Jesus.

The dance team came out. Before they began, the leader instructed everybody on how she wanted the audience to participate during certain parts of the song.

"When you hear the words, we want you to turn to the person next to you and sing the words to him or her. Then we're going to do it again so you can sing to the person on the other side of you. Does everybody understand how we're doing this?"

"Yes!" The audience's voices exploded as they clapped with excitement.

The dance team, dressed in a variety of pastel-colored chiffon outfits of the same design, was dancing to "I Need You to Survive" by Hezekiah

Walker. Fatima knew this was not good at all. And just as she suspected, Darius made an extra effort for her to feel his heart when he shook her hand during the appointed time in the song.

He smiled at her, purposely making his eyes dance. He caressed the back of her hand in a subtle, circular motion with his thumb. He held her hand longer than was necessary for that portion of the song, causing her to have to pull it out of his hand without making too much of a scene. When they came to the second verse, which was about praying for each other, he forced her to look back into his eyes as the words, "I love you; I need you to survive" were now being sung. He knew the connection they shared whenever they gazed into each other's eyes, and he played it for everything it was worth. She watched him pucker his lips softly and send her a kiss without anyone else being able to detect he'd just done it.

Fatima was messed up for the rest of the service. She didn't understand how a person could take a perfectly nice song and use it the way Darius had just done on her. He had rattled her, and what was worse: he knew it. It didn't seem to faze him in the least that he had been practically flirting with her in church literally right in front of his own wife without her ever suspecting a thing.

"You're sick!" Fatima said to Darius when he called her after she arrived home from church. She had been so upset with the stunt he'd pulled today. She literally snatched the phone off its base on the first ring after she saw his name pop up on the caller ID. "You should be ashamed of yourself! But I already know that you're not."

"Well, you wouldn't talk to me. And it's not like I planned it. We just happened to arrive around the same time as you. And the ushers made us sit pretty much where they wanted us to sit, you included. You know all of this. But I do thank God at least I got to tell you in person what I've been leaving in messages on your machine for the past six weeks. I love you," he began to sing the song again, "I need you to survive." He paused, then quickly spoke again. "Dumping me the way you did and then refusing to talk to me about it is not going to change how I feel about you. And I suspect you feel the same way about me. We have a bond whether we want it to be there or not." He let out a loud sigh. "The question is: What are we going to do about it?"

"*I'm* trying to do the right thing. You're a married man, Darius. Has that fact somehow slipped your mind, even now, after having gone to *church* with your *wife*, might I add?" She put emphasis on the words *church* and *wife*. "The fact remains: you belong to someone else. This is not right to her, or to me, for that matter."

"Oh, so I suppose you don't believe this affects me in any negative way?"

"How? Oh, you mean the fact that you're committing adultery? It affects you? You're getting the best of both worlds. You have a wife that you're building a life with. You have a family. . . . Then you *had* me on the side. Had, mind you. *Had*. Past tense. Your wife wasn't getting everything she was entitled to. And as for me . . ."

"What about you?"

"I got the leftovers, the crumbs. I was the one

who—at the end of the day—had no one. I was the one who had to wait for you to make or find some time for. You couldn't care less if I needed you. I was on my own."

"That's not true. I cared. I still care. I just couldn't always get away. And you're being a big baby about it. Goodness, Fatima, you just need to grow up. You should understand how life works by now. We don't always get what we want when we want it."

"So, what's your point? I should be happy for whatever I get? Is that the way you think I should live my life? Waiting days . . . weeks . . . possibly a month for you to be able to slip away and give me an hour or two of your stolen time? Is that all I deserve?"

"What was wrong with that? It's the quality of time, not always the quantity, that matters most. And you definitely got quality."

"Of course you would say something like that."

"You know I love you." His voice was softer.

"I won't argue that you don't. But you know what? I think Tina Turner may have put it best: 'What's love got to do with it?' "

Darius paused for a second before he answered. "So, what are you trying to say? You really don't want to be with me? Do you really expect me to believe it's over between us just because you can't have what you want when you want it?"

Fatima started laughing. "You know what, Darius?"

"What?"

"I have someone in my life who truly loves me. He loves me enough that there's nothing He wouldn't do for me. He gives me flowers every day, floods me with them year round, but especially during the summertime. He hung the moon and the stars for me. Do you hear me? He loved me so much He gave His life to save *me*. Me, Darius. Do you hear me? Me. And I want to do right by Him."

Darius started laughing. "Oh, my goodness. Will you just listen to you? Sounds like you've gone over the spiritual edge like so many others these days. Now I suppose you want me to believe that you have Jesus in your life and that's enough?"

"No. I'm not expecting you to believe anything. In fact, see if you can believe this." And she hung up. She tossed the silenced phone on the couch and flopped down next to it as she began to cry. She did have Jesus. So why was that not enough?

Darius looked at his now hushed phone. "Oh, my dear, Fatima, it's not over. You might think it's over but it's not. You see, if you didn't care, you never would have answered the phone like you did. And you wouldn't be exhibiting such intense emotions. I see what I need to do for you now. We just need some alone time together." He smiled. "Just me and you, person to person. And we can straighten this all up in no time flat. You and I are not over, definitely not. We're a long way from being over." He smiled, put his cell phone back inside his pants' pocket, and walked back inside the house.

"Find what you were looking for out there?" Tiffany asked when he came back in the kitchen.

"Not yet. But you know me; I won't give up until I do. I know I put that drill somewhere. I thought it might be in the storage house. Guess I was wrong. I just need to keep searching until I can put my hands on it again." He kissed his wife on the cheek and grinned. "Dinner smells de-li-cious! Just like you." He puckered up and kissed the air.

Chapter 16

*Seek good, and not evil, that ye may live:
and so the Lord, the God of hosts, shall be
with you, as ye have spoken.*

—Amos 5:14

Bentley walked into the bedroom and lay across the bed. "I called to make an appointment with Pastor Landris," Bentley said.

"What did they say?" Marcella asked as she continued to roll her hair.

"He's booked solid for the next three months."

"Did you tell them it was an emergency?"

"I asked them to put me on the waiting list in case of a cancellation, but I don't think you could truly classify my problem as a real emergency."

"So how are you holding up? Honestly."

"It's a challenge. The Internet is really wearing me down. I get e-mails upon e-mails with filthy words . . . taunting me. Activating and planting thoughts in my head, and it's just hard to control those thoughts sometimes. Before I know it, I'm thinking about things I shouldn't be."

"Well, I don't think you should wait for Pastor Landris. There are other ministers available at the church. Make an appointment with one of them," Marcella said.

"I told you, Marcella, I'm not talking to just anyone about this. It's hard enough for me as it is discussing it with you. You know I don't trust everybody with my business. I don't feel like having folks looking at me funny or treating me like I'm some kind of pervert."

"I've told you; I don't believe the people on staff at this church will do that."

"But you don't know that for sure. I don't want to chance it and find out I was right all the time."

"Okay, Bentley. If you like, we can go see somebody not connected to the church. I did some research on the Internet, and there are other alternatives we can look into to get you help."

"The last thing I need is to join a group of strangers and put my business in the streets. I'm trying to be the next Bill Gates. I don't need something like this out there coming back to bite me later." He rubbed his head. "No, if I'm going to seek help, I'd rather start with the spiritual. I realize this is spiritual warfare."

"I just can't understand why you have to wait so long to talk to someone at church," Marcella said as she paced in front of him a few times. "Maybe you can schedule an appointment with Xavier when he gets back from his trip to Florida."

"Oh, I definitely don't want your friend's husband knowing my business either. I'm sure you've already told Avis everything though."

"That's what Xavier does, Bentley. He listens to people's problems and helps them. He's a doctor." She didn't even acknowledge his last statement.

She stopped pacing. "Fine. Then I think I'll call the church and see what I can do to get you an earlier appointment with Pastor Landris," Marcella said.

Bentley stood up and looked at Marcella. "So, what are you trying to imply? You don't think I really called for an appointment?"

Marcella looked at him and frowned. "That's not what I'm implying at all. I just said I would call to see what I can do."

He hunched his shoulders. "If I couldn't get an earlier date, I don't know what makes you think you can. See, that's what's wrong with us. You treat me as though you think I'm some kind of an incompetent child or something."

"I do not."

"Yes, you do."

"Bentley, all I said was that I would call and see what I might be able to do. But if it's going to cause an argument, then forget it. Wait months to get help then. The baby should be here around that time. That will be perfect. You can be dealing with your problem when you should be enjoying our new baby."

Bentley grabbed Marcella as she started to walk away. "Hey, hey. I'm sorry. I'm sorry, okay? I was out of line. I know you're just trying to help. I'm just on edge these days. I'm trying not to think too much and it's messing with my head."

"I know, Bentley. And it's okay."

"Look, if you believe you can get me an earlier appointment with the good Reverend Landris, then by all means go for it."

"I was only thinking about how ridiculous it is

that you're having to wait so long. I don't understand what the problem could be. Maybe whomever you spoke with just didn't know how to handle the situation. I'll call tomorrow and if three months is the earliest time you can see him, then at least I'll feel we did all we could at this time. We'll just deal with it the best way we know how."

"I'm sorry. If I wasn't so particular about my situation and just would take the first available appointment, I could get started. But I suppose the wait time tells you a lot about who the best person to see down at the church must be."

"Why do you say that?"

"The best ones are always the hardest to get an appointment with. It's the ones nobody likes that are generally available."

Marcella shook her head. "I don't think that's the case here. I guess everybody just feels like you; they'd prefer Pastor Landris. They won't give the others a try."

"Well, we'd better hurry and do something soon. I don't want to alarm you, but I'm having some real challenges in fighting this. I really need some help here. I'm even paying more attention to the commercials with the sexual overtones oozing everywhere. And surfing through the channels, those rap videos with half-naked, booty-shaking women. It's just hard on any man, saved, sanctified, or otherwise. But I suppose that's their whole point. Oh yeah . . . makes me want to run right out and purchase their various products. Let me hurry up and go get that CD." He let out a short laugh. "I'm kidding, you know, about going out to purchase their bag of chips because a half-dressed woman was eating some, or the CD ad I just watched of half-naked women bouncing around."

"I know you're just being sarcastic." Marcella took his hand. "We can still pray ourselves."

"Yeah, you're right. We can do that. We don't need a preacher or anyone else to help us do that." He squeezed her hand. "Will you lead it?"

Marcella smiled. "Sure."

They bowed their heads and she began.

Chapter 17

*Or when saw we thee sick, or in prison, and
came unto thee?*

—Matthew 25:39

"Charity, how are you?" Johnnie Mae asked.

"I believe I'm making progress. Thank you
so much for coming," Charity said.

"I told you I'd check on you when I got a
chance. I wasn't just saying something to be saying
it. So things are progressing?" Johnnie Mae asked
as she looked around the room located in a hospital-
type facility that had the feel of a small hotel room.

Charity looked down at her hands. "Sapphire
says I'm doing well. I am beginning to come to real
terms with certain things. Still can't seem to get
Faith to cooperate with us, so I don't know. You'd
think I'd have more control over her since it appears I am the one who created her in the first
place. This is so crazy."

Johnnie Mae touched Charity's hand. "Don't be
so hard on yourself. You know we're all pulling
and praying for you. And I believe you're going to

be completely healed and delivered from this very soon. Some things just take time."

"Okay. Enough about me. How is your mother?" Charity readjusted her body.

"Now, that's a loaded question for sure. Mama's not doing so well. To be honest, she's had a difficult time ever since you left. You were so wonderful for her."

"I'm sorry."

"No, please don't. I'm not telling you this for you to beat up on yourself. You can't help what's going on with you, no more than Mama can help what's going on with her." Johnnie Mae sat back in the chair. "I just wanted you to know how much of an impact your life had on her in that short time you were with her. It was amazing. She seemed to thrive with you. None of us has been able to create the atmosphere you did with her."

"She loves music."

"Yes, she does. We tried that, but there must have been something different with you, because she was just not the same after you left. In fact, she got so bad we couldn't leave her home for even a few minutes. I really may just have to put her in a home soon."

"Is your sister Rachel living with her?"

"No. Rachel decided to move to another city. She sort of got upset with me because she wanted to continue living in my old house, rent-free, of course. I may have not minded that so much, but she got to where she didn't want to do a thing for Mama. She just thought she should be able to sit around the house all day. Listen, I don't want to burden you talking about my problems either."

"It's not a burden. I'd really like to think about something other than what's going on in my life. Besides, I really care about you and your family. I don't get to visit with anyone much outside of the folks in here. I am happy I get to go to church some Sundays, even if I don't get to stay long. The doctors associated with my case don't want me getting too stressed out or overdoing it. But I'm so thankful whenever Sapphire comes by and checks me out to take me to a service. I enjoy Praise & Worship and Pastor Landris's teaching so much. I'm having to stay here until my doctors agree it's okay for me to live at home. They're not sure what might happen if my other personalities come out and I'm home alone. Especially now that they're aware I know of both their existences."

Johnnie Mae smiled. "I know it's been hard on you. And not having any family around to help you go through this can't be easy. That's why I promised you I'd come by and see you from time to time. I suppose you haven't been able to convince your mother to come up here yet?"

Charity leaned forward. "No. Things have really been tough for my mother. Maybe in a few months she'll be able to come. You think it might be okay to bring your mother by some time? I mean, if you don't think it's a good idea, I truly understand."

Johnnie Mae cocked her head to the side and gave her a warm smile. "You know, that might be a great idea. I'll check with her doctor and see what he thinks. I do believe she'll love seeing you again whether she remembers you or not."

"I just don't want to do anything to upset her or set her back."

"To be honest with you, it's very possible this could help her feel better. It sure won't hurt for her to get out, and I know in the past you two seemed to have such a positive effect on each other."

Charity smiled. "You look so radiant these days."

Johnnie Mae grinned. "You haven't heard? Maybe it's because I'm expecting."

Charity's face lit up and she clapped her hands. "Oh, that is wonderful! So that's why you're glowing. I should have known. When is the baby due?"

"August fourteenth. I'm almost five months now. The baby is kicking and everything."

"Do you know what you're having?"

Johnnie Mae smiled. "No, in fact, I decided I didn't want to know. My doctor almost slipped and told me what she thought it was during the sonogram, but I caught her before she blurted it out and reminded her that not everybody cares to know in advance."

"You and the baby are doing okay?"

"My doctor wanted to do an amniocentesis when we first learned I was pregnant."

Charity had a puzzled look on her face. "What for?"

"Because of my age. She wanted to be sure the baby was healthy and not possibly a baby with Down syndrome."

"Did you have it done?" Charity quickly clasped her hand over her mouth. "Oh, I'm so sorry I'm just getting all in your business. Sorry. You don't have to answer that."

Johnnie Mae leaned over. "It's okay. I don't mind you asking." She sighed. "I considered it for about one hot second. Then I told her I didn't want to do it. Pastor Landris and I talked about it and we agreed that should the amnio test have found anything wrong with the baby at the two-month pregnancy stage, we wouldn't act on that." She looked at Charity, who didn't seem to be totally following what she was saying. "If something was wrong with the baby, according to the doctor at that stage, they would have given us the option of continuing on with the pregnancy or terminating it."

"Oh, I see."

"Yeah. So we decided if we had the amnio done and learned anything negative, it wouldn't change our decision about having the baby one way or the other. So why put myself and Pastor Landris through all of that and possibly risk harming the baby in the process? We believe this baby is healthy. But regardless, we're not going to play God and make a decision that a baby mankind may deem inferior doesn't deserve to be born. In God's sight, this baby is still one of His creations."

"Wow, that's deep."

Johnnie Mae smiled as she spoke. "Pastor Landris and I are trusting God through all of this. I make sure I eat right and I'm taking care of myself. So far, I've been feeling really good. I'm not huge yet, as you can tell." She pressed her dress against her stomach.

"No, you look fantastic. I can see you're pregnant now. I really appreciate you taking time out to come see me; you'll never know just how much. It's hard not having family or friends in town and being stuck in a place where you rarely ever get to go outside its walls. But I'm more concerned about getting better so I can live a productive life in the future. I do feel special, though, that you cared enough to come see about me."

Johnnie Mae sat back in her chair. "Others at church have asked about you, but we know that you don't need a lot of people parading in and out. We just want you to concentrate on getting well. I'm rather fond of you and I know God's heart and desire for you is to walk in healing, health, deliverance, and perfect peace. This might be your test for now, but it will be your testimony later, when the Lord brings you through it."

Charity smiled. "Yeah, I tell Sapphire what started out as a mess, when God gets through turning it around will become a message of deliverance for those who don't believe God is able to do all things, including putting broken minds, lives, homes, and even split personalities back together. I'm glad I convinced Sapphire to be my therapist. She turned me down at first, said it was a conflict of interest. You know, Faith having dated her ex-boyfriend. God is good."

Johnnie Mae stood up to leave. "We want you to have this." Johnnie Mae handed her an envelope.

"What is it?"

"It's a love offering from myself and Pastor Landris."

Charity's eyes watered up. She opened the envelope and pulled out a check along with some cash. The check was for $2,000. The cash amounted to $200 in small bills. Charity started wiping away the tears that now flowed. "Thank you, but you shouldn't have done this. This is too much."

"Why shouldn't we? I know you're not making any money while you're going through this. And trying to get on disability, I hear, can be a nightmare. You still have bills and obligations even if you have money saved up. Pastor Landris and I just wanted to do something to help you not be so worried while you're getting better. That's all. It's hard enough already for you without having financial worries. That cash is for knickknacks and such while you're here."

"I just don't know what to say. How will I ever be able to repay you both?"

"Just get better." She hugged Charity. "And if you need anything, you make sure you give me a call. I'm going to see what I can do about bringing Mama by one day when both you and she are up to it. I think it will be a good thing. I'll call you."

"I look so forward to being able to see her again." Charity stood back and looked at Johnnie Mae. "Thank you. Thank you. You don't know how blessed I am to have people like you and Sapphire in my life. Sapphire has gone above and beyond trying to help me. If I could just manage to get a rein on this personality called Faith, I believe I'll be close to a breakthrough, and this can be over."

"It's coming. Just believe that and have faith—"

Charity laughed. "I know: no pun intended."

Johnnie Mae let out a loud laugh. "Yeah. Right. Faith. No pun intended."

Chapter 18

And why beholdest thou the mote that is in thy brother's eye, but considerest not the beam that is in thine own eye?
— Matthew 7:3

"Avis, you must tell me everything. I mean everything!" Marcella said over the telephone.

"Oh, girl! Xavier is like a totally different man. He actually took off from work for three and a half weeks. Do you hear what I'm saying? Not three and a half hours, which was a job trying to get him to do in the past, three and a half whole weeks. I feel like I'm having an affair with another man, he's just that different."

"That sounds like real love to me. But the man's not crazy even if he deals with folks with crazy issues from time to time on his job," Marcella said.

"Marcella, don't say that. The people he helps have problems just like the rest of us, only theirs can be more magnified on scales we can't begin to imagine. Many of them deal with their problems differently than maybe you or I, and they may, sometimes, need help reeling things in."

"You're right. I'm sorry. I was trying to make a joke, but it was a bad one and in bad taste. Tell me though, did you guys rekindle any of your old flames?"

Avis laughed. "Rekindle? Girl, we almost burned the house and a few hotels down! I told you it's been like cheating on my husband with another man. He and I got away by ourselves for a few days, and were I to write a book about it—all I can say is: MM had better watch out!

"Speaking of MM, have you finished reading her latest book yet?" Avis asked, referring to one of the hottest authors of fiction burning up the best-sellers' charts with number-one books one right after the other.

"Finished it?" Marcella said. "Girl, there were places in that book where I had to set it down, do you hear me, walk to the freezer, stick my head inside just to cool myself off. And I was not having hot flashes either. I got so turned on, I tell you what—I was glad I was married. Bentley didn't know what got into me that night! I will say though—I do feel for the single women who read MM's work, because that girl knows she can paint a picture that leaves *nothing*, do you hear me, nothing for the imagination to have to fill in. When that dark-skinned, chocolate, fine brother walked in and saw that woman on the couch without a stitch of clothes on and only those pink, fluffy, high-heel, house shoes, girl, I was right there with them, do you hear me," Marcella said. She looked up right into Bentley's face. He stood there, staring at her, not cracking a smile.

"Well, MM can flat out write some scenes,

that's all I can say," Avis said. "However, I have been feeling a little guilty about reading her work here of late. Especially being a Christian and taking my walk with the Lord more seriously than I did in the past. But then I picked up this Christian fiction book the other day, and some of those scenes in that book were just as hot; it didn't leave much for me to fill in either. So I figure it must be okay. People say we should keep it real and tell the truth. The truth is this stuff happens even in Christian homes. Ask Xavier; after these past weeks he can testify."

Marcella had become a bit distracted by Bentley's stare. "I'm sorry, what did you just say? My mind wandered there for a minute."

"Look, I've got things to do here, so whatever it is that just grabbed your attention, maybe you should go and handle your business." Avis laughed. "Yeah, and while you're at it, tell Bentley I said hello." She laughed again.

Marcella gave a halfhearted laugh. "Yeah. I'll do that." She placed the phone back in its holder after saying good-bye. "That was Avis," Marcella said to Bentley. "She's back home now. They came back earlier this week. She said to tell you hello."

"That's nice. So she and Xavier have worked things out? I know you said she'd sort of left him to go visit with her mother. Then Xavier showed up down there."

"Yeah, they worked things out. And it sounds like they had a great time doing it, too. She sounds more like a teenager in love for the first time than some old, married woman with four children."

Bentley moved his head as though he were trying to pop a kink out of it, first to the right, then the left. "So, you two were talking about some dark-skinned, fine, chocolate brother making out with his woman, huh? Is that from the book you've been reading the past few nights? The one on your nightstand with the half-naked man and the extra-sexy, barely covered woman on the cover?"

Marcella smiled nervously. "It's just a book, Bentley. Fiction. It has this great story line. It's about this woman who is a Christian living a double life no one knows about. You know, the same-old-same-old kind of stuff you find in books these days."

"Books that cause you to see other people naked and doing the 'do' only using your mind?"

"Look, Bentley. This is not the same thing you're dealing with. And I don't even feel like trying to defend a novel with *words,* not real pictures. There is a difference."

"Yeah. A lot of guys I know say they only buy *Playboy* and *Hustler* magazines for their great articles. Just like you, only you buy your books strictly for their great story lines."

"Bentley, there is a difference!" Marcella said it more piercing than she had meant to.

"If that's what you want to believe, Marcella. But in my world, pictures in a person's head are just as real as the pictures my natural eyes see outside my head." He leaned down and kissed her. "But you know what? I'm not trying to get the splinter out of your eye. Not while I'm working on the plank in my own. I have an appointment with Pastor Landris in three weeks—"

"Oh, Bentley, you were able to get an earlier appointment? That's wonderful!"

"Yeah. They say a bunch of people decided to schedule with other counselors and that freed up Pastor Landris. If you still want to go with me, you're welcome to come."

"Of course I want to go with you. I'm your wife. I want to support you through this."

He smiled. "Yeah. Okay." He kissed her again, grinned even more, and walked out of the room. "In the meantime, I think I'll go check out the book on your nightstand," he yelled back. "I need a quick fix!"

"Bentley? Bentley?" Marcella said, chasing behind him. "What do you mean by that crack? Bentley?! You come back here and tell me exactly what you meant by that!"

Chapter 19

Let me be weighed in an even balance, that
God may know mine integrity.

—Job 31:6

"Edwin, where's your paycheck for this week?" Desiree asked Friday afternoon after having waited the whole day yesterday for him to hand it over. He got paid on Thursdays every two weeks. "Did you deposit it yourself?"

"Don't you worry about my check. I worked for it, so I'll hand it over when I'm good and ready."

Desiree looked at him and began to make a slow, sucking noise with her teeth. "I suppose you also wouldn't happen to know why our bank account just *happens* to be overdrawn either, now would you?"

He shrugged his shoulders. "Don't look at me; you're the one taking care of the bills these days, remember? You believed you could do a better job than what I was doing." He started to walk away. "It's your baby now."

She grabbed him by the wrist. "Wait just a minute,"

she said in a quiet voice. "Where are you going? We haven't finished talking just yet."

He looked down at her hand holding him. "Woman, *what* is your problem?"

"Our account is overdrawn by fourteen hundred dollars. Our house note check bounced as well as about six other checks. The bank charges thirty-five dollars every time a check bounces, as I'm sure you already know. That means in addition to the penalties all these people are going to charge us for our bounced checks, we also have charges for seven insufficient fund checks at thirty-five dollars a pop that the bank added to our growing deficit."

"Like I said, don't look at me. You handle all of that now."

"But I balanced the checkbook and we had plenty of money to pay all the bills I wrote, with some left over. I don't understand what could have happened."

He pulled his wrist out of her grasp. "Then I'd suggest you check with the bank and see what kind of computer error they plan to blame this one on. Because I don't have a clue why you're overdrawn," Edwin said.

"What about your paycheck?"

He turned and walked up closer to her. "You know what, Desiree? You are really starting to grate on my nerves. You're starting to sound like a broken record. I don't have to stand around here getting the third degree from you all the time. If you're grumpy because you want a cigarette or you're hungry, then go smoke or get you something to eat other than rabbit food. Just don't try and take your frustrations out on me. I truly don't have the time or the patience for this." He walked over to the table, snatched his baseball cap off it, and started toward the door.

"And just where do you think you're going? We're not finished talking yet."

He made a snorting sound. "Oh, that's where you're wrong, Baby-cakes. I'm done. Now if you want to carry on with this nonsense conversation that's going nowhere, then *knock yourself out*. I'll be back. Maybe by then, you'll be done."

"Edwin, don't you dare go to the track! You get back here so we can talk this out!"

"I don't know if you realize this or not, but I'm a grown man. You don't tell me where I can and can't go. If I want to go have some fun at the track, then that's what I'm going to do. If you don't like it, nobody's holding you here. That same door I'll be walking out in a few seconds can swing the same way for you. Like I just said, I'll be back." He walked out, practically slamming the door behind him.

Desiree sat down and looked at the insufficient notice again, with the individual checks and amounts listed, and shook her head. "I don't understand how this happened," she said as she stared at the paper. Looking at her watch, she realized the bank would be closing in about forty minutes. She had to hurry if she planned to get there before six o'clock. "It's times like these when I wish I had opted for on-line banking. Then I could just check it from here." She got up and headed for the bank to see what could have possibly happened and hopefully to get things straightened out before the day was over.

Desiree wasn't positive yet, but she felt in her spirit: *Edwin will somehow be somewhere in the midst of all of this.* What she wasn't sure about was: *If he is, what am I going to do about it?*

Desiree came home from the bank practically devastated. *How could Edwin do this to me?* She knew one thing: she would be waiting up for him when he came home this time around. And when he returned, it would not be pretty. Not pretty at all.

Chapter 20

Her princes in the midst thereof are like wolves ravening the prey, to shed blood, and to destroy souls, to get dishonest gain.
—Ezekiel 22:27

Edwin paced the floor. This last race had to pay off or he was done for. This was all the money he had left, and there was no way he could go home totally busted. Desiree had asked him about his check, which he had spent the majority of Thursday night at the track. He didn't understand what could have happened. Never had he lost like that before. Sure he had bet more than he normally would on the races last night and tonight, boxing six out of eight dogs almost every race, which cost $120 each time he did that. But that was because he needed desperately to win some big money.

This evening, Desiree questioned him about all her bounced checks. Of course he denied knowing anything about them. He wasn't stupid. But come Monday, when she talked to the bank, she would learn just how much he really did know about those missing funds. He had only a few days to make things right, or she would know he had been the one who had caused the account to be grossly insufficient.

"Come on, you stupid dog!" he yelled as the last group of dogs raced toward the finish line. "Get up there, three! You sorry dog, what's wrong with you! Get up there! Yeah, come on! That's right! Go! Go! Yes! Yes! Yes! Thank You, Lord! Thank You!"

Edwin let out a yell, which was something most bettors tried not to do too often following the end of a race. People watched you to see if you won, and you never knew who might try to jack you later in the parking lot on your way to your car. But he couldn't hold his joy inside. This race would be paying some big money, and he could take these winnings home to Desiree to replace the paycheck money he'd lost, plus cover the bounced checks, fees, and the penalties. If it paid what he thought it would, he could even give Desiree a little extra, which would probably be the only way he'd be able to smooth over her anger. He looked at his ticket and smiled. "Eight-four-three," he said as he kissed his ticket and shook his head. "This should pay big! Really big!"

"Ladies and gentlemen, please hold all tickets. We have a photo finish for third place. Please hold all tickets while we review the photo finish."

"What?" Edwin said. "Photo finish?" He turned to his friend, who had come and stood next to him. "What are they talking about? That three dog clearly beat that one dog. This is a rip-off here.

They just know they're going to have to pay some big money if that three dog came in third instead of the one. These folks need to quit!"

"So you have that one?" his friend asked.

"Yeah. I boxed six numbers. I just didn't have a one in there anywhere. Where did that one dog come from anyway? They must have juiced him up or something. That sorry one dog has come in last place the last five races he's run. And now all of a sudden, tonight, he decides he wants to try to win?"

"So you didn't have the number one dog?" his friend asked as he pointed to the monitor. They were showing the replay of the race again.

"No." He looked over at his friend. "Don't tell me you had it?"

His friend smiled. "Yep. I had it. I figured it was about time that dog did something. Besides, the last five races he ran, he was out of his position. That one dog is an outside dog. They had him on the inside all those other races. That's why he lost when he did. I had the eight, the four, and the one."

"I still say the three beat him," Edwin said.

Just then the monitor flashed up the winning numbers: 8-4-1-3. "Ladies and gentlemen, we have the official results for this last and final race. Eight-four-one-three."

"Oh, they're full of it!"

"There's the photo finish on the screen. The number one dog beat the three by a nose." His friend grinned as he started walking toward the tellers' windows.

Edwin couldn't believe this had happened. How

could he have lost? What was he going to tell Desiree? She wasn't going to let go about the missing paycheck he hadn't put in the bank yet. On top of that, now he didn't even have enough money to buy gas to get back and forth to work the next two weeks. As he walked past the ATM machine, he stopped and pulled out his wallet. He could take out an advance on one of their credit cards. It wasn't like he hadn't done it before. He had three cards; one of them had to have enough cash left on it to make up for his squandered paycheck and the money Desiree needed to make those bounced checks right. It wasn't like he didn't intend to put the money back in two weeks after he got paid, and then go down to Mississippi, where he was sure to win.

He looked at how close he'd come to winning this last race. It paid $6,183 if you had the trifecta straight, $3,091.50 any other way. He almost had it. All he needed was one good win, and he would be back in the game. Tomorrow, he would come back during the matinee. He would stay all day if that's what it took for him to win at least some of his lost money back. If he could just break even with what he'd lost, he would be happy.

Edwin put the credit card in, keyed in his pin number, keyed in the amount he wished to withdraw, and waited. When it came back that he couldn't get that amount, he tried a lower figure. That didn't work. Finally, he put in for $20 and learned he couldn't even get $20 off that card. Same thing with the other two cards. He thought about the number of times he had withdrawn money from those accounts and realized he had probably already maxed them to the limit. These may have also been the checks paid that bounced.

There had to be a way to get some money from somewhere until he could find his winning streak again and straighten out this whole mess.

Meanwhile, there was Desiree. He would still have to deal with her first thing in the morning. What was he going to tell her? Another lie? Try to bully her again?

"Hey, man," he said with a huge smile to his friend as he walked past him. "So you got that trifecta. Congratulations."

"Thank you."

"Listen, can I talk to you for a second?" Edwin said with a rather serious look.

His friend smiled. "If it's to hit me up for a loan again, forget it. I don't know if you remember, since you've been pretending like you don't, but you haven't paid me back from the last time you 'talked to me for a second' and 'borrowed' a few bucks."

"I know. But you know I took off from being here a while and when I returned, I've had a little trouble getting back into my groove. My stride is a little off, that's all."

"What stride? You were losing before you took off on your little hiatus. That was when you had to borrow that money from me, remember? Well, my brother, the GOOD BOOK says you reap what you sow; you didn't sow my money back to me, so you don't have any grace to reap from my harvest now. Good luck with your old lady, though, when you get home. If you ask me, man, I'd say you have a serious gambling problem, and you need some help." He laughed loud and hard. "I'll put in a little prayer for you on my way home. 'Cause from the look on your face, I'd say you're going to need all the divine help you can get from above." He strolled away with an extra pep in his step.

Edwin looked around to see if there was anyone else who either owed him money or would be willing to spot him a few bucks until he could win some when he came back tomorrow. Everybody he did see that he knew, he realized he owed them money as well.

"God, how did I get myself in this mess? Look, Lord. If you'll help me out this time, I promise you, I'll start going to church every Sunday. God, please. Now you know Desiree is going to hit the ceiling. Have a little mercy on me down here."

He left the building and headed for his car. He didn't walk fast; no reason to be in a hurry to get home. He had a pretty good idea what probably awaited him when he woke up in the morning. And in all likelihood it wouldn't be loving, forgiving, or pretty.

Chapter 21

And by him all that believe are justified from all things, from which ye could not be justi-fied by the law of Moses.

—Acts 13:39

Edwin slowly opened the front door. He walked quietly into the house as though he were a bur-glar. Tonight he had to be extra careful not to awaken Desiree. It was bad enough he hadn't given her the money from his paycheck. It was bad enough he had caused all those checks to bounce. Now it was almost two o'clock in the morning, and he didn't need her mad about that as well. *If there is a God in heaven*, he thought to himself, *Desiree will have gone to sleep around eleven and she'll already be in never-never-land.*

He took off his shoes, then tiptoed into the bed-room. It was dark, but he knew the layout of the room so well from all the times he'd sneaked in late like this, so he didn't make any unnecessary noises. He didn't even want to chance waking her by going into the bathroom to brush his teeth. So he peeled off his clothes and slid between the sheets ever so slowly.

Done! He let out a long, quiet sigh and closed his eyes.

The light on Desiree's nightstand suddenly came on. She was sitting up in the bed now.

Edwin could tell she was staring at him, so he tried to pretend he was already asleep.

"No need for you to try to act like you're asleep," Desiree said. "I know you just crawled your sorry self in the bed."

"What?" Edwin said. "I'm trying to sleep here." He turned his back to her.

"Edwin, stop playing. I wasn't asleep when you came in. I heard you open the front door downstairs. I knew when you tiptoed your cigarette-laden self in here. So sit up. We have things we're going to get straight right now. This morning."

Edwin sat up and peeked around at the clock perched on Desiree's nightstand. "It's after two in the morning, Desiree," he said as though he didn't know it. "Whatever you want to discuss or fuss about can surely wait until we wake up. I'm tired, and I'd like to get some shut-eye."

"Oh, you're going to get some shut-eye all right. First off: where's your money from your Thursday paycheck, Edwin?"

"You know what?" He sat up straighter and looked boldly at her. "You have some real issues. All you think about is money. In case you've forgotten, I worked for that check. It belongs to me. And I can very well do with it as I please. Normally I bring almost all of it home to you. But there's nothing written in stone that says I have to do that. And I'm about tired of you taking me for granted. Do you know how many women wish they had a man like me? Maybe I'll just keep my entire pay-check this time so you can learn to start appreciat-ing me better."

"Where's the money, Edwin?"

"We can talk about this in the morning when we wake up."

"It's already 'in the morning.' I'm up, you're up, so let's talk. Let's get it on."

"I don't want to talk about it now," Edwin said. "I'm tired, Desiree. I don't feel like doing this right this minute. When we wake up, we can dis-cuss this like two civilized human beings."

"Well, we could have discussed it earlier this evening except you decided to leave and go to the track. Is that why you don't have the money from your check? Did you gamble it away at the track?"

"I'm telling you, woman. If you keep this junk up, I'm going to get up and find me somewhere else to sleep. I'm tired, and I'm not in the mood for this."

Desiree made a short, crazed, laughing sound as she started nodding her head. "Okay, so I'll take that as a yes. You gambled away your paycheck you received this week. Next thing: the overdrawn checking account."

He slumped a little, but tried to still act confi-dent. "I told you, the checking account is your baby now. If you can't balance the checkbook any better and you have checks bouncing all over the place, you can't blame me."

"Uh-huh. Well, now. I've already checked with the bank. Right after you left."

"You did?" He sounded surprised, but quickly composed himself. "So."

"So I learned something very interesting. According to them, there seems to have been a rather large check written and cashed on Monday from our account," Desiree said.

"You write the checks. And last I heard, that's what a checking account is good for—to write checks. If you have a point, I really wish you would hurry up and make it. It's really late, and I'm really tired."

"Oh, of course. How inconsiderate of me to keep you up when you were out so late already." She cocked her head to the side. "Anyway, it appears that a check for two thousand dollars was written to, signed by, and cashed by you this past Monday."

"Couldn't have been me. Must be a forgery or something. I don't have access to the checks anymore, remember? If I need a check written, you are the one who usually writes it now. You have the checkbook, wherever you have it hidden these days." He rubbed his forehead. "I don't have a clue where it is."

"Edwin, you took a check out of the checkbook, I can only assume, before you turned all the checks over to me."

"That's not likely, because you would have noticed if a check was missing."

She clapped her hands. "Very good. You are so right. I would have noticed if a check was missing, except you are way too smart for me," She reached over on the nightstand and picked up a piece of paper. "Here's a copy of that check." She handed the paper to him. "Well, aren't you going to look at it?"

He shook his head. "I don't need to see a copy of some check. I told you it couldn't have been me because I don't have access to our checks anymore."

"Oh, you should look at this one." She shook it at him. "The bank went to a special effort to get a copy of this for me to see so quickly. Take it and look at it."

He looked over at her and took the paper from her. "Looks like my signature, but as I said, I didn't have access to our checks so I couldn't have done it. I suggest you file some kind of a report with the bank and let them know somebody has accessed our account and that they are counterfeiting checks. You may need to close that account until things can get straightened out."

"You know, I don't think you really want me to do that. You see, you could go to jail for perjury if the law has to get involved. Although, seriously, they can't charge you with robbery since you actually stole from us." She picked up a new pad of checks.

Edwin started to get up out of the bed.

"Where are you going?" Desiree asked.

"I'm tired, and I'm going to sleep on the couch. Anything to get away from you with all your ridiculous, paranoid accusations."

"Edwin, the check on this copy matches the check that happens to be missing from this group of checks." She got out of the bed and stood in front of him. "You took a check out of here because you knew it would be months before I reached that check number."

"Yeah, okay. So I took the check. I'm tired of being broke all the time! I'm tired of you trying to tell me what to do with my money. There's no harm in me gambling. It's not a sin. Yet I have to listen to your mouth all the time about it. I'm tired of it, Desiree!"

"There's no harm in you gambling? Is that what you just said? Edwin, you *stole* a check out of our checkbook—"

"I can't steal what already belongs to me, remember? That money in the bank is just as much mine as it is yours. We have all these bills, and it's like I'm working for other people. Every dime I get my hands on goes into someone else's pockets. Working out there in the hot sun, laying bricks day in and day out, having some dumb guy I happened to have trained trying to boss me around and tell me what to do. Then I come home, and what do I come home to? You with all your nagging and your 'honey do' list of things you want done or you don't like."

"I am not like that. Once again, you're trying to steer the subject away from you and what you've done. You have a problem, a serious problem, Edwin. Not only are you taking money from our household to gamble with, now you're thinking of ways to steal money so you can go gamble. My ring . . . the one I couldn't find last year, did you take it and do something with it to get gambling money?"

Edwin started to walk out of the room. Desiree ran and stood in front of the door.

"Move out of my way," Edwin said with a scowl.

"No. You answer me. I turned this house upside

down looking for my ring. You know how much that ring meant to me. Did you take my ring and pawn it?"

"Pawn it? No," he said with an even meaner look.

"Edwin?" Desiree turned her head up slightly and frowned at him. "Please tell me you didn't do it?"

"Tell you I didn't what?"

"Tell me you didn't sell my two-carat diamond ring," she said through clenched teeth.

He snickered. "Well, you wanted to do this now, so I suppose we can just do this." He took a few steps away from her. "Okay, I sold your precious ring. Are you happy now?"

She wanted to hit him. It took all she could to hold back her fist, but in her heart she wanted to beat the devil out of him. "How could you do that? And how could you let me look all over this house for a ring you knew wasn't even here?"

"Kept you out of my hair, didn't it? Besides, you didn't check with me before you bought that ring. That was too much money to spend on some dumb ring that you couldn't even wear because of all the weight you'd gained."

She shook her head as she bit down on her bottom lip.

"What, Desiree? You want to hit me?" Edwin then laughed. "Go ahead. Hit me. My day can't get any worse than it is right now anyway. Okay, I gambled most of my paycheck away on Thursday night and the rest of it tonight trying to get back the money I lost from the check I cashed on Monday out of our checking account that I also lost, all at the good old dog track. Which means if you wrote other checks counting on my paycheck to be in the bank, then you're going to bounce even more checks."

"Ugh! I cannot believe this is happening to me."

"Why does everything have to be about you? Do you have any idea how it feels to have to come home every day to someone who is so self-centered?"

"I am not self-centered. How can you stand there and say such a thing? I'm hurt. We have worked too hard to get this house and all these other things. I don't want to lose what we've worked for because you have a problem you can't control," Desiree said as she shook her hand in his face.

"See what I mean. I, I, I. 'I don't want to lose.' 'I'm so hurt.'" He stepped back from her some more. "Well, what about me? Don't *I* deserve some happiness, too?"

"Are you saying you're not happy with me?" Desiree looked at him hard.

"I'm saying that you crowd me."

"How can you say I crowd you when you're never home? We don't do anything together for you to get crowded by me."

"Why do you think I started gambling in the first place?" Edwin asked. He walked back toward the bed and sat down.

Desiree walked over and stood right in front of him. "I don't know. Why?"

"I needed to get away from all our problems. You wanted a baby right after we got married. I didn't because I knew things were already tight with just the two of us," Edwin said.

"Well, you got what you wanted. I haven't been able to have a baby even after you reluctantly agreed it was okay for us, no matter how hard I've tried."

"There you go again: I."

"What do you want from me, Edwin? You complained about my smoking after we were married. I quit smoking. It was hard, but I did it."

"Yeah, well, I didn't know giving up the cancer sticks was going to cause you to eat yourself into oblivion."

"You are so cruel. Why am I not ever good enough for you? Why? Why can't you love me enough to want to spend time with me the way you spend time with those dogs at the track? Oh, you can leave here at five in the evening and not come home till almost two o'clock in the morning. But when it comes to spending an hour or two with me, you act like you're being nailed to a cross or something."

"That's because I don't feel like anything I do pleases you. I go to the track and to the casino because I need to feel like I'm worth something to somebody. Don't you get it? I don't make enough money to please you. Whatever I do is never enough. At least when I go to the track, I feel like somebody thinks I'm important. At the casino, people actually smile at me and make me feel like they're glad to see me coming, as opposed to here."

Desiree got closer to him. "I don't believe you. I work just like you do to help out. I've told you how much I love you and how much I appreciate you. Deep down, Edwin, you're a good person. But just

like those little white sticks called my name and
made me think I had to smoke them, that's what
gambling is doing to you. It's the high you seek."

He stood up and grabbed Desiree by both her
shoulders. "No! I gamble because I like feeling like
I beat something for a change. I like the feeling of
winning, since I don't ever seem to win when it
comes to you." He flopped back down. "I like it
when people treat me nice because they think I
have something to offer! I like it! Okay?!"

Desiree sat down next to Edwin. She took his
hand in hers. "You already have something to
offer, Edwin. You have the love of a God who
thinks you're so special He sent His Son to die on
the cross for your sins. That's how much you're
worth to God."

He took his hand out of hers. "Please, let's not
bring God into this conversation. If God loves us
so much, then why haven't you been able to have a
baby? You're the one who wanted one so bad, and
I know you go to church and stuff on a regular
basis. You pay your ten percent. Why hasn't God
given you what you wanted the most?"

She took his hand again, and lifted it up, and
pressed her lips against it. "I didn't know you felt
this way about things. Why haven't you ever said
anything before now?"

He looked into her eyes. "How can you be so
loving to me right now after all I've done and said
to you? We don't have any money in the bank. The
credit cards are maxed out, so we can't even float
ourselves a loan by taking an advance off them."
He dropped his head down. "I even took the
money we had out of our savings account, not that

there was that much still in it. So we can't even use our savings to tide us over until I can straighten this mess out."

Desiree touched his face. "You're a good person in spite of all these horrible things you've done. You just need some help. But don't you see? You can't get help if you refuse to admit you need it."

"I went to that church altar over two months ago to be released from this stronghold. And look at me, I'm worse off now it seems than when I first went up there. At least before, I won sometimes."

"That's because you went back and wallowed in your mess. You were doing so well, but you just had to tempt it by going right back into what you had walked away from. You can't blame that on God. You have to learn to die daily to your flesh. I have to die daily to my flesh," Desiree said. "Every day I wake up I have to choose to do the right thing. And I pray to the Holy Spirit to help me. I want a Nutty Buddy bar so bad right now it's not even funny. I could devour a whole bag of potato chips today, this very minute, if I get started eating just one. Cigarette temptation is not so bad for me now, but I know I can't try and smoke one because that one could lead me right back to my two-pack-a-day habit."

"I'm sorry," Edwin said to Desiree. "I'm so sorry!" He kissed her. "Oh, Lord, please forgive me. I realize, God, that you desire to bless me with your best. I can't do this anymore. But I can't walk away on my own. Please, Father. Please. Deliver me from this hold. I don't want to do this anymore!" He looked into Desiree's eyes. "I don't want to do this anymore. Look at what I've become. I'm not sure whether I can ever stop. I really can't say that I will ever be delivered from my desire to gamble. So what do I do?"

She smiled. "Yeah, but God can turn things around. We just have to come to Him and allow His Spirit to reign in us. That's the only way I've been able to do this. I told you: I die daily, and I'm refreshed with a new breath of God's Holy Spirit to lead and guide me."

"So," Edwin said as he stood to his feet. "What are we going to do about this mess I've made? And it's a real mess."

"We're going to have a nice prayer to the Father. We're going to get in the bed and get some rest. Then after we get up, we're going to put our heads together and figure something out. With the leading of the Holy Spirit, He will direct us on what we need to do. If we need to go get you some help from outside—counseling, Gambler's Anonymous, whatever—we'll get you help. But you have to really want to do this. If you don't, nothing anybody else does will make a difference. You have to want things to change. It's on you."

Edwin reached down and pulled her up. "I'm going to make a promise to you. I'll do whatever I need to walk away from this. I just thank you for loving me with the love of the Lord. I know it has to be His love. I promise I'm not going to mess this up." He pulled her into his arms and held her. "I love you too much, Baby-cakes. And I love God too much. I don't intend to let either of you down ever again."

They kneeled down beside their bed, he took her hand and held it, and they prayed. Really prayed. And before they got up, he squeezed her hand three times.

Desiree smiled as tears flowed down her face. "Thank you, Father," she whispered. "Thank you."

Chapter 22

And deliver them who through fear of death were all their lifetime subject to bondage.
　　　　　　　　　　—Hebrews 2:15

"Dr. Holden, it's good to have you back," Sapphire said when she walked into his office. She had an armful of folders and an electronic gadget on top.

He smiled. "You don't have to be so formal when patients aren't around. Xavier is fine."

"Habits are hard to break, you know."

"Yes," he said as he closed a file he held in his hand. "That's why I was gone for over three weeks. I had to follow our 'it takes twenty-one days to break a habit' philosophy."

"After you break it, you know you're supposed to replace it with something better."

"True. That's why I'm making a new habit of leaving this place in a timely manner: no later than five o'clock, no matter what's going on or who 'desperately' needs me. And, I'm not planning any Saturday appointments, no matter how many more people I believe I can help. No more running to the hospital when someone's in trouble and 'only Dr. Holden can help me.' No more taking on other colleagues' clients at the expense of time with my own family."

"Wow, looks like you're a changed man for real." Sapphire set the files she had brought back to him on his desk, then sat down in the chair. "Those are the files you asked me to bring back first thing this morning."

He picked them up and placed them on top of the credenza behind him. "I'm more of a delivered man now," he said. "Work had a stronghold on me. But a transfer of power has taken place, and now I'm the one in charge instead of it being the other way around. Where I used to work to live, then live to work, now I live to live."

"That's huge. Really. What a wonderful way to put that. I may have to use that one myself."

"So, would you like to bring me up to speed on Trinity?" Dr. Holden asked as he leaned back in his chair and rocked it slightly.

"I feel bad hitting you up so early after you got back. But I'm getting nowhere, it seems. Charity wants so much for this to hurry up and start moving toward some type of closure. Whatever it is that's buried deep inside her, truly has her in total disconnect."

"What do *you* think happened to her?" Dr. Holden leaned forward.

"Naturally, most people would think it was some type of sexual abuse. But I don't know. Faith, who seems to be the most dominant of the three of them, doesn't appear to have been sexually promiscuous when she was in charge of Charity's body. But there does appear to be some kind of a link to what happened and Charity's grandmother's death, though."

"Do you believe it would be in Charity's best interest to know the truth no matter how ugly or hard it might be? Or should we just leave it alone and concentrate on working to integrate the three of them back into one, regardless of whether Charity recalls what happened that caused these different manifested personalities in the first place?"

Sapphire sat back in her chair and shook her head slowly. "That's what I keep asking myself. Especially after the last conversation I had with Faith."

"I take it Faith hasn't made an appearance for you since we talked last month?"

"No, she hasn't. She said she would wait for your return to talk to you, and so far, she has been true to her word."

Dr. Holden picked up his pen and started writing on a pad in front of him. "So when would you like me to see her? And will it be you and I in there together?"

Sapphire picked up her portable digital assistant. "Yeah, like Faith would give me the satisfaction of being in there," she said while pressing buttons on the handheld electronic device.

Dr. Holden leaned back in his overstuffed burgundy leather chair again. "What happened between you and Faith?"

"I almost said 'she's crazy,' but what would that indicate about me. Calling a person who really doesn't exist crazy. Let me see if I can explain this. Pastor Landris's brother and I were like a couple—"

"Thomas Landris."

"Yeah."

"He's one of my patients. Remember?"

"Yes, I remember. I was the one who diagnosed him as having a bipolar disorder and urged him to get some help," Sapphire said.

"And he got it not a minute too soon," Dr. Holden said. "He was in the throes of a serious episode when I first saw him. He had to stay in the hospital almost a month, but I finally got his medicine dosage to the right level, and he's doing remarkably well."

"Yes, I know. I've seen him, and he seems to be doing well. Much more functional and not as volatile as he was last year."

"Sorry, I didn't mean to interrupt your story. I just didn't know if you remembered I'm his doctor. I wouldn't want you divulging anything you believe should be kept confidential about him to me."

Sapphire shook her head. "There's nothing I can't tell you concerning this. Anyway, Thomas and I were sort of dating, if you can call it that. We had some problems because of his untreated bipolar disorder. Our relationship started going bad around March two thousand and three and by early two thousand four, was completely over. I believe Faith hooked up with him in September of 2004. They had a brief courtship and were about to be married—"

"Wow, this is some heavy stuff. I had no idea. So she must be the woman he was telling me he was about to marry in December 2004 before things fell apart during their ceremony. He never told me who she was. Talk about a small world."

"Yeah. Wow is right," Sapphire said. "Anyway, Charity stopped the wedding, from what I hear, and that's when Thomas realized he needed help as well as Charity."

"So Faith doesn't like you because you were the woman before her?"

"Technically. I think she also hates that Charity and Hope like me. It's like I'm a threat to her or something."

"You are. She probably knows you're going to be the death of her, so to speak. She's fighting for her life right now, and you, Sapphire, are the arch-enemy."

"I've tried to explain to her that I'm not her enemy. I'm just trying to help all of them be whole and well. I didn't want to treat Charity because I felt it was a conflict of interest because of Faith. Charity insisted she wanted me only. Faith refuses to cooperate with me."

"Do you think Faith will tell me what we need to know, or do you think this was just a ploy to get under your skin?"

Sapphire stood up. "I think she enjoys toying with me. I guess she thinks choosing to talk to you over me will make me feel bad. Who knows what she thinks?" Sapphire paced a few steps.

"Well, if we're ever going to treat her success-fully, we'll need to know." He pointed at her elec-tronic gadget. "What date are you looking at?"

She went back and sat down. "I have a session scheduled for Charity this coming Wednesday. I realize that's probably too soon for you. So what-ever time is best for you, we can accommodate. I'm aware you're just getting back and you have your own catching up to do. Folks were filling up your calendar just to see for themselves that you really did come back."

Dr. Holden pulled up his calendar on the computer. "The earliest I can possibly squeeze in a session with my new schedule would be next Tuesday around ten. But you would need to bring her here. That way, I'll be ready for my next session, and I won't have that drive downtime."

"Of course. I'll pick her up and bring her here myself." Sapphire gathered her PDA. "I appreciate this, Xavier. I wouldn't have asked so soon after you got back, but I feel we're so close to a breakthrough for Charity. She's such a sweet person. I hate seeing her being tortured like this." Sapphire walked toward the door. Placing her hand on the doorknob, she turned back to Dr. Holden. "If you need me to handle any of your clients while you get caught back up, and if they'll let you, just let me know. You know I have your back."

He smiled. "Yeah. I know. But I think I'm going to be okay. Some of my clients are doing great and they need to move on with their lives. I'm going to work on doing a better job of conveying that to them and help those who really are well, to start believing it."

Sapphire opened the door. "Open or closed?"

"Closed, please."

Sapphire walked out the door and closed it behind her. "Please, God. Please. Let Faith cooperate with Xavier this time around. Please."

Chapter 23

And the Lord God said, It is not good that the man should be alone; I will make him an help meet for him.

— Genesis 2:18

"Landris, I've made a decision," Johnnie Mac said when she walked into his office at church. She leaned down and greeted him with a peck on his lips.

"Do tell. You've finally decided on the baby furniture you want for the nursery?" Pastor Landris said as he watched her sit down.

"No. I've decided I'm going to help you with your workload. I know you have people on staff as counselors, but I've taken the classes already, and I am equipped to do it. You poured your life into all of us last year, showing us how to be as compassionate and passionate as you are about helping those in need of spiritual guidance. So I'm ready."

"Stop. I appreciate you wanting to help, but like you said, there are already people on staff to do this. And you, my love, have more than enough to keep you busy." He leaned forward.

"I don't have to do this full-time, or even part-time. I finished writing my last book and turned it in, so I don't have that on my plate. It will be next year before they even release it, so I'll not have to do much by way of promotions until then."

"What about Princess Rose? You know how much your daughter loves spending as much time with you as she can. Then there's your mother." He leaned back. "She's not doing so well right now. I know how that has been getting to you."

"See, that's what can be great about what I'm proposing. Princess Rose is in kindergarten all day. And I can still go by and check on Mama like I've been doing every day. Her doctor says there's only so much I can do for her at this point. I'll still be able to do that. I'm not talking about being here at the church all the time." She picked up a pen off his desk and began to spin it. "Here are my thoughts about how we can do this. You can add my name to the list. That way if you have some women who might not feel comfortable discussing their problems with a man, I can help with those."

"We have a woman on staff already precisely for that reason."

"I know," Johnnie Mae said. She set the pen back in its holder. "But can we be honest here? A lot of folks don't care to schedule with her. I know she's really good at what she does, but people are funny about who they let their guard down to."

"So what are you saying?" he asked with a smile. "Some people will feel better talking to you and that will help me with my workload?"

"Well, you did that great talk with the congregation about scheduling with other people. And I'm sure many of them took what you said to heart because you told me a lot of people did call and rescheduled with others on staff. Not everybody. But enough to help alleviate your load."

"Which was great. That cut down on the wait time for a lot of folks who were on my calendar some six months away. Now I'm able to get to them within about three weeks to a month. We'll see how long this lasts. I just don't understand how anyone with a problem will wait so long to get a resolution merely because they have a preference in who they want to discuss it with." Pastor Landris stood up and walked around to the front of his mahogany desk. "I'll tell you what, though. If you like, I will have them put your name on the list of available counselors with a notation that you're taking appointments on a limited basis only. Nothing heavy. We'll see how that works."

Smiling, Johnnie Mae stood up, face-to-face with him as he sat back against his desk. "Just trying to help my pastor in any way I can. Besides, you're going to see. This is going to be a blessing for somebody out there. I just know it. It just feels like God is leading me to do this for a specific reason. I don't know. I just want to be obedient."

"Well, you already have blessed me. Just knowing you want to help like this—"

"Oh, I'm kind of being a little selfish. I don't want all these people wearing my husband out. This way, I can be sure I'm doing my part to keep that from happening."

"I will turn your name in to Sherry today and have her do the necessary things to have you added. We'll go from there and see how it works out." He grabbed her gently by the shoulders. "But now, don't get your feelings hurt if no one requests you. It's not you, it's just the way some people are. I've had to say this to the others on staff who at one time were taking it personally when hardly anyone wanted to schedule appointments with them. It's not you. Okay?"

"And don't you take it personally when I get more than you thought I would calling and asking for me specifically. It won't mean, dear Pastor Landris, that they don't think you're still awesome." She laughed. "They just might believe I've been around much of the anointing by being around you, and I'm okay to talk to."

He laughed, too. "Okay. Again, I appreciate what you're doing. But I don't want you overdoing it. I mean it. The first sign that it's too much, you let me know."

"Well, I'm officially six months now. I'm not as tired as I was early on in my pregnancy, so I'll be fine. If a problem comes up, then I'll let you know I can't do this anymore."

"I have an appointment this afternoon to counsel a couple. Would you like to sit in with me?"

"A couple?"

"Yeah." He picked up the printed schedule from off his desk. "Bentley and Marcella Strong."

"I think I may have met Marcella before, but I'm not sure. Her name sounds familiar, anyway. Do you know what they want to discuss?"

"No. We don't have people disclose that information when they make an appointment. I just figured this would be a great opportunity for you to get the feel for what you're volunteering to do. Besides, this will probably be great for them, having the two of us in here together regardless of what their problem is."

Johnnie Mae nodded. "Sure. What time?"

"Four-thirty."

Johnnie Mae picked up her purse. "That'll work. Princess Rose will be home from school and I can either bring her with me or drop her off at her little friend Shannon's house."

"See, that's what I mean. This is going to be hard for you to do. Princess Rose should not have to suffer with time she'll be missing with you."

"What, missing me? Princess Rose was begging me, just this morning, to let her go to Shannon's house and I told her I'd have to think about it. Of course, she pouted about it. But when I pick her up from the bus stop, I'll tell her she can go and everybody will be happy. No, I want to do this one with you. And school will be out for the summer soon, so Princess can spend lots of time with me." Johnnie Mae headed for the door.

"All right. I think it's going to be kind of nice having you sitting in on this counseling session. It's usually just me. I don't get a lot of couples coming in together initially. Typically, it's one or the other. Most times, I have to convince them to bring in the other spouse after a few sessions if I see the problem still persists and it affects or involves the other spouse. Bentley Strong's problem must be something if it caused them both to decide to come in together for the initial visit."

"I'll be back around four o'clock," Johnnie Mae said. "No later than four-fifteen."

"I'll see you then," Pastor Landris said as he smiled.

"What are you smiling about?" Johnnie Mae asked with a playful look.

"I don't know. There's just something about you that automatically causes me to smile."

She smiled back. "Yeah. I know. Maybe we should see someone about our condition."

"It doesn't bother me in the least."

"Me either." She winked and then left.

Chapter 24

That your faith should not stand in the wisdom of men, but in the power of God.
—1 Corinthians 2:5

"Don't forget our appointment with Pastor Landris is at four-thirty this afternoon," Bentley had said to Marcella on his way out the door as he left for the office. "We need to be ready to leave here no later than three o'clock." Which is why he couldn't understand when he got home at three, that she wasn't ready.

"You know how Pastor Landris is about being on time. He doesn't play," Bentley said through the bathroom door at 3:15 P.M. "He says being on time is a matter of integrity. The last thing we want to do is to show up late. Then I'd have to tell him all the other issues I have on top of that," Bentley said.

"I'm hurrying," Marcella yelled back from the other side of the door. "We still have plenty of time. It's just a little after three. It only takes twenty minutes to get there."

"But you can never tell what problems we might

run into on the way there. We could get stuck in traffic. That could make us late and would not be a valid excuse in Pastor Landris's eyes. He'll just likely reiterate what he usually says during Sunday services: 'You should always factor in enough time for the unexpected.'" Bentley paced the floor in their bedroom. "This appointment was difficult enough for me to get as it was. If we're late, he may not even see me. What were you doing all day today that kept you from being ready already, anyway?"

Marcella walked out of the bathroom and turned around for him to zip her. "Sorry. I don't move as fast as I used to. Maybe it's because of this baby I'm carrying around. Maybe if you were the one to have to carry all this extra weight, you would do a better job than I happen to be doing, and I would be ready. Look at me, Bentley, I'm huge!" She looked down. "I can't even see my feet without bending forward."

He finished zipping her and she hurried to step into her new Jimmy Choo shoes.

"You're not huge. Marcella, look. I'm not being critical; I'm just asking what you were doing that kept you from being ready." He stopped and thought a second. "Oh, I know what you were doing, watching soap opcras. That's it, isn't it?"

"Bentley, I don't have time to argue with you about this. I'm trying to finish getting ready." She was looking in the dresser mirror, putting on her lipstick. She turned around, popped her lips at him to set her lipstick, and said, "There! All done."

"Good." He looked down at her shoes. "Do you really think you should be wearing heels that high? I mean, being pregnant and all."

"These heels are a compromise for me. I don't like flats, yet I've put my five-inch heels away until after the baby comes. Three-inch heels are as low as I plan to go, baby or no baby. It was hard finding something cute like these in three-inch. I don't do ugly or cheap shoes. You know that about me."

"I was just asking."

Marcella grabbed her purse and walked toward the door. She turned around. "Well, don't just stand there. You were in such a hurry to get me out of here. Let's go." She continued walking. "You know it's going to take me a minute to get to the car with these heels and being pregnant. I told you I don't move as fast as I used to."

They arrived at Pastor Landris's office at 4:27.

"See, I knew it," Bentley said under his breath as they walked back from the secretary's desk and he saw the clock. "We were almost late. You never know what you'll run into on the freeway. I told you."

"How were we supposed to know they would have only one lane opened today? Traffic was practically at a standstill." Marcella lowered her body slowly down on the couch. "It took us fifteen minutes just to cover two miles. Was that my fault?"

Bentley sat down next to her. "How are we supposed to know? That was the whole point of leaving early enough. You have to factor in extra time for just these such things."

"Mr. and Mrs. Strong?" Sherry said, still seated. "You can go into Pastor Landris's office now." Sherry pointed to the door on her left with a smile.

Marcella and Bentley began to stand at the same time. Bentley let out a deep sigh once he was standing upright.

"Ready?" Bentley said to Marcella as he helped her finish getting up.

"Ready."

"Well, okay. Let's do this." Bentley placed his arm around his wife's expanding waistline. She briefly wrapped her arm around him but found it too difficult to do that and be able to walk comfortably at the same time.

As they went into Pastor Landris's office, Bentley's arm was still linked around her.

Chapter 25

And be not conformed to this world: but be ye transformed by the renewing of your mind, that ye may prove what is that good, and acceptable, and perfect, will of God.
—Romans 12:2

"Good evening," Pastor Landris said as Marcella and Bentley came in and sat down.

"Good evening," the couple said.

"You both know my wife, Johnnie Mae?" Pastor Landris nodded as he smiled at his spouse, who was seated at his right-hand side.

"Of course," Marcella said, smiling at Johnnie Mae. "You came in the conference room when we came forward to become members here. Sister Johnnie Mae Landris, a.k.a. Johnnie Mae Taylor. I've read a few of your books. I happen to be an avid reader."

"That she is," Bentley said before she got the words out of her mouth.

Marcella flashed him a disapproving look.

"So you're Bentley and Marcella Strong," Pastor Landris said.

"Yes," they replied lovingly, and in unison.

"Is that the name you'd like for us to use during

our conversation today? We just want you both to feel as comfortable as possible."

"Marcella and Bentley is fine with us. Neither one of us has a nickname or anything like that," Marcella said.

"When is your baby due?" Johnnie Mae asked Marcella.

Marcella smiled and smoothed down the tight-fitting dress that barely disguised her basketball-looking tummy. "August nineteenth," she said with enthusiasm. She looked over at Johnnie Mae and nodded. "Yours?"

"August fourteenth."

"That's something," Bentley said as he shifted his body a little and crossed his leg. "Our babies could end up being playmates in the church nursery."

Johnnie Mae smiled. "Absolutely."

"Okay, let's first have prayer and then we'll get started," Pastor Landris said. They bowed their heads as he prayed for God to lead and guide them into all truths and His perfect will.

Pastor Landris looked at Bentley, then Marcella. "Bentley, according to my file here, you were the one who scheduled this appointment. Also, you asked if it would be all right if your wife came along with you. So what seems to be the problem you've come here to talk about?"

Bentley uncrossed his leg, resituated his body, and sat up straight. "Well, Pastor Landris. This is a bit difficult for me to talk about. Also, I wasn't expecting your lovely wife to be in here with us." He nodded in Johnnie Mae's direction.

Pastor Landris raised his hand to stop him from

saying another word. "Does my wife's presence bother you? I asked her to come today because I felt it would be good having a woman here with your wife—"

"Oh, no, no. I'm sorry," Bentley said. "I'm a little nervous, so I guess that didn't come out quite right. I'm glad she's here. It's just been hard for me to talk about this with anyone. I really didn't want to come in and talk about it with you, but I know I need help. I don't want to lose my wife and family over something like this."

"I understand. You do know whatever we discuss in this office will stay strictly between us. It is not our policy for anyone associated with Followers of Jesus Faith Worship Center's staff to ever disclose confidential information or discussions with anyone outside of possibly another counseling staff member if additional advice is needed. That begins from the time you make your appointment until your last good-bye out of whoever's office or presence you were in. We don't betray a confidence here. And should I find out someone has breeched a confidence, they will be dealt with," Pastor Landris said as he alternated his fixed eyes between the two of them. "I hope this puts you a little more at ease."

Marcella glanced over at her husband, then back to Pastor Landris. "That's what I told him. He does have another concern as well." Marcella glanced quickly over at Bentley. "You might as well tell him that, too."

Bentley looked as though he didn't know what she was referring to.

"About his judging you harshly . . ." She bobbed

her head, trying to prompt him to take it and run. "You know . . . by not allowing you to possibly ever work in the church or ministry or be over a ministry you may be qualified for even after you overcome this."

Bentley turned his gaze from his wife to Pastor Landris and cleared his throat. "I'm concerned you may view me negatively after you hear what I'm dealing with."

"Is it that bad?" Pastor Landris said.

"Well, it may be in your eyes."

"I'll tell you what: you tell me what it is, and we'll go from there."

Bentley began to iron both legs of his pants down simultaneously with his hands. He looked over at Johnnie Mae, then Marcella before looking back at Pastor Landris. "Okay." He took a deep breath and exhaled slowly. "When I was around thirteen years old, my uncle introduced me to pornography by way of magazines. Somewhere along the way, I got hooked on porn."

"I see," Pastor Landris said.

"When you had that special altar call after you finished your teaching series on strongholds, I came forward and was prayed for. I've even been to the special Wednesday night Bible study and the Deliverance support group, but nothing seems to be working. At least, not the way I'd hoped and prayed."

Pastor Landris picked up his pen and wrote something down. "Well, something is working, because you made the step to come here and confess all this to me. Now, have you gotten rid of the various temptations out of your house and from on your job?"

Bentley laughed a little, mostly from being nervous. "Oh, I did that right after I came to the altar. I stayed up until the middle of the night so Marcella wouldn't find out I had all that stuff in our house to begin with. I drove to a Dumpster in somebody else's neighborhood, if you can believe that, and dumped every bit of it."

"How did you feel when you did that?" Pastor Landris asked.

"Honestly? Like I had just lost someone I loved deeply," Bentley said. "I almost drove back and climbed inside that Dumpster to get all my stuff back."

Marcella gave him a look as she began to visibly frown at him. "Someone you loved deeply?" Marcella asked. "Someone you loved deeply?! You've got to be kidding me. I just know you are kidding."

"Marcella," Johnnie Mae said. "Allow him to get this all out without you judging what he's saying. He needs to feel free to tell the truth, because the truth will help set him free." Johnnie Mae nodded at Marcella to calm her, then to Bentley for him to continue.

Pastor Landris put the fingers of both his hands together and pointed them toward Bentley. "Go on, Bentley. You were expressing how you felt when you took all that pornography to the Dumpster."

"Yeah," Bentley said as he sneaked a look at Marcella from the corner of his eye. "It's hard to explain, but having pictures of naked women somehow made me feel accepted. I felt like I be-longed, and in a strange way . . . like I was truly loved. You see, Pastor Landris, Sister Johnnie Mae, I grew up a loner. The kids in my neighborhood didn't care to play with me. I could truly identify with poor Rudolph the red-nosed reindeer and all the other misfits. I was geeky. Too smart, I guess. Too much acting like white for a black boy from the 'hood—they were some of the cruel words said about me."

" 'Acting like white.' You mean, because you were smart?" Pastor Landris said.

"That and because I spoke well. You see, my mother always emphasized speaking 'good English' as she put it. She wouldn't let me get away with double negatives, splitting verbs, using slang, or talking as if I 'fell off a turnip truck,' as she termed it when people sounded a little too country."

"So you say your uncle was the one who first in-troduced you to pornography?" Pastor Landris asked. "Why do *you* suppose he did something like that?"

"He thought I was spending too much time with my head in books and on the computer. He felt I needed to become a little more rounded . . . bal-anced . . . normal."

"How did you feel when you first saw that maga-zine?" Johnnie Mae asked.

Pastor Landris looked at her as though to ask why she would even ask a question like that. She saw his questioning look and said to Bentley, "I just want you to go back to that moment when you were choosing between life and death, so to speak, by looking or choosing not to. In this case, death being death of a certain innocence."

Marcella looked at Bentley and waited for his answer.

"I didn't like it. It felt wrong. I was embarrassed to be seeing things I wouldn't normally see. But then there was something about it that aroused me, I guess. And at some point, it made me feel good to feel like these women didn't have a problem with me like other people seemed to have. It was confusing at first. Still is, to be honest."

"But you do realize those women weren't and still aren't real, don't you? Not really. At least not to you," Marcella said in a frigid tone. "You didn't then, and you don't now mean anything to them except for all the money they can suck out of you."

"See, Pastor Landris, that's precisely the point I was making earlier about my wife," Bentley said, looking directly at Pastor Landris while seeming to ignore his wife's spoken words.

"What?" Marcella said, also directing her gaze toward the pastor. She then looked over at Johnnie Mae. "What? What did I do? Why are all of you looking at me like that?"

Johnnie Mae softened her face even more. "Marcella, men don't like for us to know this about them because they want to present themselves as the big, strong, don't need anybody type. Sometimes we women say or do things that can really bring a man down, and they won't tell us we just hit them below their belt or that we just hurt their feelings or heart deeply. What they will do though, is look for ways to bring themselves up. You telling

Bentley the women weren't real to *him* in the context in which you just did, probably hurt him and embarrassed him just now more than you will ever imagine."

"The women in those magazines don't relay the message that they don't care to the men who are looking in them," Pastor Landris added as he addressed his comments to Marcella. "Bentley is dealing with a problem that so many men and some women—in church, out of church, in the pews, in the pulpit, and in the streets—do on a daily basis."

Pastor Landris looked at Bentley. "Bentley, what I just said to your wife is not to excuse your behavior. You have a wife; you need to tell your wife what you need and allow her the opportunity to fulfill your needs instead of you going outside your marriage for that. God designed and intended for it to be done this way. You must let your wife know when you need to feel like you're 'the man.' You know what I'm saying here?"

Bentley laughed and shook his head. "I know, Pastor. And I hear you, but it's hard to do that. I feel like I have to grovel for attention or you know—"

"I don't make you grovel for that!" Marcella said with a look of sheer disbelief.

"I'm not even talking about what you're thinking about, Marcella. I'm talking about having to grovel for you to make me feel good about myself."

"How am I supposed to know you don't feel good about yourself? I myself thought you had a pretty healthy ego. You're always in the mirror, posing like you're Hercules or somebody. Hercules, Hercules," she began singing, clapping her hands and bouncing up and down the way the character did in the movie *The Nutty Professor.*

"Marcella," Bentley said, saying her name sweetly as he cut his eyes over at Pastor Landris to try and gauge what he was likely thinking right about now, "you don't have to tell *everything.*"

"And don't be cutting your eyes over at Pastor Landris," Marcella said. "You came here about a problem you have so you could get help, and we're going to stay on course. Have you ever thought about or considered how degrading porn can be for women?"

"You mean the ones who pose for the pictures?" Bentley asked.

"No," Marcella said, almost singing the word, "I mean the ones who have to learn later in their marriage that their husbands are sneaking around looking at it because they are *obviously* not enough to keep their own *husband's* attention!"

"Marcella, please," Pastor Landris said. "Let's try to keep this on as much of a civil level as possible, okay? The goal is to reach a resolution, not to inflame the situation even more."

"It's okay, Pastor Landris," Bentley said. "But since Marcella wants to go there, I'd like for her to tell me why she reads erotic fiction, and why she can't miss one of her soap operas for even one day. She tapes them if she's going to be gone while they're on. And don't let me call her while *General Hospital* is on . . . or what are those other three soaps you love so much you can't miss? Yeah, that's right: *All My Children, The Young and the Restless,* and *One Life to Live.* Call during one of these, and she won't give you the time of day. All you'll hear if she talks to you at all is, 'Uh-huh. Uh-huh. Hmmm.'"

"Now see, that's why I didn't want to come here with you," Marcella said. She turned to look at Johnnie Mae, then Pastor Landris. "I knew he was going to figure out a way to turn this around and make it about me. Reading a book or watching soap operas is not the same as watching naked women. Would somebody please tell him that? Pastor Landris . . . Johnnie Mae, will you please explain to my husband, there is a difference?"

Johnnie Mae looked at Pastor Landris; Pastor Landris looked at Johnnie Mae. He then nodded for Johnnie Mae to proceed with the answering of this one.

"One definition of porn I've come across recently," Johnnie Mae said, "is material intended to arouse sexual excitement."

"Okay, so now this little session has become about me *and* Bentley being sexually aroused outside of each other." Marcella crossed her leg and started pumping it back and forth. She crossed her arms across her chest. "According to your definition, I can't read the Song of Solomon in the Bible anymore because a few of those chapters do something for me, too."

"Marcella," Bentley said with a sound of exasperation, "now you're just being silly. No one is attacking you here. The only reason I brought up what you do is to try and get you to see things from my perspective. The way you feel about some of your books and your soap operas is the way I was feeling about those magazines, videos, Internet, and television programs. I wasn't hurting anyone. It was entertainment to me. I never thought about how it might make you feel to know I was looking at those things. Just like you probably don't think about how I feel when you read certain books."

"All right then, Bentley." Marcella turned to Pastor Landris. "Do you mind?"

"No. Go right ahead."

"Tell me how my reading a book *with words only* or my watching a soap opera or two could possibly affect you the way you looking in a magazine with photos of naked women or watching pornographic videos affects me."

Bentley looked at Johnnie Mae, then Pastor Landris before turning his attention back to Marcella and then Pastor Landris again. "I'm sorry, Pastor Landris. Maybe this is not going in the direction you had intended. I shouldn't have brought up anything about what Marcella does. This is about me, and I know that. She and I have touched on this subject about her already, and I shouldn't have brought it up in here."

"Just answer my question," Marcella said sternly. "We're here with our pastor and wife. We're putting all *my* business out there even though you are the one who originally came here with the problem." Marcella looked at Johnnie Mae. "Don't you agree he should answer my question?"

Johnnie Mae nodded. "Actually, I do."

Marcella looked over at Pastor Landris; he nodded as well. Marcella turned back to Bentley. "Everybody here seems to agree you should answer my question. So tell me how my reading a book with words could possibly affect you in the same way as you looking in a magazine with *photos or videos of naked* women affects me?"

"Okay . . . It shows I'm not good enough for

you. It tells me our marriage is not enough, not exciting enough to you."

"What are you talking about? Whoever said you weren't good enough or our marriage wasn't good enough for me? They're books, Bentley. Fiction. Fic-tion."

"You read those novels about people having 'off-the-hook-chandelier-swinging sex,' I believe those were the exact words you used to describe some of them. You watch people on television and fantasize about how you wish you and I, or maybe even you and somebody else, could be together."

"How do you know I fantasize about how things could be with us?" Marcella asked.

"The same way you claim you know I'm fantasizing about something I don't feel I'm experiencing in our relationship because of my porn addiction."

"That was a low blow, Bentley."

"Okay," Pastor Landris said. "I think you both get the point of all this."

"There's a point?" Marcella said. "There's a point?"

"Yes." Pastor Landris sat up straighter in his chair. "Taking intimacy outside of the marriage can be detrimental no matter who is doing it or how it's being done. Wrong thoughts in the mind can destroy a relationship that has such great potential. If only the parties involved would direct their energies the right way, things could be so much better for and between them."

"Okay, Pastor Landris," Bentley said. "I don't really want to focus on what Marcella is doing that I might have a problem with—"

"And I don't want to focus on you if I really have

problems I need to address myself. I just never saw it that way"—Marcella looked around the room—"that is . . . until just now. I didn't see how I was reading about things other men were doing to other women, wishing it was me. I told myself I was getting information to help me be a better, more exciting person," Marcella said. "Or that I was just being merely entertained."

"You already are exciting to me, Marcella. My porn problems don't stem from what I'm not getting from you. Pornography allowed me to live in a fantasy world where I felt I wasn't being criticized. I felt a closeness I don't always feel. And oddly enough, I felt an unquestioning sense of acceptance. None of that is real, but you are. I understand this even more so now."

"Okay," Johnnie Mae said. "It's obvious you two love each other. So I think there's hope for this relationship to not only be restored, but go to a whole new level."

"As do I," Pastor Landris said. "First off, there are some truths we need to acknowledge. Pornography is a lie. The illusions it attempts to portray as reality about women and relationships between a man and a woman are just that: illusions. It promises things it can never deliver. And worst of all, it dehumanizes another person, it dehumanizes real relationships, and it distorts the genuine definition of true intimacy. What do you have to say about these statements, Bentley?"

Bentley paused a second. "I'd say you're right. And that's why I'm here now."

Pastor Landris redirected his gaze. "Marcella?"

"Even though I now consider what I've been reading and participating in as possibly being pornographic lite—"

"Pornographic lite?" Johnnie Mae said with a short chuckle. "Well, that's cute and quite original. I may have to use that one the next time I need to get that point across."

Marcella smiled and gave Johnnie Mae a slight nod. "Yes, pornographic lite. I can see where I was filling my mind with thoughts that could lead to trouble later down the road. It truly can lead to dissatisfaction with what I do have in my real life."

"Precisely," Johnnie Mae said. "When you don't feel you're getting from your husband what you read about, that can become a real problem. But those people in novels aren't really real. When you're watching a television show about some made-up character and you get disgusted with your marriage because it's not playing out like you see on TV, remember: it's a script. It's not real. Even the sex and love scenes are choreographed."

"You have to be careful that you don't end up on a road leading to trouble," Pastor Landris said. "The people writing these books have their own problems. The people portraying those wonderful, romantic characters you see on television, most of them can't even keep their own real marriages or relationships together. You have to ask why that is. And with pornography, it's not about what's real. It's a ploy of the devil to make you lose sight of the blessings God has for your life. The God-kind of love He desires for you to experience. 'O taste and see how good the Lord is.' I can testify to how good God is when you do things the God way . . . according to His divine plan."

"It's the same for you, Bentley, looking at pictures of people who are often airbrushed to look that good," Johnnie Mae added. "Women required to pose in positions that almost break them to do it. It's a lot of work to look that sexy. It's all just an illusion merely to poison the mind, a sleight of hand. It's not true reality."

"Reality is working at a fantastic life with the one who promised to love, honor, and cherish you through thick and thin, ups and downs, the best and the worst life might throw your way," Pastor Landris said, glancing a quick look at Johnnie Mae. "My wife did a wonderful seminar last year on marriage."

"Yes, we've heard so much about it," Marcella said. "We were just saying we wished you would consider doing it again so we can attend."

"I think we're going to make it something we have every year or at least on some regular basis. It really blessed those who attended and strengthened so many marriages. From some reports I've heard from the men, their wives were all they needed and had time to fantasize about after the information they both took from the seminar," Pastor Landris said.

"And the women were calling their men Fab-i-o-So-Fab-u-lous. They weren't wishing for fairy tale romances any longer; their husbands were giving them as close to the real love thing on a daily basis as possible," Johnnie Mae said. "When we know better, we do better. One woman said what she was reading and seeing on the soaps were nothing compared to what she and her husband were writing daily. In her words: '*The Young and the Restless* may have *One Life to Live*, but the *Bold and the Beautiful* are now on *The Edge of Night*, *As the World Turns* their *Passions* toward the *Guiding Light* as she is no longer one of those *Desperate Housewives* waiting *In the Heat of the Night*.'"

Marcella sighed. "I can't say I've ever read anything that made me feel that way."

"And I know I've not seen anything in those magazines, videos, the Internet, or television that made me feel like that either," Bentley said.

"Now do you see what all you have ahead of you if both of you would merely apply yourselves to your own relationship instead of spending so much time giving it away to others who aren't even really real in your life?" Pastor Landris said.

"Well, I'm ready," Bentley said, laughing. "Fix me! Help me break my stronghold so I can live this goodly God-life."

Marcella reached over and grabbed Bentley's hand. "I'm ready, too."

Pastor Landris started writing some things in the notebook on his desk. When he finished, he tore it out and handed it to Bentley. "Here's a prescription for you. I've written down specific instructions and some scripture references I want you to get down in your spirit and into your heart."

Bentley began to read the first one out loud. "Accountability: Make your computer accountable to someone other than yourself," Bentley said.

"You say you've gotten all the porn out of your house with the exception of what comes unsolicited to you over the Internet. Marcella needs to check the computer's history log every day to see where you've been," Pastor Landris said to Bentley. "And I don't want you to become defensive about this. I want you to welcome it. Because if you slip up, someone needs to call you on it. You need someone to pray with you to stay strong. Especially if you're serious about breaking away from this."

"Marcella can do that. Can't you, baby?" He smiled at his wife, caressing her hand.

"Of course."

Bentley read another one out loud. "For both of you: Act out."

"Act out?" Marcella asked. "What do you mean by that?" She looked at Pastor Landris.

"I mean, write your own love story daily. See how creative you both can be. Then act it out. Bentley, I want you to begin to act like you've found this woman you have to have and you're going to do everything in your powers to ensure one day, she's completely yours," Pastor Landris said with a smile that seemed to dance. "I don't care that you're already married to her."

"I can do that."

Pastor Landris looked at Johnnie Mae and nodded for her to take over.

"Marcella," Johnnie Mae said. "You need to loosen up a bit and give your man a little show every now and then. Let him see what he has at home, and you won't have to worry about him going to strange women to get *anything* That's in the Bible: Proverbs chapter seven. Read the whole chapter, in fact."

"You sound like a woman who knows what she's talking about," Marcella said.

"Let's just say our baby was not from an immaculate conception. And when you really love someone, it's not hard to want to please them," Johnnie Mae said as she looked over at Pastor Landris and smiled.

"But it should work both ways," Pastor Landris said. "You hear me, Bentley?"

Bentley saw the look exchanged between Pastor and Mrs. Landris. "You two are for real," Bentley said. "It's funny: I can feel the love and respect you have for each other. That's what I want for Marcella and me. We love each other, but there's so much we're missing out on." He looked at his wife. "That ends today. Today, I'm a new man."

Marcella looked at Bentley. "Wow, that was so romantic."

Bentley licked his lips and smacked them. "Just perfecting my love script here. Practice, they tell me, makes perfect. I'm going to start practicing what our pastor preaches." He turned his attention back to Pastor Landris. "Well, Pastor Landris, I believe we get it. Why waste your life and time on fake, when you can enjoy the real deal? But you have to work at it. Anything worth having is worth working for. I get it. Oh, I get it."

"I'm not saying it will be easy, Bentley, but you *can* overcome your stronghold. It's about the mind. Transform yourself by the renewing of your mind. Take on the mind of Christ." Pastor Landris got to his feet. "Let's join hands and have a word of prayer."

They all stood and Pastor Landris ushered them into the presence of the Lord with a powerful plea to the Father for restoration, deliverance, healing, and mending of those things that were once sick, twisted, and broken but are now being changed forevermore.

Chapter 26

*For I know that in me (that is, in my flesh,)
dwelleth no good thing: for to will is present
with me; but how to perform that which is
good I find not.*

—Romans 7:18

Fatima's doorbell rang. She had been in an especially somber mood today. It was May 14th, her birthday, and she had grown conditioned to dread this day. It wasn't because she didn't appreciate being born or the fact that she had made it to yet another year. It was because few people ever really remembered or seemed to care that it was her special day. Sure, her parents and siblings usually called sometime before the clock struck midnight. All except her baby brother, who traditionally never did. He was too much into himself to notice other people existed on the planet if they didn't act like the world revolved around him. And a few friends usually called, here and there.

Today, she turned 32, and she was still alone. *What was there to celebrate?*

She opened the door.

"Delivery," the flower man said. He handed her a huge bouquet of exotic, mixed flowers.

"They're beautiful," Fatima said as she carefully took the lead crystal vase.

"Top of the line." He smiled. "Hope it brightens your Saturday."

"It's my birthday," Fatima said, although for the life of her, she didn't know why.

"Well, happy birthday," he said with an even bigger smile as though he really meant it.

Fatima smiled. He turned and strode quickly back to his van and drove away. Admiring the flowers, she walked into the house, anxious to see who could have sent her something so nice. Her parents didn't do flowers. They always sent a card with money in it. Always.

"What do we get for a person who has everything or can buy herself whatever she wants whenever she wants?" Fatima's mother would say every year. "I hope you don't mind, but we know money will always fit."

"Thank you, Mother," Fatima always politely said. "And the card is lovely as always."

The mailman hadn't delivered yet, so who knows, maybe her mother had decided to break with tradition and send something different this year. Fatima couldn't think of anyone else it could be from. Her three sisters and one other brother who usually called on her birthday weren't flower-sending types either. And her daddy, when it came to gift giving, usually went in with her mother.

She put the vase on the table and removed the small card tucked snugly inside of its miniature, cream-colored envelope.

"You are so beautiful to me. Happy Birthday!"

It wasn't signed. Without a signature, she couldn't

imagine who they could be from. Maybe it really *was* from her mother. That was one of the sayings her mother constantly hammered in her head: that she was indeed beautiful. Fatima started to call her mother to see if they were in fact from her, but there was another tradition her mother and father had: they always called her at the exact time she was born. If she called them now, it would ruin things for them. They would be calling right at 1:02 P.M. That was only some thirty minutes away. She could wait thirty more minutes to find out.

The doorbell rang again. Fatima went to answer it, wondering who *this* could be.

"Delivery," the same man who had brought the flowers earlier said again. He held out a long, white box secured together by a yellow ribbon tied into a lovely bow.

"Weren't you just here?" Fatima said. "Are you sure those are for me?"

"Yes, ma'am. You're Fatima Adams, right?"

"Yes, that's me."

"Then these are for you."

She took the box and cradled it under her arm. "Thank you. I feel like I should tip you or something, especially since you had to come twice."

"No need, ma'am. It's all been taken care of. You just have a nice birthday."

"Thanks," she said again. She went back inside and hurried to open the box.

"Yellow roses," she said. She found the card inside and read it.

"You light up my world. You're the sunshine of my life. Happy Birthday, Fatima."

Now she was really confused. This card wasn't signed either. The doorbell rang once again. She couldn't help but to beam. *Now who?*

When she opened the door, another man stood with a large rectangular box. "Special delivery for Fatima Adams," he said in a high-pitched, slow drawl.

"That would be me."

"Sign here please, ma'am." He held up a gadget with an electronic-like pen attached to it for her to sign. She scribbled her name; he handed her the box.

She looked for a return address, but there was only a dress shop address. After she walked back into the house, she had to find a pair of scissors to cut loose the tape that held the box together. Inside the box was an A-line, beaded, knee-length, form-fitting dress.

"Purple," she said as she took the dress in her hands and held it up to see the front and back of it in its full splendor. "My favorite color. This is beautiful." She carefully laid it on the couch as she searched the box for a card or some clue as to who had sent it. There was nothing nestled in between the tissue paper that had blanketed the dress.

The phone rang. She glanced at the clock: 1:02 P.M. on the dot.

Right on cue! It was her parents singing happy birthday to her. This was such a highlight for them.

"That was so nice," Fatima said. "Thank you, both."

"You're welcome," her father said.

"So how has your day been so far?" her mother asked.

"So far it's been great. And of course, this call just made it all that more special, as it always does every year."

"Has our package arrived yet?" her mother asked.

Fatima smiled. "Yes, I suppose. I'm just not sure which one might be from the two of you."

"Which one? We only sent one," her mother said.

"Yeah. I figured that. I just received three deliveries almost back-to-back, and there was no card saying who anything was from. So I'm not sure which one is from the two of you."

"Well, we signed our card just like we always do," her father said. "And Mother put the signed check inside the card, just the way she always does. Didn't you, Mother? You shouldn't have to guess, Fatima, which one is from us."

"You sent a card with money?" Fatima sounded surprised and a bit disappointed.

"Well, yes," her mother said. "I told you, Fatima. We don't have a clue what to ever buy you. With money, we don't have to worry about you needing to exchange it because you don't like the color or you already have something like it. I know our gift will always fit, and it's something you can always find a use for. I know it might seem insensitive, but it works great for us. We don't ever have to worry about our feelings being hurt because you didn't like your present."

"Well, the mailman hasn't come yet, so I haven't gotten your gift, Mother and Dad." Fatima looked again at the purple dress that seemed to twinkle in the sunlight.

"Maybe one of your sisters or your brothers sent the other package."

"I doubt that *very* seriously," Fatima said. While she talked, she walked over to the box holding the roses and took it to the kitchen to put the roses in a vase.

"Now see, Fatima you always act that way about your siblings. They don't ever buy you a gift because they're barely making it with their own families. It's hard on them, on all of them. You and your baby brother are the only two who don't have any real responsibilities."

"Mother, I can't speak for your baby boy, but I have responsibilities." She turned on the faucet, filled the vase with water, and poured in the contents of the packet enclosed to keep the flowers alive longer.

"You know what I mean. You don't have a husband or children. And at the rate you're going, being so choosey and all, who knows if or when you'll ever have anyone in your life. I don't know if you realize this, Fatima, but you're not getting any younger."

Fatima smiled at the phone. "Okay, Mother. Dad, thanks to both of you for calling and singing happy birthday to me. Thanks for the card when it does arrive. I know I'm going to just love it. I love you both—"

"Fatima?" her mother said.

She let out a sigh. "Yes, Mother."

"Baby, I hope you do something fun today. Why

don't you go out and try not to be so . . . so . . . well, you know."

"What, Mother? So stuck up? So diva-ish? So what, Mother?" She took the knife and sliced the ends of each rose stem so water would be able to flow freely to the buds.

"So antisocial. You know, you can be a bit uppity sometimes. Try to be a little more friendly. Maybe you'll run into a nice young man, and who knows, maybe you'll finally be able to settle down and have a family like your sisters and brother."

"Oh yeah. And I'll be sure and make a wish when I blow out my candles today."

"You have a cake for your birthday?" her mother asked.

"No, Mother. I really don't need a cake. There's nobody here but me. Remember? That means there would be nobody here to eat it but me. And you know where that could lead—weight gain, yet one more thing you'll be able to point out that's wrong with me and my life."

"Baby, I'm not pointing out things that are wrong with you. I love you. I just want you to be happy."

"Well, I'm happy, Mother. I am *so* happy I don't know how to contain myself."

Fatima put the roses in the vase and started arranging them with the greenery and the baby's breath. "I have a great job, with great pay, and great benefits. I have a three-thousand-square-foot house, a luxury car that I can afford to keep both the maintenance *and* repairs on, all the designer and otherwise fancy clothes and shoes I can stand.

I attend a church where the Word of God goes forth every week. I even have money saved up in the bank so when my wonderful siblings *with* responsibilities, mind you, and those without, let us not forget him, need something, they know they can come to the Bank of Fatima twenty-four/seven because my *mother* is going to hammer at me about what the Bible says I should do when people ask me for a loan that's never really a loan, since a loan generally means you're going to be paid back, which has yet to ever be the case with them. I am *happy*, Mother. Hap-py!"

"Well, you don't sound very happy, Baby. Did I say something to upset you? I didn't mean to upset you if I have, especially not on your birthday."

Fatima carried the roses into the other room as she released a sigh. "I'm not upset, Mother. I'm glad you called." The doorbell rang. "That's my doorbell. I have to go."

"All right. We love you!" her mother said.

"Love you, too. Bye," Fatima said. She hung up and walked to the door. "Yes," she said to the man standing with a Kangol hat on and his back turned toward her.

"Delivery," he said in a deep, slightly muffled voice. He then turned around with a slightly large, square box in his hand.

Her gaze went from the box to his face. "Darius?" Her voice was laced with surprise. "What are you doing here?"

"Happy Birthday," he said with a mischievous grin. "Surprised?" He smiled as he continued to hold the box out to her.

"You remembered my birthday?" Fatima smiled as she slanted her head slightly toward him and tried not to let him see she was now blushing.

"Of course, I remembered your birthday."

"But you never seemed to have remembered it before."

"That was then; this is now. Are you going to take this, or are you waiting for my arm to fall—"

She laughed. "Don't you dare do that."

"Do what? That scene from the movie *Mahogany* with Billy Dee Williams and Diana Ross? One of your favorites, right?"

"Yes."

"Well?" He started lowering the box as if it was becoming harder and harder for him to keep holding it in the air. "Are you going to take this or what?"

She took the box and found herself smiling even more, no matter how hard she tried not to. Through the plastic window, she could see what was inside it: a beautiful cake with her name scripted in purple with purple and yellow flowers surrounding it.

He rubbed his hands quickly together and blew into them as though they were cold, which they couldn't be since it was the middle of May in a very hot Alabama. His eyes traveled unhurriedly from her head down to her feet. "May I come in?"

"I don't think that's a good idea," Fatima said, standing her ground.

"Why not, beautiful? You do know you are so beautiful to me. You light up my world. You are a queen, a woman of royal distinction. Purple for royalty, for her majesty the queen." He bowed before her, then stood back erect while shaking his head and grinning.

She looked at him as her eyes began to widen. "You? That was you who sent me all those things today?"

"A bouquet of flowers in a lead crystal vase. Yellow roses because you really are the sunshine of my life. You, without a doubt, light up my world. And a dress fit for a queen going out to celebrate one of the most important days of *my* life—the day you, Fatima Adams, graced this earth with your presence and blessed all those who have had the fortunate pleasure to meet and know you." Somehow on cue, his eyes twinkled.

"Darius . . ."

"Can we please just go inside and talk? I won't do anything inappropriate. I won't pressure you. I just want to talk . . . somewhere other than outside for your nosey neighbors to see. And you know some of them are looking. If after we talk you want me gone, you just say the word, and I promise I'll not ruin your special day today by fighting you on it."

Fatima pushed the door open and let Darius pass inside. She carried the cake to the table in the kitchen. When she came back, Darius had taken off his hat and put it on the coffee table. He was holding a small velvet box in his hand. He patted the place next to him. "Come sit next to me. Please," he said.

She stood where she was.

"Please. I have something for you. A birthday present. Come on, sit by me."

She walked over slowly and slid down cautiously next to him.

He took her hand. She felt electricity instantly and snatched her hand out of his.

"I'm not going to hurt you," he said as he reached to take her hand back. "You felt it, too, didn't you? There's a connection between us, positive and negative charges that cause sparks and a steady current to flow through your body." He slowly and gently brought her hand up to his lips and planted a soft kiss on the back of it.

"I don't think this is such a great idea."

"And I think I've missed you so much all of these months. I can't stand this, Fatima. I can't stand not having you in my life. I love my wife, but I'm not in love with her. She doesn't make me feel the way you do. It's different with us. When I turned around and saw you just a little while ago, my heart literally did a flip and then skipped a beat. I've never known a woman to cause that type of reaction in me. You're very special, Fatima, and I'm not going to let us go by the wayside without at least putting up a fight."

"You . . . are . . . married, Darius. How many different ways can I say that to you?"

"But for how long? You met my wife that Sunday. There's nothing between us anymore. Couldn't you tell? Didn't you feel it? We don't have anything in common. Not like you and I seem to."

"You don't really know me, Darius. All you know are the stolen moments we've shared. Sure it's easy for you to compare a woman you're with day in and day out to one you see only briefly, and most times, when she's at her best . . . when I'm at the top of my game. You don't know all the bad things about me. And for that matter, I don't know all your negative junk either, except for the fact that you *will* cheat on your wife. I do know that."

"Ooh, low blow. Score one for you." He picked up the small box he'd held earlier, which was now resting on the couch beside him. "I want you to have this," he said as he handed her the box.

She didn't reach to take it. "What is it?"

"Open it and see." He nodded his head once and pushed it closer toward her.

"I don't like what that box looks like it might be."

He turned the small box around in his hand as he pretended to examine it better. "Looks like a blue velvet box to me. People get them every day. It seems harmless enough. What does it look like?"

"It looks like a ring box to me."

He laughed. "Very good. I see you are at least familiar with jewelry. Now, do you think you can take this box and open it so we can see if you like what's inside or not?"

"I really don't want to."

"Fatima, why are you being silly?"

"I'm not being silly, Darius. I don't know what kind of game you're playing, but this is my heart you're playing it with. This stuff hurts." She looked into his eyes. "Do you understand this at all?"

"Of course, I understand. I've been hurting for the past two months. I called and you wouldn't even answer. I think about you day and night, but I can't do a thing about my feelings or thoughts. And believe me, I've tried. I submerged myself in my work. I spent extra time with my children. I tried doing some of the things you and I at least wanted to do together, with my wife. Like going out and having fun, for example, which she doesn't want or care to do. Ever. But no matter what I did, nothing would take the place of my thoughts of you."

"That's why you need to stop doing stuff like this. Every time you do it, it's just like having a wound that's on its way to being healed and somebody comes along and starts pulling and picking at it until it opens up and starts bleeding again."

He took her hand. "Don't you think if I *could* stop, I would? This is not easy for me either. Woman, you've got some kind of a stronghold on me. Yeah, okay. I'm a man; I'm supposed to be tough. But men want and need to feel love, too. We men want to feel like someone out there thinks we're somebody special just like you women do. But we can't go around spouting off junk like that. Not out loud. We can't ask for it like you women are allowed to. We look weak if we do. And let's face it, women just don't care for weak men." He held the box out to her once again. "So please, take this and open it."

Fatima pressed her lips tightly together and shook her head slowly but continuously. "I'm scared. I just can't. This hurts too much." She began to cry. "I don't want to love you, Darius. I promise I don't. And every time I believe I am finally getting over you, something happens, like this, and I'm right back where I started with you."

He took his thumb and alternately and gently began to wipe the tears from each side of her cheeks and face. "Do you want me to leave?"

She continued to cry. He leaned over and pulled her into his arms as he held her. "Fatima, do you want me to leave? Because I didn't come here to hurt you today. It was a special day for me because I realized this is the day you were born. And I was thinking about what that really meant in my own life. I knew those other years I was not here for you on your birthday. I knew you had to spend your special day without me in the past. But today, I was determined I would make it up to you. I wanted you to know how much you really do mean to me. Whether we're just friends or whatever, I care deeply for you."

She looked up at him. "You always know the right things to say, don't you? You always seem to know what I need, when I need it. So if I open that box, what am I going to find inside it? A friendship ring? Or the ring you know would mean the most to me even if it means nothing substantial to my life?"

"Do you think I'm trying to play you right now?" Darius tried to appear sincere. "I love you, Fatima. I can't help that." He leaned down and kissed her. Then he kissed her again. "Why don't you go upstairs, take your new dress, put it on, and let's you and I go to Anniston or Tuscaloosa or Huntsville or Chelsea . . . somewhere where no one knows us. And let's celebrate your birthday the way you've always wanted us to."

"You mean dinner . . . a movie . . . spending time together without having to be anywhere at any particular time or having to watch the clock?"

"Yes." Darius kissed her on her nose. "That's exactly what I mean."

"Then we come back here and spend some more time together, just you and I. And we make wild, passionate love or you just hold me . . . like you're doing right now?"

He smiled even more. "Whatever you want. Whatever happens. Just the two of us. Together."

She looked up at him the way a little girl who was shy would look up at an adult. "Yeah. That does sound good, doesn't it? Really good."

"Oh yeah, girl. Now you go on upstairs and get ready so we can get this birthday party started."

She stood up, walked over to the bouquet of flowers and inhaled deeply. She went and caressed the buds of the roses that were still tight-lipped. She picked up the dress at the end of the couch with all its fine, beaded work, ran her hand over portions of it, and smiled. She looked over at him. "And after we've been together and confessed our undying love for each other, then what?" she asked, still maintaining her smile.

The smile on his face began to drop. "Then what?"

"Yeah. Then what?"

"Then we go on with real life. I mean, I don't understand what you want me to say right here. Then you and I go back to reality. To our real lives."

She smiled. "Oh. You mean, then you get up sometime during the early morning hours—before the sun breaks—and you hurriedly put your clothes back on. You kiss me on the lips, then the cheeks, and you tell me how hard it is to leave. But you have to get home before it's too late. After all, you *are* a married man; we both knew that fact going in. . . ."

"And you know I won't want to go, but that's the

way it has to be. For now anyway. Not forever, just for now."

"Right. Because you love me. And you would never do anything to hurt me."

He stood up and walked over to her. Wrapping his arms snugly around her, he whispered softly, "Girl, you know that. That's why I'm here right now. Your birthday is special. You're special. Do you know what I had to do to even be here today like this? And then, for me to be available for us to do all the things we're planning on later today and tonight. I had to lie to my wife who, incidentally, is now three months pregnant. But I'm here for you. My wife thinks I had to go out of town on some important family business, and that I'm doing all I can to get back home before daybreak just so we can make it to church together as a family tomorrow. I'm going to be worn out."

"Your wife is pregnant again? So you're having another baby? Well, I suppose congratulations are in order." She let out a small laugh, then pulled it back in. "And yet, you're here with me? You're doing all of this . . . for little ole me."

"Yes," he said as he scrunched up his face, wondering what Fatima was really trying to say. "I'd do anything for you. You know this. So quit using up all our valuable time with all this nonsense about how I feel about you, and let me show you just how much I really *do* care."

She smiled, pulled the dress closer to her body, and started slowly walking up the curving staircase. She stopped and turned around to look back down at him just once more.

He winked as he shook his head slowly, scanning her body again as he bit down hard on his bottom lip . . . just before he moistened both his lips and grinned. "Hurry up now. I can't wait." He rubbed his hands together, puckered up his lips, and kissed the wind in her direction.

Chapter 27

Learn to do well; seek judgment, relieve the oppressed, judge the fatherless, plead for the widow.

—Isaiah 1:17

"Charity, it's good to see you. You look well," Dr. Holden said as he sat down in his chair next to the chaise lounge.

Charity smiled at him as she paced around his office trying to walk off some of her nervous energy. "Thanks."

"How do you feel you're doing?"

"I feel better about a lot of things. Some things still bother me, though."

"Like?"

"Like how I could have two other personalities and didn't realize they even existed. I mean, you would think if we're all sharing the same body, I should know when something is off like that. Yet, I didn't. Or maybe I did, but I chose to pretend I didn't. On top of that, it looks like I am the one responsible for the two of them being brought into existence. How do you even handle something like that?"

"It's not like you did it on purpose," Dr. Holden said.

"No?"

"No. You were a little girl. Something happened. You didn't know how to cope. It was overwhelming. A large part of the development of defense mechanisms is unconscious. . . . What you did is called splitting. It's a way to deny reality, a way to ultimately survive."

She let out a slight laugh. "Yeah. And the best way I knew how to survive was to create two people who otherwise wouldn't exist? I mean, I've heard of make-believe playmates, but that is carrying things a little too far."

"Maybe not. It was the way your mind chose to deal with the pain and stay sane. I admire you for being as strong as you are right now."

She started wringing her hands. "Yeah, I'm strong all right. So strong that I can't even control Miss Faith and make her tell me what happened so this nightmare can be over. I'm not a little girl anymore, Dr. Holden. Whatever happened that I couldn't deal with back then, I'm old enough to be able to deal with now. At least I would think."

"Yet, you have Hope and Faith who, to this day, seem to still exist."

"From what Sapphire tells me, not so much Hope. I think Hope understands I'm a different person now, and I don't need the two of them anymore. Not separate from me anyway. This is so crazy, Dr. Holden! I just want this to be over with."

"When you're ready, you can come over, sit or lie down, and we'll get started."

"Sapphire is not going to sit in with us on our session?"

"No. But she's outside. Unfortunately, we've not been able to get 'Miss Faith,' as you call her, to co-operate with Sapphire when she's around."

"Yes, I heard she says she'll only speak with you. See, that's what I mean. I really like Sapphire. So how can I have a side of me that hates Sapphire? And why can't I control her? Why can't I just turn Faith off? I should be able to make her talk to Sapphire or to me, for that matter. Flip a switch and presto."

"Let's not dwell on that," Dr. Holden said. He turned on the tape recorder and got his notebook in position. "The object of all this is to get Faith to talk and tell us what she knows, then help you toward the path of complete healing. Whatever we need to do to accomplish that, we're all committed to doing it. Especially if it will release you from what has been oppressing you all of these years."

Charity laid back against the lounge. She nodded to Dr. Holden that she was ready to begin.

"Okay, Charity. From here on out, I want you to relax. And I want you to listen to my voice and go where I tell you to go in your mind." He spoke about general things until she was more relaxed. Then he said, "Charity, do you remember being a young girl in your mother's house in New Orleans?"

"Yes."

"How was that for you?"

"It was great. I remember my father, but just barely. He went away and never came home. I didn't totally understand how that worked back then, but Motherphelia said we would understand it better in the by-and-by." Charity's eyes were closed. She seemed calm and really relaxed.

"Tell me about that day."

"Which day?"

"The day you walked in the room and that bad man was in there."

"Are you talking about Mr. Lucious?"

"Was that the name of the mean man Hope talks about?"

"I guess. He hurt my mother and he hurt me. He could be mean."

"Was he always mean to your mother and you?"

"Stop it! Stop it! Don't you do that!" Charity cried out.

"Charity," Dr. Holden said in a quiet voice, "what's happening now?"

"Don't you tell! He said he would hurt us and our family if you ever told it!"

"Charity? Charity? Charity . . . can you hear me?"

Charity suddenly became calmer. "No, doctor. Charity is no longer here."

"Is that you, Hope?"

"Two strikes. One more and you can't help but to get it right."

"Faith." He exhaled ever so quietly.

"Right-o, Doctor H. Give the man a gold star," Faith said as she popped open her eyes and grinned.

"How are you, Faith?"

She snickered. "Like you really care. Look, let's not play games, Doc. I like you all right, but I am not fond of people who think I don't see through their psychobabble education."

"Is that why you won't talk to Sapphire?"

"Oh, Sapphire's not that deep. She's not a real doctor, at least she's not like you. Just a psychotherapist. Is that what she's called? Anyway, I just don't like her because she thinks she's smarter than me. But she's not," Faith said. "Must I lie here, pretending I've been hypnotized or something, or can I get up while we have this conversation?"

"You can sit up if you prefer."

Faith sat up and smiled. "I think Sapphire has Charity drugged too much. It's difficult for me to do anything with so much medication flowing through this body."

"You do understand why she has to be on medication, don't you?" Dr. Holden maintained full eye contact with Faith.

She stood up and started walking around his nicely furnished office. "I understand you think everything you're doing is helping Charity, when in fact, you're really not." She picked up a picture off his desk. "Your family? Cute," she said, setting it back down.

"Why do you think what we're doing won't help Charity?"

"Because what happened was really bad, Dr. Holden. Really bad. You think she can handle it being a grown woman? I'd say you'd have a hard time handling this right now being a grown man with your fancy doctorate degree." She touched his framed certificate hanging on the wall, then continued to casually stroll around his office, picking up and setting down things at will.

Dr. Holden followed her moves by adjusting his

body as she walked. "I believe not only can Charity handle it, but she can also work through it and be well on her way to a full recovery and a wonderful and productive life."

"She had a productive life before Sapphire stepped all up in our business and decided 'we' needed help. Now look where Charity is—in a facility that's literally guarded twenty-four/seven. Oh yeah, that sounds like the good life to me. Before all this great help came along, we worked, provided for ourselves, had a home where we could come and go anytime we pleased without having to have somebody come 'check us out' and 'bring us back' or stop us when we want to go out and have a little fun. Now we're praying for financial handouts here and there in order to pay the bills that don't stop coming just because our income has." Faith flopped back down on the chaise lounge after her short tour around the office.

"Charity admitted herself for help and her own protection of her own free will."

"Protection? Protection from whom? From me?" Faith let out a menacing laugh. "I hate to break this to you, Doc. But you guys locked her up with the person you think you're protecting her from. How insane is that? That's equivalent to a person stealing from someone and you locking them in the same cell with their thief. Hope is in here." She pointed at her body. "Charity is in here, and I'm in here. Do you really think I don't have any power over what either of them does or remembers or says?"

Dr. Holden wrote something down. "So do you consider yourself a thief?"

She stopped and stared at him. "What?"

"You sort of stole Charity's body. And since you're the only one who seems to totally recall what happened that day that caused all of this to transpire, I'd say you've also stolen Charity's memories as well."

"Are you smoking something that's frying your brains?" Faith asked.

"I'll take that as one of your jokes you're famous for." He waited a few seconds. "So, are you going to answer my question?"

She folded her arms across her chest. "I didn't steal her memories. These memories are mine, so I get to decide who can know and who can't."

"No. Those memories belong to Charity and you stole them from her."

"How do you figure that?"

"On that day, whatever it was that happened, you didn't exist. And if you didn't exist, then you couldn't have had a memory to store those facts in. Therefore, the only person who existed at that time was Charity; thereby they were Charity's memories. After it happened, you and Hope came along. And if I had my guess, I would say Hope came even before you."

Faith hunched her shoulders. "Okay. I'll concede that. Hope did come before me, but Hope is never enough to do what all needs to be done. Sure, Hope will get things started for you, but in the end, it takes Faith to get the job done. Not everybody can go the distance. But now Faith, Faith will be there until things are manifested. You can believe that, Dr. H."

"And Charity?"

"What about Charity?"

"Where does Charity fit in the scheme of things?"

"Charity, like love, can be—in my humble opinion anyway—somewhat wimpy. Charity allows too many people to get away with things they should have to pay for. I say if you do the crime, you should pay the time. I don't believe in letting people get away with doing things. And there are some evil people out there, Doctor H. You know it's true." She held out her hand.

"What?"

"May I have some paper and a pen, please?" Faith said with a smile as she relaxed against the chaise lounge.

Dr. Holden got up and went to his desk. He pulled out a stenographer notebook, took a pen out of the holder on his desk, and handed both to her. "Here you are."

She took them. "Thank you." She flipped opened the notebook and turned it to a random blank page.

"So what are you going to write?"

"Oh, I just decided since you want to take notes on me, I'd take notes on you."

Dr. Holden sat back against his chair. "Why don't you just tell me what happened that day? And if I think it's too much for Charity to handle, we'll just drop it and find another way to help her."

Faith started writing in the notebook. "If I tell you what you want to know, I'm out of here, aren't I?"

"Do you really want to stay?"

Faith continued to write. "There was a time

when I thought I did. Not immediately after this happened, of course. It was a lot for me to handle even if I do act like I'm so tough. Knowing what I knew, then dealing with it later, made me become this hard, seemingly heartless person. But that was the only way Charity could have survived. We all have that type of personality somewhere deep inside of us." She turned the page and continued to write as she talked.

"It's just that most folks don't have them to separate out the way Charity had me. Charity, when all of us were one, couldn't have done what had to be done, I don't think. But breaking me away from her the way she did, and me not having to deal with that love factor being mixed in with what needed to happen . . . I could do it. She knew that; she trusted me."

Faith flipped to another page as she paused a few seconds, then continued to write. "Doctor H., somebody had to protect us. Granted, I didn't do a fantastic job. And unfortunately, Motherphelia died. But we were only seven, Charity, Hope, and I. Seven-year-olds don't possess the tools to always plot things out to the very end. Seven-year-olds can only see so far ahead. We didn't see past that one moment in time. We couldn't see past that one day. We didn't foresee what would happen a few weeks . . . months, even years down the road. Charity loved Motherphelia and Motherphelia loved Charity . . . deeply. After Motherphelia died and Charity realized she had somehow been the cause of it, she gladly allowed me to take possession of those memories."

Faith closed the notebook. She looked deep into his eyes. "Therefore, Doctor H., I did not steal Charity's memories. Charity *happily* and *willingly* turned them over to me for safekeeping."

"Nonetheless, they *are* Charity's memories, and it's time things were set right."

"Of course you'd say something like that," Faith said. "What do you have to lose? But me, should I comply with that, I'll be history. No, not even history. A mental disorder, a mere figment of Charity's mind, a make-believe person held over from a little girl's childhood. No thanks. I refuse to go out like that."

"But you do realize that you don't have a right to be here any longer? Charity desires to have her life back. She wants to be whole again."

Faith smirked as she looked at him. "And how would you know? You don't know one blessed thing about Charity. You fancy doctors with your fancy degrees act like you know so much more than the rest of us, when in fact, all you know is what you've read and retained from a book. You don't have a clue about Charity or what she's been through. She's not a mere case study to me. Charity needs me! She needs my protection. I won't sit back and let people run over us. I won't let people abuse or misuse us."

"Technically, you would still be a part of her, Faith. You just shouldn't be the one in control anymore. Charity has the right to make her own decisions. But the fact is you are and you can't help but be a part of her."

Faith laughed. "Oh, yeah? What part? The part, in your educated mind, that went bad? Poor Charity needs help because she has other personalities taking over her body. Faith is bad. Faith has to go." Faith mocked what she felt Dr. Holden was trying to say.

Dr. Holden was calm. "I don't think of you as bad, Faith. In fact, I think you did what you felt needed to be done to keep Charity sane and safe through difficult times."

"You're just saying that. I'm on to you. You're trying to pull that bad cop, good cop routine. Acting like you're on my side. But it's not going to work. I'm not falling for any of your psychobabble or reverse psychology junk." Faith opened the notebook back up and began writing again.

"Faith, do you love Charity?"

Faith stopped writing and looked at him, narrowing her eyes. "What?"

"Do you love Charity?"

"What kind of an asinine question is that? Of course, I love Charity."

"Then why won't you cooperate? For these past months, Sapphire has been doing everything she can to help Charity get better."

Faith commenced to writing again. "I don't like Sapphire," she said.

"Why not?"

"Because she'd like nothing better than for me to completely disappear. She wants me destroyed. She doesn't care about Charity. She only cares about how she looks."

"I believe she cares," Dr. Holden said. "And she cares about you as well."

"Yeah, okay." Faith flipped several pages and wrote some more, slower now.

"No one wants to destroy you, Faith. But it's time for you to give Charity back her life. She's not a little girl anymore. I'm certain you helped her more than anyone will ever know. But it's time for you to let go."

Faith looked at him with a softer look. "I did help her, you know. Everything I've ever done was for Charity." She looked back down, turned the page, and tilting her head slightly, she continued to write in silence, her body no longer as tense as it had been.

Dr. Holden sat back against his chair. "Faith, Charity is ready to move forward with her life. *Her* life. And it is her life. If you really care about her, I mean if you truly want to help her, then why wouldn't you give her what she needs in order to do that?"

Faith relaxed completely on the chaise lounge. "If Charity really wants her memories back, then fine. She can have them, as far as I'm concerned." She continued to write, tapped the page with the point of the pen, closed the notebook, then stuck the pen in the spiral portion. "Tell Charity I really *am* sorry. Hope has resolved herself to leave. But like I've always said: Hope is good for getting you started, but it takes Faith to bring you to the door of actual manifestation." Faith closed her eyes. "Tell Charity that all of us did what we thought was right at the time." Faith's voice was beginning to fade. "All of us. Tell her I only hope she has the faith to walk in love after all is said and done."

Dr. Holden studied Faith as a strange but peaceful look appeared to overtake her. She was serene now. "Faith?" Dr. Holden called her name gently. "Faith?"

Her eyes began to flutter. She opened them. "Dr. Holden?" She looked around the room. "What happened?" She pressed her fist against her forehead.

"Faith?"

She placed one hand over her face and breathed in deeply, then removed it. "No. It's Charity. Don't tell me—Faith never showed up, did she?" Charity looked at him.

Dr. Holden reached over and helped Charity as she sat up. "She showed up."

"Did she tell you anything? Did you get what you needed from her?"

Dr. Holden shook his head. "She told me some things. And she also told me to tell you she was sorry for everything. But no, she didn't tell me what happened."

Charity popped her lips. "Figures." She ran her hand over the closed notebook she still held. "So what is this for?"

"Just a notebook. Faith insisted if I was going to take notes on her, she would take notes on me. She is quite a personality, I will give her that much. The classic 'mess with another person's mind' game."

Charity handed the notebook with the pen stuck in the wire part back to him. "Well, I suppose we can try again another time. Unless you think it's useless and we need to try a different approach. Maybe you can hypnotize me to try and remember."

There was a knock on the door. Sapphire peeked inside. "Is it okay if I come in?" she asked.

"Sure," Dr. Holden said. "As you probably saw from the monitor, Faith came, but she's gone now."

"Yeah. I saw and heard. I guess it was a good idea to put a camera in here during this session. Do you think she knew I was watching, and that's why she didn't cooperate?"

"With Faith, who knows? Maybe she never intends to tell us anything. Faith likes the game," Dr. Holden said as he stood up. "We can't hate the player. We'll just have to pray about this and try something different." He took the notebook and lightly tossed it onto his desk. Glancing at his watch, he said, "Well, ladies, I hate to have to rush you out, but I have another appointment in less than five minutes."

"Oh sure," Charity said. "I just appreciate you for seeing me with your schedule."

Sapphire nodded to Dr. Holden as she started out the door. "Thanks anyway."

"We'll talk later, okay?" Dr. Holden said to Sapphire. "Take care, Charity."

They left. His secretary was waiting to bring in his next patient's chart. He picked up the notebook Faith had written in, wrote her name and the date on the outside of it, and placed it in his desk drawer to possibly review later. He wasn't certain whether or not he even wanted to read the observations Faith had made about him. *It's a different matter when someone turns the tables and starts analyzing and observing you.*

He felt bad that he hadn't been able to get

more out of Faith. They all would need to pray mightily about what to do next. But at least Charity wanted to be helped. The question now was how to do it?

Chapter 28

Rejoice not against me, O mine enemy: when I fall, I shall arise; when I sit in darkness, the Lord shall be a light unto me.
—Micah 7:8

Johnnie Mae was unpacking a cardboard box when she ran across a cigar box that looked familiar but she couldn't remember where it had come from. As she peeled off the gray-colored duct tape and opened it, she realized it was the box Angel Gabriel's great-grandmother had given her. Opening it, she began to flip through some things that at first made no sense to her. There was information on a child recorded in a book Johnnie Mae assumed was done by a midwife—one lonely entry. Johnnie Mae remembered Pearl had been a midwife, as had Pearl's mother. But Johnnie Mae didn't have a clue why Pearl had thought it important to give this book to her. There was also other information pertaining to the child, a little girl, inside that box.

Johnnie Mae picked up the phone and called Angel. "Hi, Angel. This is Johnnie Mae Landris."

"Hi there. It's been a few weeks since we talked."

"Yes, it has been a while. Everybody is so busy these days."

"So what's up?"

Johnnie Mae looked at the midwife book as she spoke. "Do you remember that box your great-grandmother left for you to give to me?"

"Vaguely."

"Well, I guess what I really want to know is did she happen to tell you why she wanted me to have it?"

"No. She just asked me to give it to you and said you would know what to do with it," Angel said.

"Hmmm. That's interesting, because I don't have a clue what to do with it. Maybe she thought I'd like to have it for research purposes or something on that line. But there are some things in here about a little girl named Rebecca."

"Rebecca?"

"Yeah."

"Rebecca was my mother's name. But she died when I was around five. We didn't know it at the time, but I think she probably died from AIDS. My daddy, I hear, was a drug addict and he probably passed it on to her after having used contaminated needles. Back then, people didn't know what we know now about shared needles spreading that virus. He overdosed, so who knows if he had AIDS or not. That's how I ended up being raised by Great-granny."

"I didn't know that."

"It's not something I go around talking about. It was kind of hard growing up without my mother."

"Where's your grandmother?"

"I don't have a clue. I don't even really know

who my grandmother is. She was an off-limits subject for everybody in our house. Like she did something and the whole family completely disowned her or disavowed her and wrote her out of existence—wiped her name off everything, including the family Bibles. And back then when black folks didn't want you to know something, believe me, they didn't tell it. Not like it is today where people will get on television and air all their business to the world and whoever else wants to hear it."

"I would think you could find that information out if you really wanted to," Johnnie Mae said. "There has to be some kind of record out there."

"I guess I never really wanted to," Angel said. "She wasn't there for my mother or Great-granny. She sure never came home to see Great-granny, which would have been her own mother, during all the years I was there. I just never thought about her. Great-granny had that way about her. Somehow, even as old as she was, I never felt like I was missing anything in my life."

"So when your Great-granny died, your grandmother didn't come for the funeral?" Johnnie Mae asked as she rifled through the few papers and other things inside the box. This was starting to sound much like Lena and her mother, Memory's story.

"Johnnie Mae, I'm not even sure if my grandmother is still alive. I would think not. It's like I said, I've never given much thought about her until you just mentioned it right now. Maybe I should have. But you don't tend to miss something you've never had."

"And you don't know your grandmother's name?"

"No. Don't think I've ever heard it before. Ever. All these years, not one person has said anything about her."

"Well, okay. I just opened this box and all this was in here. It didn't make sense to me why she asked you to give it to me, so I thought maybe I was missing something." Johnnie Mae straightened up the things in the box and closed the lid. "I'll just put it up and maybe look at it later to see if I can figure out why she thought I should have this or even would want to have it."

Johnnie Mae and Angel chatted about other things, among them, Brent's recent proposal of marriage and her not having given him an answer yet. Johnnie Mae hung up and took the box to put it away until a later time, a time when she felt like maybe trying to solve the puzzle. Pearl had a lot of wisdom, and from what Johnnie Mae saw when she met her, Pearl never did anything just to be doing it. There had to be a purpose behind it.

"Pearl," Johnnie Mae said as she slid the box on a shelf in her walk-in closet, "if you were trying to tell me something, you'd better give me a little more direction here."

"Mommy, who are you talking to," six-and-a-half-year-old Princess Rose asked as she peeked into the closet.

"Oh, no one in particular, baby girl. People do that from time to time. We talk when we think no one is listening, to no one in particular." Johnnie Mae stooped down and kissed Princess Rose on her nose. She couldn't help but think of Solomon,

Princess Rose's father, and how much he would have enjoyed seeing how beautiful and smart his daughter was growing up to be.

"You mean like when I talk to my friends that other people can't see?"

"Yes, just like that." Johnnie Mae tapped Princess Rose's nose lightly.

"Mommy," Princess Rose said as she cocked her head to the side and smiled, "can I feel the baby kick again?"

"Well, the baby's not kicking at the moment," Johnnie Mae said as she placed her daughter's hand on her stomach. "See? I think the baby's asleep."

"Can we wake the baby up and make the baby play?" Princess Rose rubbed her mother's stomach in a circular motion.

"I think we should let the baby stay asleep for now. It takes a lot of work to become a baby forming inside there."

"Did it take me a lot of work when I was becoming a baby inside your stomach?"

"Yes." Johnnie Mae took her by the hand. "And you see how wonderful you turned out."

"I hope this baby is as good as I am when the baby comes. Some of these babies get on my nerves. They act just like a baby about everything."

"Your nerves?" Johnnie Mae said with a laugh. "When did you get nerves?"

"I've always had nerves, Mommy. Just like you."

"Oh." Johnnie Mae smiled. "Let's go fix some dinner. I'm getting hungry."

"Yes, and the baby is probably getting hungry, too."

Johnnie Mae pulled Princess Rose's plait. "Your hair is getting so long."

Just then the phone rang. Johnnie Mae answered it before walking out of the bedroom.

"Sister Landris, this is Monica from the church. I have a woman who wants to schedule an appointment to talk with someone. I see where your name was listed and when I told her who we had available, she wanted to schedule with you. Can you check and see if tomorrow is okay for you?"

"What time tomorrow?"

"She said anytime—morning or afternoon—is fine for her. She's flexible tomorrow. Said she just desperately needed to talk with someone as soon as possible."

"Great. I like the flexible kind. Let's schedule her for in the morning at 10 A.M."

"Done. If anything changes, I'll let you know. Otherwise, I'll have a conference room secured for you, and we'll see you tomorrow morning."

"Oh, Monica?"

"Yes?"

"What's the person's name?"

"I'm so sorry, Sister Landris. I'm trying to do too much in a hurry, I guess. Her name is Fatima Adams, and she's a member here already."

"Fatima Adams. All right then, Monica. I'll see you tomorrow around nine."

Chapter 29

If any man among you seem to be religious, and bridleth not his tongue, but deceiveth his own heart, this man's religion is vain.
—James 1:26

"Listen, I told you that if you continued to go over to that church you had to leave this house," Arletha said. "I wasn't just saying something to hear myself talk. There are evil spirits lurking out there, and I refuse to allow them access to my home."

"That's just ridiculous," Memory said. "I don't see anything wrong with that church. In fact, I see what a difference it's making in my life. You just don't understand the person I was before I started going there."

"I'm sorry I ever took you to that place with me. Had I known all of this was going to come out of it, you'd better believe, I never would have asked you to step foot in that church that first time. In fact, had I known what that church was really all about, *I* never would have stepped foot in there myself and wasted my time."

Memory stood there. "Well, I don't understand

how you can profess to be such a Christian with the attitudes you seem to have."

"What attitudes? I believe certain things, and there ain't one thing you can do or say to convince me otherwise. I should have known you were just the devil trying to get access into my house."

"Oh, so I'm the devil now, huh?" Memory asked. "I went to church. Do you hear that part at all? You're upset and wanting me to leave because I attended a church you don't approve? How religious acting is that?"

Arletha put her hands on her hips. "This is my house. I told you months back how I felt about that place. You can go to any church you please, but then I can have whomever I please living or not living up in my own house."

"Okay, fine," Memory said as she threw her hands up in the air. "I'm tired anyway."

"Tired of what? Running from the law?"

"What would make you say something like that?"

Arletha turned up her nose. "Some man came by yesterday asking about a woman who fits your description to the tee. Yeah, that's right."

"A man?"

"Yes, and from the looks of him, I'd say he was some kind of law enforcement agent . . . maybe a bounty hunter. Said he was looking for a Memory Patterson. I told him I didn't know nobody by that name. Then he proceeded to throw out what he called aliases this Memory might be using. He says there's a reward out for information leading to her whereabouts. Pretty nice one, too. It would be great to be able to bless a good church with it, as soon as I find one good enough, that is."

Memory sat down and looked up at Arletha. "So what all did you tell him?"

"I told him the truth: that I didn't *personally* know anybody by that name. But first thing in the morning, I might just give him a call and let him know you're here . . . the one he seeks. Elaine Robertson, Memory Patterson, or whoever you really are."

"You can't do that."

"And why can't I?"

"I don't know who is looking for me or why, but I know I've not done anything to cause anyone to be searching for me like that."

"Yeah, I bet you haven't," Arletha said. "When you first showed up here, I felt sorry for you. Couldn't understand how your own child and grandchild could turn you out, an old, feeble woman, like they did. Thought we elderly people needed to stick together. Take care of each other. But since you've been here, I guess I understand better now. I'm missing a ring. You wouldn't happen to know what happened to it, would you?"

"I don't steal."

"Sure you don't. So why is Mr. Big Shot hot on your trail? You're too old to be selling drugs. Did you kill somebody?"

"I told you, I don't know why this person is looking for me."

"Well, I'd suggest you get your things and get up out of my house before tomorrow. I can't have nobody living with me that's teamed up with the devil."

"Where am I supposed to go on such short notice? And what about the rent money I paid you for this month already?"

"I don't know where you're going to go, and frankly, I don't care. As for the money you've paid, leave me a forwarding address, and I'll gladly mail you a refund. The Good Book says for us to come out from among them, meaning sinners and heathens like you. It's apparent to me now, you're not saved. So you have got to get up out of here."

"And what makes you believe I'm not saved?"

"You don't act saved."

"Well, I am. And being saved is not based on works, 'lest any man should boast' anyway," Memory said.

"Yes, well . . . I don't believe in that once saved, always saved way of thinking either. I believe you can lose your salvation. Your name can be blotted out of *The Book*. Backsliders, adulterers, murderers, thieves, whoremongers, liars, fornicators . . . they're all going to hell. They might have confessed with their mouths the Lord Jesus, and believed in their hearts that God raised Him from the dead, but if people were really saved, they wouldn't be living and carrying on like they do. I say, they couldn't have ever been saved. Else, they wouldn't slide back into sin and reside there. So yes, if anybody asks me, I do believe a person can lose their salvation after they have been saved. That I do."

"I don't believe that. We're not saved by what we do. We can never be good enough! That's why so many people stay away from ever coming to get saved—they think they have to get right first. That's just wrong. We are saved by grace. Jesus is the reason we're saved. He saves us. The Holy Spirit helps change us . . . refines us, after that."

"See! See! That's what I'm saying. You running down there to that heathen's church and listening to him talking about coming to some altar to be released from strongholds. I can assure you most of the folks who went up there went back home just like they came up, still being held strong. They weren't changed a lick."

"I changed," Memory said.

"Yeah. Of course you did. You found some of your heathen buddies to hang out with at church. These churches are just becoming like country clubs now anyway. 'Woe unto those who call good evil and evil good.' All y'all gonna burn in the fiery furnace, sho' as we're all born to die!"

"Who died and made you judge and jury?"

"The Bible says I'm going to get to judge. I can see things right now. I see the sin running rampant through this land. I see those who profess to be saved but their lives are far from it," Arletha said as she pointed her finger at Memory.

"What about the sin that can't be seen? The sins of the heart? Are there big sins and little sins to God? Is one sin worse than another?" Memory said.

"Don't be trying to preach that junk to me. I'm living right, trying to be perfect, unlike most folks who call themselves Christians these days. And I can't wait until God finally smashes all these pretend-to-be Christians. I pray for Him to take a lot of folks out. Preachers, like that Pastor Landris down there telling folks what they want to hear instead of what the Good Book says and means. 'Nothing but the pure in heart shall see God.' Now, that's scripture. So how pure are you? How pure are most Christians?"

"How perfect are you?"

"Oh, I don't sin."

"Well the Bible says otherwise. In fact, the Bible says all have sinned and come short of the glory of God. The Bible says in First John, the first chapter and the eighth through the tenth verse: 'If we say that we have no sin, we deceive ourselves, and the truth is not in us. If we confess our sins, he is faithful and just to forgive us our sins, and to cleanse us from all unrighteousness. If we say that we have not sinned, we make him a liar, and his word is not in us.' You," Memory said as she pointed back at Arletha, "forget that sins are not merely the outward ones everybody sees. But they are also the ones we do inwardly that only God can see and judge, sins of the heart. Those hidden sins, that nobody knows about but you and God. God sees and God knows all of it."

"What are you trying to say?"

"I'm trying to say that before you start judging others, you'd better be careful. Because you might see what I'm doing wrong on the outside, but God sees what you're doing wrong on the inside: sins of omission and sins of commission. To God sin is sin. There are no big sins and little sins in His eyes. Yes, I have sinned, but today . . . today, I'm going to make some things right. Today, I'm going to go down to that church you have a problem with me going to, and I'm going to confess my sins to some man or woman of God." Memory went and got her purse and started for the door. "I'm making a change today."

Arletha rushed and stood near the front door. "You can't go down there!"

"Why not? Because you forbid me to? Well, guess what—you've told me to get out of your house. And I'm going to do just that. But before I leave here, I'm going to make peace with my God. I'm going to confess my sins, unlike you who believe you have none. I'm going to allow God to wipe my slate clean. And I can only pray that God truly will have mercy on my soul."

"I tell you what. Why don't you just go pack all your things, and I'll gladly drop you and your stuff off at that fancy church for good."

"I told you I would leave your home as soon as I got back," Memory said as Arletha continued to stand in front of her.

"No, ma'am. You will pack your stuff, and you will be out of my house for good now. I don't want you here, and I don't want you having any reasons to step foot back in here after you're gone this time. So go on and get your stuff. I'll get my car and drive you to that unholy place myself. Let's see what *they* do for you down there when you really need some help."

"Fine," Memory said as she headed up the stairs. "I don't have much to pack, anyway."

"Yeah, I know. I went in your room yesterday while you were out, and I could see where most of your things were already packed up in your no-matching suitcases."

"Why did you do that?"

"Why? Because of that man who showed up snooping around about you. I have every right to know what's in my house." She began to tap her foot. "So get your stuff and hurry up about it. The sooner I get you out of here, the better things are going to be for me."

Memory packed the rest of her things. She said a prayer as she knelt down beside her suitcases before going down the stairs.

"Lord, I don't know what the future holds for me, but I sure know who holds my future. Guide me, O thou great Jehovah."

She made several trips downstairs, carrying her suitcases one at a time by herself. She loaded her things into Arletha's car without a clue, other than stopping off at Followers of Jesus Faith Worship Center first, where she would go or what she would do next.

Chapter 30

Let your light so shine before men, that they may see your good works, and glorify your Father, which is in heaven.

—Matthew 5:16

Johnnie Mae arrived at the church right at 9 A.M. She stopped by Sherry's office first and spoke to her before finding Monica.

"Oh, you're early. Just like you said you'd be," Monica said.

"Yes. My motto is, 'Early is on time and on time is late.' I can't remember where I heard that, but I adopted it in my life, and it's made all the difference in the world. Pastor Landris has often said people don't have a problem showing up late even to church. They feel people ought to be glad they came even when they get there late. What we don't realize is that we really are sowing something when we do that. And we do reap what we sow. When we pray to God about things, we want our relief or help to be on time. Actually, we'd prefer it if it came early, but at least on time. When it takes longer, it never occurs to us that maybe we sowed lateness and we're reaping lateness. Not from God, because whenever God shows up, He's always on time. But with others who may be late doing what they were supposed to just like we were late. It's a principle of life, sowing and reaping."

"That's good. I need to adopt that one myself. 'Early is on time and on time is late.' Got it." Monica looked down. "I have you in Conference Room C: 'Come unto me, all ye that labour and are heavy laden and I will give you rest.' Matthew eleven twenty-eight."

"Thanks, Monica. I suppose, if it's okay, I'll go on in, pray, and anoint the room before Fatima Adams gets here."

"Yes, you can go right on in. You have the room until noon. If she arrives early, do you want me to hold her until ten or what?"

"No, I'll be ready when she gets here. So should she arrive early, just send her in, and she and I can get started. It's not like I'll be in there with anyone else, so it will be fine whenever she's ready."

Johnnie Mae went into the conference room. She set her things down on the table and began to walk around. After about fifteen minutes, she began to pray. "Lord, I thank You that everywhere my feet tread is now anointed. I thank You for anointing my mind with the right words to say. I thank You that I am blessed to be a blessing. I thank You that I have the mind of Christ. I yield my thoughts, my opinions, my mouth, my tongue, my heart, totally to You, Father God, Let the words of my mouth and the meditation of my heart be acceptable in Your sight. Lord, I thank You today, captives will be set free. I pull down every stronghold that tries to exalt itself above the knowledge of You and Your

Word, O God. Guide me O thou great Jehovah. Anoint me with thou free spirit. Help me to help Your people. I now decrease so that You may increase in my words and my deeds. Let Your light so shine in me that the lives I touch today may see Your light shining through me. It's not about me, Father. This is all about You and You getting the glory. These blessings I pray and thank You for, in the name of Jesus who is our Advocate and who sits on Your right hand making intercessions for us. Amen."

"Amen," a voice said.

Johnnie Mae turned around. "I'm sorry, I didn't hear you come in."

"I hope it's all right," Fatima said. "I know I'm early, but Sister Monica said it was okay for me to come right on in."

"Oh, it's fine. I was just setting the atmosphere."

"Just from what I heard, I think I may already have been ministered to." Fatima walked closer to Johnnie Mae. "Sister Landris, I'm Fatima Adams."

"Please, just call me Johnnie Mae. It took me long enough to get here." Johnnie Mae motioned for her to sit down.

"Excuse me? Get here? I don't mean to pry, but what do you mean by that?"

"My name. I used to be hung up on people not calling me Johnnie Mae. There was a time, after I was grown, when I wouldn't let anyone call me that. It had to be J. M. or don't call me anything." Johnnie Mae smiled as she took a seat. "Thank God for deliverance."

"Well, I know a lot of people who will insist that you call them Sister or Brother, Minister, Reverend, Doctor, Pastor, Evangelist, Prophet, Prophet-ess, Bishop, or whatever title to the office they happen to be holding. It can be so confusing and so paralyzing when you're trying to remember who is what and you don't want to offend them."

"Yes, I've known some people who have gotten pretty hot if you didn't address them by their title. But I suppose to them it's a matter of respect. And I respect that. Me, personally, just call me a servant of the Most High God. The only thing that sometimes bothers me is when people try to hyphenate my two last names when it's not hyphenated. No matter how many times I tell them otherwise, they still do it."

"Two last names?"

"Yes. You see, I'm an author—"

"I didn't know that," Fatima said. "You write real books for a real publisher?"

Johnnie Mae smiled. "Well, yes, if you put it like that. I write real books, and I have a real publisher who publishes them." Johnnie Mae didn't want to get into so much about her career, but it seemed to make Fatima more relaxed before they began.

"Wow, I can't believe I'm getting to meet a real live author. I write, but my stuff is mostly poetry. I'm not trying to get anything published or anything like that. I just do it for my own benefit."

"I meet a lot of people who tell me they write or are working on a book."

"So what do you write?"

"Mainstream fiction, although people are starting to classify me as being more of a Christian fiction writer lately. In fact, my publisher just decided they want to release my next book as a Christian novel. They were looking into getting into that market, so it looks like I'll be launching their Christian line next year."

"That's great. I'm sorry, I interrupted what you were saying about hyphenating your name, but it's just I didn't realize you were an author. I knew you and Pastor Landris have a book out there that's here at the church, but I thought that was the extent of your published work."

"I was just saying that when people hyphenate my name when it's not to be hyphenated, it changes my name completely. When people go into a bookstore and ask for a book by Taylor-Landris, there's no such author name, so they are told they don't have my book. It can really mess an author up, especially when the books are not readily available on the shelf. Then there are some people who don't realize I'm still using Johnnie Mae Taylor as my publishing name instead of Johnnie Mae Landris. So they go in and ask for a book by an author named Landris. I have no idea whose book, if anyone's, they end up with."

"Johnnie Mae Taylor?"

"Yes."

Her eyes widened. "I've read one of your books before. I can't believe it. I didn't realize you were *the* Johnnie Mae Taylor who wrote books. Wait till I tell my friend Gia."

Johnnie Mae smiled. "Well, enough about names and what I do. We're here today to talk about what's going on with you."

"Where do you want to begin?"

"For you and me, we will begin with a short prayer. And then wherever you'd like to kick this off, we'll begin from there. The middle, the beginning, whatever it was that caused you to feel the need to come in today for counseling. Wherever it feels right to you, I'm here. And between me, you, and God, I believe you're going to leave here different than when you came in."

Fatima tried to smile but only nodded. With heads bowed, Johnnie Mae prayed.

"Okay, whenever you're ready." Johnnie Mae fixed herself to make Fatima as comfortable telling her story as possible. Her goal was not to appear judgmental or shocked about anything she might hear over the course of this counseling session.

Fatima, on the other hand, wasn't sure how what she was about to say to the pastor's wife—no less—would play out. She just knew she had to tell *somebody*!

Chapter 31

Let him know, that he which converteth the sinner from the error of his way shall save a soul from death, and shall hide a multitude of sins.

—James 5:20

Fatima told Johnnie Mae about a man she had been seeing for over three years. How much she loved and cared about him. How much she believed he really did care about her. How hard it had been having a relationship with him. The fact that he was married with small children. How he began early on in the relationship telling her how awful things were for him with his wife. How he was planning to get a divorce. How hard it is for men to leave because of the negative things men have to deal with after a breakup or divorce.

"Negative things?" Johnnie Mae said. "Did he say what?"

"Like not being able to see his children the way he would like. Women traditionally get the children and men only get to see them on weekends. He seems to genuinely love his children, and he said he wanted to be with them every day while they were growing up. That's important to him.

They're expecting another baby now," Fatima said as she fidgeted with one thing and then another. "And he said then there's the baby-mama-drama he hears about from his friends who are dealing with divorce. Well, I know a lot of that to be true from some of my friends. But if you ask me, I'd say from a spiritual standpoint, he thinks divorce is wrong based on certain scriptures he's read in the New Testament, 'in red' as he says, 'which means Jesus said it.' So that's another thing I think that's messing with his head and his decisions."

"Hold up. Now, I know we are not here to address him and his problems since this is really about you and what you need to do. But you're telling me he has a problem with divorce because it's something Jesus spoke about in the New Testament, but he doesn't have a problem with committing adultery or looking upon a woman with lust in his eyes?"

"I know, I know," Fatima said. "When I say it out loud, it sounds crazy even to me. But I'm having such a hard time because I really do love him and it's hard to stop. I came forward a few months back when Pastor Landris prayed for people to be released from their strongholds, and I seemed to have been doing okay for a while. I was attending the Bible study and the support group. But then he would call and my heart would react and break all over again. Then . . . came my birthday a few weeks back."

"So do you want to tell me what happened?"

"Not really, but I suppose that's what caused me to call yesterday to talk with somebody here at the church. I can't do this on my own anymore." She started crying. "I just need some help. And I don't know who to turn to. I don't know how to fix this. It just hurts so bad! It feels like my heart is being ripped apart daily."

Johnnie Mae handed her the box of tissue. "It's going to be okay. Just get it out so Satan can't keep using this against you. It's apparent you're being tortured. Jesus came that you might be set free, but you're not free. Look at how this is affecting you."

"No, I'm not free by any means. And this does have me all messed up."

"Do you need some water?"

"Yes, please," Fatima said as she dabbed at her eyes and tried to compose herself.

Johnnie Mae got up and poured water from the pitcher on the other end of the table. She handed it to Fatima and rubbed her gently on her back to comfort her. "Feeling any better now?"

Fatima nodded. "I'm sorry. I didn't mean to break down like that. It's just people have no idea how hard something like this can be. I know it was partially my fault. That's the thing: when you start into something of this nature, and it doesn't always matter what sin or stronghold it is, it's hard to stop. You don't get in it thinking it can be this complicated or heart-wrenching, and by the time you figure it out, it's almost too late to stop the snowball that's now rolling out of control and faster down the hill."

"Well, I'm going to sit right here for as long as you need me, to get this all out so you are able to go from here."

"But don't you have other appointments? Other things you need to do?"

"No. So far, there's nothing keeping me from giving you all the time you need."

Fatima looked down at the tissue she clutched in her hand. "Before my birthday, whenever he would call, I just wouldn't answer the phone. If he left a message, I wouldn't return the call. Once I even ran into him at church—"

"So he's a member here?"

"Yes."

"Wow, Pastor Landris has a lot of work to do, I see," Johnnie Mae said. "Is he in a leadership position?"

"No."

"I'm sorry. Please, go on."

"As I was saying, I ran into him at church one Sunday, and we ended up sitting next to each other with his wife on the other side of him. Of course, we acted like we barely knew each other." Fatima took another sip of water. "After I got home, he called me."

"And you answered."

"Exactly. I was so upset with him, I didn't know what to do. But it was so hard doing that."

"Doing what?"

"Sitting by him and trying to keep my mind on Jesus and what the pastor was saying while my emotions were literally kicking me in the stomach. I couldn't situate my body comfortably in the seat and every now and then he would 'accidentally' touch my hand if it was not firmly planted in my lap or 'accidentally' rub up against my arm or leg if I wasn't totally still. So as you can imagine, I sat the whole time squeezed up trying not to let any of our body parts touch each other. It was dreadful!"

"I can imagine," Johnnie Mae said as she looked sympathetically at Fatima.

"No, I don't think you really can." Fatima wiped at her tears again. "After I told him to leave me alone that Sunday after church when he called, and that I meant it, he seemed to honor my request."

"How did that make you feel?"

"Horrible. Because even though I told him I wanted him to leave me alone, deep down, I really think I wanted him to keep trying. I wanted him to want me enough. It's so stupid—"

"Don't say that."

"I'm not talking about me being stupid, but the rationale behind my thinking is stupid. I really wanted him to leave me alone, but deep down, I think I really wanted to know I meant enough to him that he wouldn't be able to leave me alone. That contradiction just makes no sense. So even though he was granting me my wish, I would catch myself staring at the phone, willing it to ring still, like back when I used to want him to call when we were first together. I was hoping I would answer the phone and he would have called from another number to get past my screening of his number just so I would have to answer it and he could talk to me." Fatima held her head all the way back and looked up at the ceiling.

"I wanted him to really want me. And what I figured out was that he didn't want me that much." She let her head back down and released a short laugh. "Back up a second and let me say he wanted me, but he really did want to have his cake and eat it, too. So he kept his cake—his wife—but got to consume extra cake on the side—me. Still it was bad for his wife because she was being cheated on. It was bad for me because I didn't really have that special person to care about me and only me."

"And for him?"

"Yeah, and for him, how did it affect him? Let's see . . . His biggest problem was trying to figure out how to juggle his family and his woman on the side and keep us all happy. His biggest problem was deciding who would get him and when. Poor thing. What a problem to have to deal with." She took another drink of water.

Johnnie Mae noticed her glass was almost empty. She picked up the pitcher of ice and water and poured some more into Fatima's glass.

"Thank you." Fatima took yet another drink. "So on my birthday this year, which in the past I usually spent alone or with a few girlfriends if they didn't have anything else planned with their boyfriends or husbands, which most times they did, he sent me flowers. And not just one bouquet of flowers, but a dozen yellow roses in addition to this gorgeous, exotic mixed bouquet. Had them delivered within thirty minutes of each other. Then I received a box from this exclusive designer shop located in Mountain Brook, and it had this stunning hand-beaded dress that I would have never purchased for myself. Believe me, I will spend money on clothes, but I don't know if I would have ever spent that kind of money on a dress like that one. Trust me: he put out a good chunk for that dress for sure."

"So he sent you flowers and a dress for your birthday?"

Fatima smiled. "Yes, he sent me those, and then another delivery came. This wonderful birthday cake, delivered by none other than him."

"And you let him come inside." Johnnie Mae said it as though she was telling the story now.

"Yes, I let him come inside." Fatima looked into Johnnie Mae's eyes. "I hope you're not thinking I'm this horrible person."

Johnnie Mae touched her hand. "I'm not judging you right now. I'm allowing you time to judge this for yourself. But it's important that you face some truths, and the only person who can do that is you."

"But aren't you allowed to judge me . . . to call me an adulterer, a fornicator, some loose woman with no morals, a husband stealer, a home wrecker, Jezebel's daughter?"

"Some people believe they have that right to judge others. Personally, I'm working on some things I need to get right about myself. I figure I have my hands full just keeping my own flesh under the subjection of the Holy Spirit. With me walking in the Spirit, which is the only way I know of to not walk in the flesh, that's a full-time job, right there," Johnnie Mae said with a smile. "When do I have time or a place to judge others? You just need to make better choices. And to really think about what's going on."

"You're just being kind."

"No, I'm just being honest. You see, there are sins of the flesh and sins of the spirit. Were I to glory in your problems, thinking I'm so much better than you because I'm not doing what you are, then I'm walking in a sin right there. My sin then becomes one of the heart. Not one that people can see outwardly, but it's inside. But guess who sees my thoughts, when I don't think the right way?" Johnnie Mae shook her head.

"You may not know it or see it, but God sees when I sin inwardly and no one else has a clue," Johnnie Mae continued. "You're getting an opportunity right now to make your outwardly sin right. But people with sins of the heart, sometimes they don't feel that accountability factor to do anything about sins they may be committing over and over again. But God knows it. And I want to be right with God always. If there's something there— whether inside or out—I want God to help me get it right. Not because I'm saved by my works, but because I want to grow in Him. Because I don't want to be a stumbling block to anyone who may be looking at me and seeing me in my sin. I don't want someone to miss heaven because my light wasn't shining and people weren't able to see the glory of the Lord shining through me. I don't want to be a hindrance to someone else's getting into the kingdom."

Fatima started to cry again. "I'm so glad I came today. I called yesterday to get an appointment with Pastor Landris. When they told me the waiting time, a month, I didn't know what to do. Then she said there were others on staff I could talk to as early as the next day. I started to tell her I would just wait or to forget about it altogether. But then I remembered what Pastor Landris told us about a month ago regarding God's desire to meet the needs of the people. That God could do that through anyone. It's not just one certain one. I know God loves me. When she started telling me the people who were available, I felt in my heart I wanted to talk with a woman about this. I'm not putting the men down, but I just prayed God would send me to a woman who might really be able to minister to me and help me."

Fatima sipped some more water. "When she spoke your name, I knew I *definitely* didn't want to talk to you."

"Really," Johnnie Mae said with a smile.

"Oh, don't get me wrong. I felt like you were capable and you would be really good. I just didn't know if I wanted to tell the pastor's wife that I've been messing around with a married man. You know?"

"I know."

"But God spoke to me and said for me to make the appointment with you," Fatima said. "I was still a bit apprehensive. That's why I got here so early. I was so nervous. Then I walked in on you praying, and I knew God had me come here on this day to talk with you."

"I'm glad I'm here as well." Johnnie Mae touched her stomach. "Sorry. My baby just kicked pretty hard there."

Fatima laughed. "Do you think your baby was telling you to tell me to hurry up so the two of you can get out of here?"

Johnnie Mae laughed a little. "I think I just need to stand up for a second to stretch." She glanced at her watch. They had been talking for almost an hour and a half now.

Fatima saw her glance at her watch. "Do you need to go? Have I exceeded my allotted time? I'm already feeling much better."

"No, no, no. We're fine. I was just looking at my watch to see how much ground we've covered and the amount of time." Johnnie Mae placed her hand behind her back and arched it. "You can talk if my standing up doesn't bother you. I just need to take a little pressure off from sitting down."

"Your standing doesn't bother me. I just don't want to keep you too long."

"I'm fine. Really I am. Please, go on with your story."

"There's not a whole lot left to tell. He was standing there with this beautiful cake. He had sent me all those flowers and that dress. But the greatest thing of all: he not only remembered my birthday, but he showed up for the first time in the three years we've been together, on my actual birthday. And he wanted to give me the whole day. Just me and him. For the first time ever, I would get an entire, uninterrupted day and night with him. That had to mean I meant something special to him . . . that he loved me, right?"

Johnnie Mae smiled and waited. "So what happened?"

"What happened? Well, he told me to go change into that stunning dress he'd bought me. We were going outside the city limits so we could go out in public and have a romantic time together without having to look over our shoulders. We were going to come back to my house later that night, and I don't have to tell you what was planned to top the night off. And he would get up early in the middle of the morning, before the sun could break the day, and get back home to his wife and family without her ever being the wiser." Fatima started to cry again. She grabbed up a handful of tissues and tried to plug the holes that seemed to be pouring tears now.

"It's okay. Get it all out. Let the Holy Spirit purge you. Just let it all out."

"I took the dress, headed up the stairs for my best birthday in years. And I suddenly stopped midway on the staircase. I turned around and looked at him. I mean, I really looked at him. And I heard the Spirit of the Lord say: 'That's not love, and that's not my best for you.' Then the Spirit said: 'I would never do something like this to someone I love. This is not of me. I have better waiting for you.' And I knew that man standing there didn't truly love me. Not really. Love doesn't hurt like that. I know that now. But I also knew from having read the scriptures profusely over these past few months, how much God loved me and what love really felt like. And it didn't feel like that." Fatima stood up just as Johnnie Mae sat down. She leaned on the back of her chair.

"So, I walked back down those stairs. He was looking at me like I had lost my mind. And I gave him back that beautiful dress with all its tags still intact. I walked over to where the flowers sat, and I combined them into the one vase. It wasn't as pretty that way, but it would be easier for him to carry. And I said to him: 'I think your wife will appreciate these.' Well, of course, he didn't appreciate me saying that. But I told him I already had a date for my birthday with someone who truly loved me. And that I wouldn't dare disappoint or disrespect the love shown me by continuing on with him. If he wasn't married, it might be a different matter altogether. But he was. If his marriage wasn't working out, it wasn't my problem to solve or to try and make things better for him. That's between the two of them. It was an A and B conversation, and I was C'ing my way out of it." Fatima sat back down and stared into nothingness as she continued to speak.

"I opened my front door. I didn't say another word. And I let him walk out of my life. I then realized my stronghold was finally being broken. I was no longer being held captive. Does it still hurt? Yes. Like I can't tell you how much. But for now, I'm working on me and being a better me. I realized I needed to become the woman I want *my* wonderful husband to be married to. And I've decided not to wait until my husband gets here to become that woman. I'm going to already be her when he finally does show up."

Johnnie Mae leaned over and pulled Fatima into a hug. "That was so good. That was so good."

Fatima sat up straight after the embrace. "And you know what? Until I sat here with you today, I didn't realize those words were even inside me. I was holding all this in, but you said for me to get it out. Satan was torturing me because deep down, I felt he had something to hold over me. But being here with you like this, feeling the love of God the way I believe God intends for Christians to be with those who are hurting . . . you have no idea how much you have ministered to me *this* day. The scriptures I've been reading over these months, meditating on day and night—today, they became *alive* for me!"

Johnnie Mae wiped away a tear that had started a journey down her own face. "Romans eight-one says, 'There is therefore now no condemnation to them which are in Christ Jesus, who walk not after the flesh, but after the Spirit.' Yes. Oh, yes. God is good. And I thank Him right now for showing me how He would have me to be with His people. Now, Fatima, the scripture says, I believe it's in James . . . hold on a second."

Johnnie Mae opened the Bible that sat on the table and flipped the pages. "Yes, it's James five-sixteen: 'Confess your faults one to another, and pray for one another, that ye may be healed. The effectual fervent prayer of a righteous man availeth much.' I believe that, and we will pray together in just a moment. But I just scanned the rest of this chapter, and it says in verse seventeen, 'Elias was a man subject to like passions as we are, and he prayed earnestly that it might not rain: and it rained not on the earth by the space of three years and six months.' Just look at what God will do when we pray earnestly and fervently. Verse eighteen: 'And he prayed again, and the heaven gave rain, and the earth brought forth her fruit.' Nineteen: 'Brethren, if any of you do err from the truth, and one convert him'; twenty: 'Let him know, that he which converteth the sinner from the error of his way, shall save a soul from death, and shall hide a multitude of sins.' And this . . . this, Fatima, is what you and I will do."

Johnnie Mae smiled. "We will pray it doesn't rain, in the sense of your feelings for this man, and we will pray that God will open up the heaven for it to rain, which is to say God will send you the man who will treat you the way you should be treated and love you the way Christ loves the church. Don't you settle. Do you hear me? Don't settle for anything less than God's best. And one day, before you know it, the earth," Johnnie Mae touched her stomach when she felt the baby kick, "will bring forth *you* fruit."

Fatima laughed. "I can actually feel the joy of the Lord," she said. "I really do."

"Now," Johnnie Mae said as she turned her chair squarely in front of Fatima, "I do have one Word God just placed on my heart to tell you: 'Fatima Adams—Go, and sin no more.' Now, what say you and I have that prayer?"

They bowed their heads and fervently and reverently prayed.

Fatima and Johnnie Mae walked out of the conference room.

"Thank you so much," Fatima said as she hugged Johnnie Mae again. "I feel, for the first time in a long time, free."

"Well, you know what they say: 'Whom the Son sets free . . .'"

"'Is free indeed,'" Fatima said, finishing the sentence. "I feel so different. It's like I'm in expectancy or something."

"Sort of like me," Johnnie Mae said as she looked down at her expanding waistline. "One thing about expecting: you know something has to happen soon."

"That's the truth. When is your due date?"

"August fourteenth."

"Are you tired yet?"

"A little. But it's been a good pregnancy. I didn't have a lot of morning sickness. Some . . . but not a lot. And of course, Pastor Landris has taken such great care of me. I've gotten to indulge in a few things I usually try to stay away from, like chocolate cake."

Fatima moaned. "Aaah, you too? That's one of my weaknesses as well: chocolate cake. And I'm talking the fudge, rich, dark, glistening, semisweet chocolate kind, not the confectioner's sugar, shortening or butter mixed with cocoa kind."

"Oh, you know it. Now look what you've gone and done. Made me hungry." Johnnie Mae glanced at her watch. "Well, it's eleven forty-five, almost lunchtime. I could stop by and see if Pastor Landris is available for lunch today. Or if he's not and you want, we could go grab a bite."

"Sounds like a plan to me. I hope Pastor Landris can go with you, though, especially since I held you longer than my allotted time. You just don't know how much I appreciate you for allowing me that extra hour or so. God is so good. And I don't intend to disappoint Him or let Him down in any way if I can help it."

Johnnie Mae reached inside her purse and pulled out a gold, metallic case. "Here's my card," she said, handing Fatima one of her business cards. "If you need me, call or e-mail me."

"Thanks. But you've done so much; you really don't have to do this. You truly *are* a jewel." Fatima was about to put the card in her purse when it slipped out of her fingers and fluttered to the floor.

"I got it," a male voice said, quickly bending down and retrieving the card for her. He promptly handed it back to Fatima. "Here you are."

"Thanks," Fatima said.

"You're Fatima Adams, aren't you?" the man asked as he looked, now standing close to her.

She eyed him with a quizzical look. "Yes."

"I didn't realize that was you standing here. We went through new members' class together, and we both attended that Hearing and Knowing God's Voice Bible study at the end of last year. Remember? I'm Trent Howard."

Fatima smiled. "Yeah, your face does look familiar."

"I'm sure you probably don't remember me. I'm usually pretty low-key. Kind of a fade in the background, behind the scenes sort of guy. I don't make a lot of noise."

"Trent is truly a blessing to the ministry," Johnnie Mae said. "I'm Johnnie Mae Landris, the pastor's wife." She held out her hand.

"Oh, yes, ma'am, everybody knows who you are!" He shook her hand. "I've met you before, but not like this. I'm sure you meet so many people it's hard to remember all of them. It's good to see you again, Sister Landris," Trent said.

Johnnie Mae took out her phone after it made a short tone. She looked at the screen. "Trent is the one who is responsible for developing and maintaining the church's Web site," Johnnie Mae said with a smile as she looked at the screen on her phone. "Pastor Landris can't say enough about this young man. So Trent, Fatima and I were just about to go to lunch, but I just got a text message from Pastor Landris asking me if I can possibly have lunch with him. I suppose he must have gotten a break. I feel bad now because I just told Fatima we could go grab a bite to eat. Looks like I'm going to have to stand her up."

"Well, Sister Landris, I was just on my way to get something to eat myself. Fatima, if you don't mind hanging out with me, I would love to have the company. That's only if you'd like to, of course."

Johnnie Mae looked at Fatima and smiled. "Oh that would be *perfect*." Johnnie Mae started making various expressions with her eyes at Fatima as she continued to smile. "But, Trent, I wouldn't want to get you in trouble or mess anything up with your girlfriend by putting you on the spot like this."

"Oh, I'm not dating anyone at the moment."

"Not dating anyone? You must be kidding me. A tall, fine-looking, God-fearing young man like you with all your talents, plus your dedication to the work of the Lord, and you don't have women practically knocking down your door?"

"No, ma'am. I'm just keeping myself busy until the right woman does come along," Trent said.

"You and Fatima look to be around the same age, maybe a few years difference. About how old are you, Trent? That's if you don't mind me asking."

"Oh, I don't mind. I'm thirty-three."

"Thirty-three," Johnnie Mae said, putting emphasis on each syllable. "Oh, I remember those days when I was in my thirties. Only, I was a pure workaholic back then. I'm sure you and Fatima have lots in common you can talk about, though. Don't you think so, Fatima?"

Fatima slowly shook her head and wriggled her mouth to keep her impending laugh from bursting forth, then nodded. "Oh, I'm sure we probably do, Sister Landris."

"Oh, please now. Both of you, call me Johnnie Mae. We're all God's children here." Johnnie Mae put her cell phone back inside her purse and smiled. "Well, I'm off. Have fun, you two!"

"We will," Fatima said. "You and Pastor Landris have a great time, too."

"Yes, yes. I'm sure we will," Johnnie Mae said as she walked off with a grin.

"Is there any particular thing you have a taste for?" Trent asked Fatima.

"Chinese sounds good," Fatima said.

"Perfect. If you like, you're welcome to ride with me," Trent said. "There's one close by, about ten minutes or so."

"How about I just follow you in my car?" Fatima said.

"Oh, yeah. Sure."

Fatima looked at him. "And maybe the next time, should there be a next time, you can do the driving."

Trent lifted his head a little higher and cocked it to the side as he smiled and nodded. "That would be great. Yeah. That would be great."

Chapter 32

Wherefore putting away lying, speak every man truth with his neighbor: for we are members one of another.

—Ephesians 4:25

Johnnie Mae sat in her husband's office. "Thank you for lunch, Pastor Landris."

"Thank you, Mrs. Landris and soon-to-be-baby Landris," Pastor Landris said.

Johnnie Mae shook her head. "You are so silly."

"I am not. I think it's just a case of"—he lowered his voice's pitch—"the love bug."

"Well, men aren't supposed to act like that," Johnnie Mae said.

"Says who?"

"Says most of the books, most of the TV shows, most of the movies, and most men themselves."

"Well, I don't know if you've noticed, but I get all my truths and information on how to act and what to believe from the Word of God," Pastor Landris said.

"Always so spiritual." Johnnie Mae shook her head. "God must really love me."

"Why do you say that?" Pastor Landris leaned forward and gazed into her eyes.

"Of all the men out there, He thought so much of me, He gave me you."

"Sorry, but you are in error. According to the Word of God, He gave me you."

Johnnie Mae squinted her eyes a little as she smiled. "Oh, is that right? Now why does it sound like you're about to make a male chauvinist statement right about here?"

"I don't know, but I'm just telling you what the Bible says. If you have problems with it, then take your concerns up with the Lord. Proverbs eighteen-twenty-two states, and I quote, 'Whoso findeth a wife findeth a good thing, and obtaineth favour of the Lord.' Sounds like the man is the one who finds the wife, so I found you and I found a good thing. Ecclesiastes nine-nine says, 'Live joyfully with the wife whom thou lovest all the days of the life of thy vanity . . .' Not that I'm vain, not *anymore* anyway. But I am told in the scriptures to live joyfully with the wife whom I love all the days of my life, and I plan to do just that. I'm not even going to quote Ephesians five-twenty-eight and five-thirty-three to you because you already know what those scriptures say regarding loving my wife like my own self."

"You're such a show-off," Johnnie Mae said, smiling.

"Yeah, well, I'm *your* show-off."

There was a knock at the door. "Excuse me, Pastor Landris, Johnnie Mae."

"Yes, Sherry."

"I don't mean to interrupt."

"Oh don't worry about it. It's nothing we can't finish at home if we have to. What do you need?" Pastor Landris looked at his watch. "My next appointment isn't for another half hour or so."

"No, it's not your next appointment. But there is a woman here. She's down with Monica right now. She's an elderly woman who has a bunch of suitcases with her. Quite a few in fact, Monica says."

"Is she here looking for money?"

"No. She says she desperately needs to talk with someone. She seems to be in a pretty bad way. All the other counselors here are already booked. There are a few people I could try to contact, but they wouldn't be able to come until later this afternoon. I know, Johnnie Mae, you had that one appointment scheduled this morning. I was wondering if maybe you could see her? She's not a member, but she says she has visited here quite a few times. Her name is Elaine Robertson."

Johnnie Mae looked at her watch. It was 1:30 P.M. She needed to be home around three-fifteen, in time to meet Princess Rose's school bus.

"I know it's short notice," Sherry continued, "and if you can't do it, I'll check with—"

"No, I can see her," Johnnie Mae said. "I'm here already and not scheduled to meet with anyone else. I should be through in time to pick up my daughter from the bus stop. Sure. Tell Monica to set me up with a conference room and I'll be there in a few minutes."

"Thanks. I'll buzz Monica and tell her you're on your way."

Johnnie Mae turned to Pastor Landris. "Well, God works in mysterious ways, they say. I suppose it was a good thing you and I went to lunch, otherwise I would have been gone by now."

"Well, if she's looking for money, just have Monica buzz Sherry and let her take it from there. We have procedures in place for those types of requests. There are a lot of people running church scams these days, trying to figure out how to get money out of various churches."

"Okay. Let me get back down there and see what's going on. And to think—you thought you didn't need my help."

"I never said that," Pastor Landris said. He stood up and walked Johnnie Mae to the door. She turned around and he gave her a quick peck on the lips as she was leaving. "I'll see you later," he said.

"It will probably be at home tonight. You have appointments until five o'clock, right?"

"Yeah, it's still pretty busy around here these days."

Johnnie Mae walked slowly out the door. "I think I just may have eaten a little too much chocolate cake," she said as she stepped outside his office. "I can barely move."

Pastor Landris smiled.

Johnnie Mae walked over to Monica's desk, "Hi, Monica."

"Sister Landris, I have you in Conference Room L: Love ye one another." Monica lowered her head and began to whisper as she handed Johnnie Mae

the file folder she had created for Elaine Robertson. "Her name is Elaine Robertson. She's not a
member here, but she has visited us. I've noticed
she's seemed a little upset."

"Okay." Johnnie Mae took the folder and started
to walk away. She noticed four pieces of unmatched
luggage sitting behind Monica's workstation and
came back. "Are all of those suitcases hers?"

"Yes."

"How did she get them up here by herself? They
look pretty full . . . heavy."

"Fortunately, when she was coming in, Trent
was coming back from lunch. He and another guy
helped her with them."

"Okay, well, I'll be back shortly." Johnnie Mae
headed toward the waiting area to get Elaine so
they could go on to the conference room.

The woman, who was Caucasion, was sitting pa-
tiently, waiting. It wasn't unusual lately to see white
people attending the church. That was a good
thing, since black people have traditionally attended predominantly white congregations, but it
appears more difficult to get many white people to
cross over in that same type way to black congregations, unless the leader happens to become mega.

"Ms. Robertson?" Johnnie Mae said with a gentle smile.

"Yes," Memory said as she stood to her feet.

Johnnie Mae walked up to her with her right
hand extended. "I'm Johnnie Mae Landris. I'll be
the one you'll be talking with today."

"Thank you. I appreciate being able to see
someone on such short notice. I wasn't sure of the
correct procedure to do this, but I just felt God

drawing me to come here today and talk with somebody."

"Sure. It's no problem. I'm just glad I happened to still be here today. It's really booked up these days, and difficult to see daily walk-ins." Johnnie Mae opened the conference room door. "You may come on in, and we can get started." She held the door open for Memory, who moved even slower than she usually did.

Memory looked around the room. She took a seat.

"Well, Elaine. I'd like to begin by us having a word of prayer. And then when we finish, you can tell me what's on your mind and your heart. We'll go from there and see where the Lord leads us."

Memory smiled. "Sounds good."

They bowed their heads and prayed. When the prayer ended, Memory seemed nervous. Johnnie Mae had learned from this morning to have the box of tissues close at hand as well as the water. She got up while Memory prepared herself to talk and brought both things closer to them.

"Well, let's see. Where should I begin?"

Memory briefly told of her childhood: her parents, getting pregnant, her rebellious period (which lasted longer than it should have). She skipped around and talked about arriving in Birmingham, how she'd wronged so many people over the years.

"I'll be seventy years old this year. I'm too old to be doing this same old stuff. I came to this church quite by accident. I really wasn't trying to attend anyone's church, actually. I sort of think I was believing the next time I graced a church again would be inside a steel box or whatever they use for coffins these days. But God is always up to something, even when we've strayed away from Him." She spoke slowly and deliberately.

"I grew up in the church," Memory continued. "There is a scripture that people quote all the time: 'Train up a child in the way he should go, and when he is old, he will not depart from it.' That never made sense to me. I've seen so many people who have and did depart from it, from what I could see. But sitting here today, I understand it so much more. To train means to mold, to point, to shape something in a certain direction. I think of a bonsai tree. If you mold it, it's set to grow in a certain direction whether it wants to or not. And I really have done as much as I could to grow in a different direction than the way I was originally trained. But no matter, it's already been set. I may grow, but I will grow in the direction I was trained early on to grow in. Regardless of how wide or how tall I try to go."

Memory began to cough. Johnnie Mae poured her some water and waited as she sipped it slowly.

"Are you okay?"

"I'm fine," Memory said. "Just old, tired, and a little worn for wear. As I was saying, I came to this church back when Pastor Landris talked about strongholds. Then he had an altar call for those who desired prayer to be released from their strongholds. You remember that?"

"Yes, in fact, that teaching has caused many to do just what you're doing today. But sometimes, your release is not immediate—"

"Oh, I'm not here to get a refund because it didn't work."

Johnnie Mae looked down at the table; her face was a little warm from a bit of embarrassment. She had almost defended her husband's prayer on that day as though this woman were coming back to complain about it not working and wanted some type of reimbursement or some other form of compensation. "I'm sorry. Please, continue."

Memory smiled. She glanced down, then pointed at Johnnie Mae's stomach. "You're due soon."

"Yes. August fourteenth."

"It's a boy."

"We really don't know or want to know until the baby comes. So I can't say."

"No, I'm telling you, it's a boy," Memory said. "You're carrying low. It's a boy. Trust me, I'm really pretty good at this. It's a boy. So is this your first?"

"No. I have a little girl from a previous marriage. My first husband died. Princess Rose is 'six and a half.' You know how they like to add that half in there."

"I have one daughter. Not a baby anymore. My daughter has a daughter. And my granddaughter has a daughter. In fact, I told my granddaughter she was carrying a girl back when she was pregnant. She didn't believe me. But I hear she had a little girl, just like I said. Born September eleventh, two thousand and one. Not a good day for America, but it turned out to be a good day after all for my own daughter. She got to live to see her first grandbaby. Me, I haven't a clue what my great-granddaughter even looks like."

"Why not?"

"Let's see. Well, all of that is part of my story and really why I made the decision to come here today.

My coming here has cost me the place where I was staying. But I got to do this for me. The woman I was living with is some sort of a religious fanatic who, from everything I've gathered about her, believes she's the only one who's right about everything. She doesn't have an open mind to anything new or different from what she was taught back in her grandmama's day."

"How could that have cost you your place to live?"

"She doesn't care for this church much. And I had the nerve to defy her and keep visiting here, first of all. She can't stand for something like defiance living under her roof. Forget that I paid her rent to live there. Keep in mind also, she was the one who literally forced me to go to this church in the first place because she was too afraid of a church this size." Memory took a few swallows of water.

"But something happened to me that day." Memory set the glass down gently and continued. "I saw who I really was, and I have to tell you, I didn't like myself very much. I came to the altar that day. You see, I was a liar and a cheat, for the most part. My stronghold was selfishness, self-centeredness, and self-destruction. I believed everything was all about me, and I lived my life just like that. I had a mother who sacrificed for me. I didn't care. I had a wonderful father who didn't run out on us. I didn't care. I had a daughter that I brought into the world who was helpless and needed me. I didn't care. If you had something and I could make a fast buck off it, it was going to be mine no matter who became a casualty when I went for it. My mother died, and you'll never guess what I did."

"What?"

"I deliberately stayed away from her funeral. Waited until she was in the ground a few good days before I stepped foot back in her house. I let my barely sixteen-year-old daughter go through all that grieving and worrying about what she was going to do, while I waited. And do you want to know what I did next?"

Johnnie Mae nodded her head, almost afraid to hear the answer.

"I came home and took everything my mother left to my daughter including the house, and I sold it. The only place my own child had to live and I put her on the streets to fend for herself. And for what? For some man who couldn't care less whether I lived or died. After all that money was gone from the sale of everything I took from my daughter, he was right behind it: gone. And there I was alone again, looking for my next big score. But I suspected my daughter might have gotten the upper hand on me. There was this piece of jewelry. I saw it when this white woman gave it to my mother. I suspected it was worth some money. The woman said it was for me. My mother denied it when I questioned her about it. She denied it up until months before she died. But I was certain of what I heard. And I was determined, if it did still exist, I was going to get it. At the time, I didn't know just how much it was truly worth."

Johnnie Mae began to look at this person who had called herself Elaine differently. *She just said a white woman, like she's not white.* There was a familiarity about this story. Hearing her talk was causing her to question what was going on here.

"Are you all right?" Memory asked as she tilted her head to try and read the expression on Johnnie Mae's face.

"Oh, yeah. It was just your story was sounding a little like something I've heard about before."

"I suppose that happens a lot in your listening line of work," Memory said. "And you look like you read a lot, too. They say there's nothing new under the sun."

"Yes. But please, go on."

"I suspected my daughter still had that necklace I saw the woman give my mother. It wasn't in those things I took. I just hoped she didn't think it was junk and throw it away. So I set out to get it, especially after I learned there was a reward for it."

"Oh, God," Johnnie Mae whispered.

"Mrs. Landris, are you sure you're okay? You don't look so good."

Johnnie Mae stood up and began to fan herself with the file folder. Memory went and got the other glass and poured Johnnie Mae some water.

"Here, dearie. Drink some of this. Do I need to go get someone for you? You don't look well at all. You look like death warmed over, all of sudden."

Johnnie Mae took a swallow of the water. "I'm fine. I'll be okay. If you could just give me a minute . . . let me get some air. I'll be right back."

"Sure, take all the time you need. There's nowhere I have to be anytime soon. In fact, when I leave here, I don't have a clue where I'll be going. I'm just tired of running, I do know that. But you go on out and take care of yourself. You probably did too much today carrying that baby, and he's reminding you that you need to take it easy."

"Yeah, I'm sure that's it." Johnnie Mae walked toward the door. She looked back at Memory one more time. *It has to be her.* "I'll be back in about five minutes."

"I'll be waiting."

Johnnie Mae left the room and closed the door. She leaned back against the door for a second, trying to figure out what to do next. "Oh, God. What now?"

Chapter 33

There is no fear in love; but perfect love casteth out fear: because fear hath torment. He that feareth is not made perfect in love.
—I John 4:18

Johnnie Mae went to Pastor Landris's office. "Sherry, I need to speak with Pastor Landris."

"He's in conference right now and gave me explicit orders he not be disturbed."

"I understand that, but this is really urgent."

"Are you okay? Is it the baby?" Sherry asked.

"I'm fine. The baby's fine. But this is really important. Now, either you can interrupt him or I will," Johnnie Mae said as she took short breaths.

"Okay. Hold on. I'll be right back." Sherry went and knocked on Pastor Landris's door.

"Come in," he said.

"I'm so sorry, Pastor Landris. But there's something very, very important that needs your immediate attention. You know I wouldn't have bothered you otherwise."

Pastor Landris nodded to Sherry, then addressed the man in his office. "Could you please excuse me for just a moment? I'll be right back. Just hold that thought," he said.

"Of course, Pastor," the man said.

Pastor Landris hurried out the door and closed it behind him. He saw Johnnie Mae standing there.

"What's wrong?" he said, panic lacing his voice.

"That woman that I'm meeting with," Johnnie Mae said as she tried to keep her voice from cracking and still breathe.

"Did she do something? Do we need to call security?" Pastor Landris asked.

"No." Johnnie Mae covered her mouth with her hands as she glanced at Sherry, who was still within hearing distance.

Pastor Landris saw her glance quickly over at Sherry, and he guided his wife by the elbow to another area so she could speak freely without the fear of being overheard.

"Tell me what has you so upset," Pastor Landris said.

"I think that woman in the conference . . . that Elaine Robertson . . ."

"Yes."

"I think that's Memory Patterson."

"You mean Lena Patterson's mother?"

"Yes, Lena's mother; Sarah Fleming's daughter."

"Oh my."

"Sarah has been frantically searching for her all of these years. I've kept in touch with both Lena and Sarah off and on. Sarah told me about two years ago she hired a private investigator to find Memory. But whenever he got close enough,

Memory always disappeared before he could really talk to her. Memory doesn't even believe it when he tells folks to tell her she's possible heir to an inheritance. So she ends up fleeing every single time."

"If you'd done all she's been accused of doing, wouldn't you? I mean, can you blame her?"

"No. And I'm not sure I would trust her knowing all the detailed information regarding Sarah either. Lena definitely doesn't trust her knowing what she may have access to now," Johnnie Mae said. She began to pace a little. "I told her I would be right back. What do I do?"

"Does she suspect you know who she is? That she's really Memory."

"No. She thinks I'm not feeling well because of the baby. Like I've done too much today. But I have to get back before she gets restless or suspicious or something and leaves. She's down there spilling her guts to me about all these things she's done to her daughter—"

"Lena."

"Yes. And she's talking about that necklace now, the Alexandrite necklace—I'm sure it is. I didn't know what to do . . . my breathing started getting shallow . . . the baby felt like he had balled up."

"He? You said 'he.' You've never referred to the baby as a gender before."

"Later about that. But I need to call Sarah and find out what she wants me to do. I mean, Sarah wants so much to see her daughter. And she's right here! The infamous Memory is right here, with me no less. I can't take a chance of her getting away.

Who knows if we'll ever find her again or if we do, whether it will be too late when she is finally found."

"Where is she staying?" Pastor Landris asked as he held Johnnie Mae still.

"She just got kicked out of a home where she was staying with this lady who doesn't care much for our church. That's why she brought all of her suitcases with her. She came here first, I suppose while she figures out what to do or where to go next. She keeps saying that she's tired. I can imagine. She's almost seventy years old—too old to be on the run, that's for sure. And she has a biological mother, ninety years old, she doesn't even know exists. A mother, who incidentally, could and would give anything to meet her before she dies."

"So what do you want to do?"

"Seriously?"

"Yeah," Pastor Landris said.

"You're not going to like it," Johnnie Mae said.

"Yeah, I have a feeling." Pastor Landris laughed. "But go ahead. Tell me."

"I'd like to take her home with me," Johnnie Mae said. "I have to pick up Princess Rose from the bus stop shortly, so I need to get home anyway. But I wouldn't dare chance letting Memory go to a hotel. We may never see her again. If I take her home with me, I can call Sarah or Lena, see what they want me to do, how much they want me to tell Memory, if anything. Provided this really is Memory. Confidentiality-wise, this is tricky. I probably shouldn't tell Sarah I've possibly seen Memory, but I can't tell Memory the truth about Sarah without Sarah's consent. It's a catch twenty-two." She sighed. "I'll just take Memory home with me first, and then, we can go from there."

"Okay."

"Okay? You mean, for real okay? Or there's just not enough time to argue about it okay?"

"Whatever you think is best, okay. Okay? You'll figure out ethically how to accomplish this."

She let out a chuckle. "Okay then. Well, let me get back down there."

Johnnie Mae left in a hurry.

When she arrived back in the conference room, Memory was gone. "Oh no. Where did she go?" Johnnie Mae ran out of the room to Monica's desk. No Monica. "Where's Monica?" She looked over behind Monica's work station—the suitcases were gone. She went down the hall looking. "Have you seen Monica?" she asked someone with a stack of copies in her arms.

"Yeah. She was helping this elderly woman down the hall about ten minutes ago."

"This way?" Johnnie Mae pointed to her right.

"No, the other way," the woman with the copies said as she pointed out the direction using her head.

"Toward the doors leading outside?" Johnnie Mae asked.

The woman nodded.

"Thanks," Johnnie Mae said. She started down the hall. She saw Monica and Memory coming toward her. She exhaled. "Hi," Johnnie Mae said in the calmest voice she could muster. "I was getting worried about you," she said to Memory.

"I had to use the little girl's room. This young lady here was helping me find my way around. This is such a big place. I was afraid I would get lost. Then somebody would have really had to come searching for me."

"We can't have that. That's great. I'm glad Monica was such a help. I didn't see your suitcases anymore, and I was thinking you'd given up on waiting for me to come back and had left me hanging," Johnnie Mae said as they walked back slowly.

"Oh, I'm sorry, Sister Landris," Monica said. "I didn't know where you went or how long you would be gone. I moved her suitcases into the storage room while we were away. I didn't want anybody to take anything, not that they would, but you never know."

"Oh, yeah. You were absolutely right to protect Ms. Robertson's belongings while you helped her."

"Yep, cause that's all I have left except for what I have in my storage unit. But it's practically all my clothes, so if something happened to those, I would be in a mess. Especially now that I don't even have a place to lay my head."

"You know, Ms. Robertson. I was just thinking about that. And I was coming back to tell you that my husband and I would like for you to come stay at our home for a few days."

"Oh, I couldn't do that. I didn't come here to try to sponge off anybody or get a handout. I just needed to talk, and God led me here. That was all."

"See, that's what I mean. I believe God sent you here as well." Johnnie Mae swallowed so hard and loud, she thought both Memory and Monica heard her do it. "I can't explain right now, but it's just something I believe God desires for me to do."

"But I would be imposing," Memory said. "And I can't do that. But if you would drop me off at a hotel, I would appreciate that."

They reached Monica's work area.

"Ms. Robertson, I believe you and I need to talk some more," Johnnie Mae said as she spoke rather fast. "There are some things God has revealed to me that I feel I must share with you. But here's the thing: I usually pick up my daughter from the bus stop around three-fifteen. I figure if we leave now, I could get her, then we could go to my house, and we could finish our conversation there. Pastor Landris and I would love to have you as our special guest for dinner tonight." Johnnie Mae shifted her weight to her other leg. "Please don't turn me down. You'll make me think you don't like me, or that I did a lousy job counseling with you so far, and you're trying to get away from me."

"Well, that's definitely not the case," Memory said. "Now, the old me would have jumped at an invitation like this: free room and board with free meals for a few days. But something's changed. I'm not the same creature I used to be."

"Ms. Robertson, I'm sorry, but I'm not going to take no for an answer." Johnnie Mae turned to Monica. "Monica, please get Ms. Robertson's luggage out of the storage closet. And if you would, could you call one of the guys hanging around here to come and take them to my car."

"Of course, Sister Landris. Maybe Trent's still

available." Monica said, speaking Trent's name just a little too lovingly.

"I don't mean to sound too bossy, but could you hurry? I don't like my daughter having to wait on me after she gets off the bus." Johnnie Mae did that more for effect for Memory's benefit than anything. She then turned to Memory. "You can't be too careful with your children these days. Things aren't like they used to be when you could trust that nobody would dare snatch them up, let alone harm or kill them."

"It is a different world we live in, that's for sure," Memory said. "So, I won't make you argue about whether I should go home with you for now. I'll go willingly, and we can finish our talk. You can always take me to a hotel or the bus station afterward."

Johnnie Mae slowly released a sigh of relief. "Absolutely."

After they picked up Princess Rose, Johnnie Mae and Memory went to her house. Johnnie Mae knew she couldn't call Lena or Sarah until after Pastor Landris came home. That way, she could be certain someone was watching Memory, until she knew what direction to take next.

"So Elaine," Johnnie Mae said as she was fixing dinner and had Memory and Princess Rose in the kitchen with her. "You have a daughter, grand-daughter, and a great-granddaughter. Where do they live?"

"Last I saw them, my daughter and pregnant granddaughter, they were living in the Atlanta area," Memory said. "I'm sure you've probably been to Atlanta many times."

Johnnie Mae smiled. "Yes. Pastor Landris used to pastor a church there several years back. I'm quite familiar with Atlanta."

"He was the pastor of a church in Atlanta? I wonder if he ever knew any of my people?"

Pastor Landris came in the house just then. "Family! I'm home," he said.

Johnnie Mae smiled at Memory.

Princess Rose ran to meet her stepfather. "Daddy Landris is home!" she said. "Hey, Daddy Landris! What did you bring me?"

"What did I bring you? You mean, I'm not enough?"

Princess Rose laughed. "Of course you are. But what did you bring me?" she said as he tickled her and made her laugh out loud.

"Good evening, I'm Pastor Landris."

"You know I know you," Memory said. "I have truly been blessed by your teachings, Pastor Landris. You prayed for me once when I came to the altar, the first time I came to the church, actually. God changed my heart. I can't explain how it happened, but it happened."

"Most folks can't explain how a microwave works either, but that doesn't stop us from using it," Pastor Landris said. "I hear you're going to grace us with your presence for a few days."

"Oh, that's your wife talking. I haven't agreed to any such thing. Dinner was the extent of my commitment," Memory said.

Pastor Landris leaned over and spoke quietly, "Now, you wouldn't want to disappoint my lovely wife, would you? We would love your company. We have several guest rooms in this house, as I'm sure you can imagine from the size of it. It's things like this that I believe God wants us to do for one another." He glanced over at Johnnie Mae as he spoke that last sentence.

Memory smiled as she sipped the hot tea. "Your wife showed me the rooms. And I wouldn't want to hurt her feelings. But I don't want anybody getting the wrong idea either. I didn't come to y'all's church trying to mooch off anybody or to run a scam. I came to confess some stuff, and to be honest, I still haven't gotten but half of it off my chest yet. But I promised God I would confess my sins so I can have that off me and I can start with a clean slate. Then I'm going to try to make some things right with some people I've wronged. Don't quite know how I'm going to manage that, but I'm going to trust God. For once, I'm going to walk by faith and not by sight and trust God to order my steps."

"Well, all right then. So you're at least going to stay the night, right?" Pastor Landris said.

"When you put it like you just did, I suppose I have to. As long as you know I'm on the up-and-up. I wouldn't dare put myself in a position to mess with God's anointed ones. Not now. I have enough to have to pay for as it is already."

"You do know that God will toss all you've done into the sea of forgetfulness. He will give you a new beginning. He is the God of a second chance and of new beginnings."

"God might forget about it, but a lot of these people I know write stuff down just to be sure they don't forget junk you've done to them." She drank some more of her tea. "But like I said, I will stay the night. Maybe the anointing here will give me the strength I'm going to need for this journey I have ahead of me."

While Pastor Landris kept Memory and Princess Rose entertained Johnnie Mae went upstairs to her bedroom to call Sarah.

"Don't be giving me hypotheticals. I believe you know where she is. Bring my child home to me, please," Sarah said after Johnnie Mae explained in her own way what was happening. "I don't know how much longer I have. But I have to see her with my physical eyes before I leave this earth. If the Lord is willing, I have to see her. So if you've found her, catch a plane first thing in the morning, or if you must drive up, then drive. But bring my child home to me."

"Okay, Sarah. But I need to know if I do see her, how much you want me to tell her about who you really are."

"Tell her whatever you need to tell her to convince her to come. Everything, if you have to," Sarah said. "I don't see any other way you're going to get her to come unless she knows the whole truth. I don't care how much you tell her, just get my child to me. That's all that matters to me at this point. I'm too old and too frail to come there, or else I would charter a plane and be there tonight. I'll get you whatever money you need to do whatever it takes to get her here, just please, Johnnie Mae . . . please, I don't have time for hypotheticals. If you know where Memory is right now, please bring my child home to me."

"Okay, Sarah. But what about Lena?" Johnnie Mae asked.

"I'll tell Lena what's possibly going on. I know she doesn't trust her mother any farther than she can throw her. But we're just going to have to work this out. I've come too far to turn around now. You know what I've been through to get to this point. I'm too close to let anything or anyone stop me. You know this has to be God working this out. And I don't believe He brought me this far to leave me now. Call me and let me know when to expect your arrival. I'll be waiting."

"All right. If I find her, I don't know whether we would actually fly or drive. My due date is not for a couple of months. And I feel fine to travel."

"I know I'm asking a lot of you. And maybe I'm wrong to be doing it—"

"No, Sarah. It's okay. I understand how much this means to you, more than you'll ever know."

"Johnnie Mae?"

"Yes, Sarah."

"Is there anything too hard for God?"

Johnnie Mae laughed. "No, Sarah. God is able to do exceedingly, abundantly, above all that we can ever ask or think. I know this much for myself. There is *nothing* too hard for God. Nothing!"

"Yeah. I'm starting to see that myself as well. Praise God from whom all blessings flow. My child is coming home. For whatever reason, you're holding back what you know. But I know my child is coming home! Thank you, Lord. After almost seventy years, my child is coming home! You're bringing my child back to me. Memory is coming home."

Chapter 34

*Is any thing too hard for the Lord? At the time
appointed I will return unto thee, according
to the time of life. . . .*

—Genesis 18:14

Pastor Landris reflected back on the past few
months. He had begun a series in January
called Strongholds. Here it was June and that message, as a Word from God should, was still having a
profound effect on people's lives. As he stood to
speak on this Sunday morning, looking at this vast
congregation, he saw more than just faces when he
looked into the crowd. These were the faces of
people hungry for God's Word, people in expecta-
tion of the Word of God to assist them in their
everyday lives.

People like Dr. Xavier Holden and his wife, Avis,
who were sitting in the front row to his right. On
the left side was Bentley Strong holding the hand
of his pregnant wife, Marcella. Pastor Landris
couldn't help but notice and smile at how happy
that couple seemed as they sat there waiting for
him to begin. Sapphire was a few rows behind
Johnnie Mae, and next to her sat Charity. Sapphire

and Charity could be seen together quite often these days. Pastor Landris believed that was a good thing. In fact, it fell right in line with his message for the day: preserved fruit.

"I happen to like fresh fruit," Pastor Landris began. "The other day, I went to the refrigerator and took out a container of strawberries. Inside the container were various sizes of strawberries, but what immediately caught my attention was how a few of those beautiful strawberries had started to go bad. My first thought was to get the bad ones away from the good ones as quickly as possible. You see, I knew the bad ones, alongside the good, would cause the good ones to go bad that much faster. I can't explain precisely why that is, although I suspect it's because of the convenience of transferring. But we do know this to be a scientific fact."

Pastor Landris paced a few steps to his right. "For the fruit that was going bad, I understood I could cut off the bad parts and keep what was worth saving. But for those too far gone, I knew my only option was to throw them away. That's when I heard God say, 'Just like the good fruit and the bad fruit here, that's how people must be attentive regarding who they hang around.' You see, although there was good fruit in there with the bad, the good fruit—as wonderful as it looked and was—could never turn the bad fruit back to good." Pastor Landris shook his head.

"But the bad fruit, if continued to be left around and with the good fruit, could definitely infect the good fruit and cause it to go bad. A few months ago and for several months, I taught a series on strongholds. Many times people who are trying to live right—those producing good fruit—believe they can hang around, run with, and even be bosom buddies with people in their environment and on their terms who are sin infected. They think they can *change* them. Now, I'm not saying those who know the way shouldn't be witnessing and ministering to those who don't know that Jesus is the way, the truth, and the life, and that no man comes to the Father except by Jesus. So I want you to hear me good." Pastor Landris walked down the steps to be closer to the congregation.

"What I'm saying is if your fruit is good, you have to watch being around fruit that is rotting or already rotten. Hear me again. Good fruit cannot turn bad fruit to good; but bad fruit can, if left around for too long, affect good fruit in negative ways and turn it bad. One little bruise. One small spot. A little mold. Another spot." He walked back up the steps. "But there is some good news! Somebody say good news!"

"Good news!" the congregation shouted.

"I'm talking good news with a capital *G* and a capital *N*; I'm talking the Gospel Good News."

Members of the congregation began to clap and stand to their feet. Pastor Landris took out his handkerchief and wiped the sweat off his forehead.

"The Good News is that the Holy Spirit is able to protect and preserve. And protected and preserved fruit can withstand being around bad fruit without being affected in the same way as good fruit that hasn't been preserved. So for all of you who have been and are still wrestling with various strongholds, you might need to check who you're choosing to hang around. Check and check often."

Fatima Adams looked to the man sitting on her right. She smiled. Trent Howard grinned back at her.

Pastor Landris began to scan from right to left as he continued to preach. "Jude verse twenty-four says, 'Now unto him that is able to keep you from falling, and to present you faultless before the presence of his glory with exceeding joy.' This verse," Pastor Landris said as he bounced, "should have you shouting right now. Oh, can't you just see Jesus presenting you faultless because all of the bad parts have been cut away? Jesus able to present you faultless because you're saved . . . because you were kept . . . because you've been preserved by His grace."

The congregation began to shout, "Yes!" "Amen!" and various praises to God.

A slimmer Desiree and a changed Edwin Houston were both shouting with praise.

"And during those times you find yourself witnessing to or around bad fruit, you don't have to worry about getting infected because of *Him,* who is able to keep you from falling. The *Him* who came into your life when you invited Jesus in as your Savior. *Him,* the third person of the Trinity, called the Holy Spirit, who resides in you, walks with you as your comforter and your guide if you'll listen to His voice. *Him,* who will restrain you with a feeling down here"—Pastor Landris pressed his fist against his stomach and turned it as he frowned to show the discomfort one might feel—"warning you not to do something or when it's time for you to leave a place, ordering your steps daily in the way of the Lord. Oh, somebody's getting this today! Somebody is being totally set free! And as the Word of God says, and I keep telling you: Whom the Son sets free, is free indeed!"

Many in the congregation were crying while others lifted their hands to heaven.

"None of us should ever get so arrogant as to believe that because our fruit is good that that alone is enough to keep us from being affected by fruit that's infected. That is the very reason why any good parent will tell his or her child not to hang around certain people. Parents understand how other people's negative ways can rub off on or affect another. I'm sure many of you have heard, 'One bad apple can spoil the whole bunch.'"

Darius Connors reached over and grabbed his wife's hand as he continued to squirm, unsuccessfully trying to get comfortable.

"So in this spiritual battle . . ." Pastor Landris said, "and church, this is spiritual warfare. Ephesians six-ten tells us, 'For we wrestle not against flesh and blood, but against principalities, against powers, against the rulers of the darkness of this world, against spiritual wickedness in high places.' It's not people we're fighting against. It's spiritual wickedness. So when it comes to good fruit versus bad, good is great." Pastor Landris smiled as he shook his head.

"But when you are preserved, you can withstand so much more. Just make sure that God is always with you. And He said He would be. He said He would never leave you nor forsake you. So that means wherever you go, whatever you're doing,

God is there. When you go to places you know you don't have any business being, you're taking God with you. Stop hanging out and around bacteria-laced fruit—sin—for so long that you end up infected. Understand that the Word of God is sharper than any two-edged sword. God's Word will cut off the bad parts in your life as well as in the lives of others. But when it comes to being preserved, I want you to know this with all assurance—Jesus saves! The question now is: Are you saved? Is your soul preserved?" He paused.

"If not, then you can be saved today. Why not come now? Now is your appointed time. Don't wait for tomorrow, because tomorrow is not promised to any of us. Today is your day. Today. Let's give God the praise today! Oh, He's worthy, He's worthy, He's worthy of all our praise! We need the Lord in our lives. And for anyone who might be questioning or doubting God's ability to do exceedingly, abundantly, above all, please allow me to set you straight right here, right now, today. There is *nothing* too hard for God. Nothing!" Pastor Landris looked over and smiled at his pregnant wife.

"If you need a Savior, come. If you're in need of prayer right now for whatever reason, then come. Come to Jesus, now. Not tomorrow—now. Won't you come?"

The people were on their feet, some hurrying to the altar while others were shouting "Hallelujah!" and other praises to an awesome and almighty God.

There's nothing too hard for God!

A young woman with a secret past
finds her faith in

Goodness and Mercy

Coming in December 2009 from Dafina Books.

Come now, and let us reason together, saith the Lord: though your sins be as scarlet, they shall be as white as snow; though they be red like crimson, they shall be as wool.
—Isaiah 1:18

"If you're here today," forty-eight-year-old Pastor George Landris began, "and you feel there's something missing in your life. If you admit that although there are billions of people on this earth, you still feel like you're all by yourself—that sometimes it feels like it's you, and you alone. If you feel as though no one truly loves you. If you're *fed up* with being fed up." He paused a second. "If you'd like to be born again . . . you want to know *Jesus* in the free pardon of your sins. Then, I want you to know that your being here today is neither an accident nor a coincidence. I want you to know that it's time for a change! You see, I've been told that the definition of insanity is doing the same thing over and over again but somehow expecting a different result." He shook his head slowly, then took one step to the side.

"Well, to that someone who's here today, your

change has come. If you're looking for change, change you can *truly* believe in, then the Lord is extending His hand to you today through me. He's asking you, on *this* day, to accept His hand. I know I'm talking to somebody today. In your life, it's time for a change." Pastor Landris nodded as he narrowed his eyes, then ticked his head three times to one side as he smiled.

"Oh, I know we heard the word change a lot last year. We *talked* about change. Some of you even voted for change. Some of you voted for the first time in your life *because* of change. Well, on November the fourth, two-thousand and eight, change took a step forward in these United States of America . . . a change that's *already* had an impact on the world. But on *this* day"—he pointed his index finger down toward the floor—"on this Sunday, January the fourth, two-thousand and *nine*, sixteen days before that embodiment of change is to be sworn in as the forty-fourth president of the United States, it's time for your own personal change. A change, a wonderful change."

Many in the audience began to clap while others stood, clapped, and shouted various things like: "Change!" "A wonderful change!" and "Thank God for change!"

Pastor Landris bobbed his head, then continued to speak. "For those of you here who are tired of fighting this battle alone, let me assure you that there *is* another way. I said there *is* another way. And in case you don't know or haven't heard, *Jesus* is the way! He's the truth, and He's the light.

"And today—just as Jesus has been doing since

before He left earth boarded on a cloud on His way back to Heaven where he presently sits on the right hand of the Father—He's calling for those who have yet to answer His call, to come. Come unto Him all you that labor and are heavy laden. Jesus desires to be Lord of your life. Won't you come today? Won't you come? Come and cast your cares on the Lord, for He cares for you. Oh yes, He cares . . . He cares. He cares. He . . . cares."

Pastor Landris extended his hand. He looked like someone waiting on a dance partner to take hold of his outstretched hand in order to continue the next step of a well choreographed dancing routine.

Twenty-six-year-old Gabrielle Mercedes heard his words. She felt them as they pierced through her heart, then later melted down to her stomach. She instantly doubled over as she sat there in her seat. Quickly, she felt the warmth wash completely over her, starting at her head. It felt as though she was being covered with pure love and peace, as though buckets of warmth were being poured out on her and were quickly making their way down to her feet. Her feet heard the music inside of the words "Come and cast your cares on the Lord, for He cares," and they began to move, to tap rapidly, all on their own.

The music that played on the inside of her was not the usual music one might expect to hear in church. It was music that no words she knew could aptly describe—angelic. Her body instinctively knew what to do; her legs summarily stood her upright to her feet. She hurriedly, but gracefully, started across—one-two, one-two, side-step, side-step—from where she'd sat, quietly excusing herself past those who shared the row with her. Then, forward she glided, with long deliberate strides down a wide center aisle—flow, extend, now glide, glide, faster, faster—toward the front of the church building's sanctuary. Everything happening before the right side of her brain was ever even able to effectively launch a logical and methodical discussion about any of this with the left side of her brain. She was moving forward, refusing to look back.

And when she shook the hand that continued to remain extended for any and all who dared to reach toward it, she didn't see the man of God's, Pastor Landris's, hand. All she saw was the Son of the living God called Jesus, Emmanuel, the Prince of Peace, the King of kings, the Lord of lords, the President of presidents. She began to leap—higher, higher.

And as she'd shaken Pastor Landris's hand, at least twenty other people also came forward and stood alongside her. But she'd only felt the hand of God holding her up as she stood there and openly confessed she was indeed a sinner. She knew—without any trumpets sounding, any special effects, and any special feelings—that in that moment of her confession, she was saved. Saved by grace. Now. Now.

Now faith is . . . now . . . faith is . . . faith is now . . . now.

And the feeling she did have? It was the Lord leading the dance of her life, whispering throughout her every being that she now only needed to follow His lead. She needed to allow Him to take her to the next step, and then the next one, and the next one, without knowing what the next step might be. Fully trusting His lead. *One-two-three.*

Oh, how Gabrielle loved to dance! But until this day, she'd never known the true grace in dancing. That amazing grace. God's amazing grace. The feelings she had now was a byproduct of the new knowledge she possessed: the knowledge of knowing Jesus Christ in the free pardon of her sins. All of her sins, every single one of them, Pastor Landris was saying, were officially pardoned. She was free!

"Pardoned—your slate, wiped cleaned," Pastor Landris said to those who came up. "Your sins, totally purged from your record. It's as though it never happened. God says your past transgressions have been removed as far as the east is from the west; the north from the south. All of your sins— the ones folks know about, and yes, the ones only God knows. Gone. Gone! Whatever sins were in your past, from this day forward, as far as the Lord is concerned, they're gone." Those standing were being signaled by a ministry leader to follow her to an awaiting conference room.

"Hold up a second," Pastor Landris said, halting them before they exited. "I want you to say this with me: My *past* has been *cast* into God's sea of forgetfulness."

They did as he asked—some of them leaping for joy as they shouted the words.

"You are forgiven of your sins," he said. "Look at me." He waited a second. "And God is saying to you, don't allow anyone . . . *anyone,* to ever bring up your past sins to you again. Did you hear what I said? Don't let *anyone* use your past against you. If they bring it up, you tell them that it's under the blood of Jesus now."

The entire congregation erupted with shouts of praise as they stood to their feet.

Don't miss the other books in the Blessed Trinity Trilogy:

Blessed Trinity
If Memory Serves

Available now wherever books are sold.

From *Blessed Trinity*

For I know the thoughts that I think toward you, saith the Lord, thoughts of peace, and not of evil, to give you an expected end.
—Jeremiah 29:11

Pastor George Landris watched her as she walked gracefully to the other side of the banquet hall of the church. He couldn't help but smile; she had that effect on him. She had to be the most beautiful woman he had ever laid eyes on. With the passing of time, that belief had only intensified. Knowing it would be inappropriate for him to act on his true impulse, he casually strolled closer.

"I hope you won't think badly of me for saying this," Pastor Landris said in a low voice only she could hear, "you are, without a doubt, the loveliest woman I've ever seen."

"Careful there, Pastor—I happen to be spoken for." She held up her left hand and wiggled the three diamond rocks that adorned her ring finger.

The two of them were standing near an empty table. Many of the people who had attended the banquet were chatting in groups as they prepared to leave.

Pastor Landris moved in closer and began to whisper softly in her ear. "Well, your man is indeed one blessed man, if I say so myself. Tell me . . . honestly. What are the chances of the two of us getting together later tonight after this thing is over?" he asked—his deep voice, velvety-smooth. "You know . . . to talk?"

"To talk, Pastor?" Skepticism laced her voice. "Just to talk?"

"Madam, I am a man of God, and I assure you, where the Lord leads, I have vowed to follow." He leaned back to be able to admire her better, then began shaking his head. "Mmm-mmm."

She tried, but failed—she couldn't help but smile. "Okay, Pastor. You know, it's hard to say no to someone like you, especially with that irresistible charm. How can one be so good, and yet be so bad at the same time?"

Pastor Landris bit down slightly on his bottom lip and grinned even more. He touched the back of the chair, as though he needed to do something to keep that one hand occupied. "Well, now, *Mrs.* Landris, I must confess—I have it bad for you. Only for you."

"Landris, you need to stop," Johnnie Mae Landris said, fanning at him while trying to keep her voice in check. "You would think after being married for three years—"

"It won't officially be three years until Wednesday." He grinned, his eyes again performing a quick scan of her petite body from head to toe as he slowly shook his head.

She smiled at him as he watched her before she

swatted him playfully. "I told you, you need to stop."

"What?" he asked innocently.

"Flirting with me in public." Johnnie Mae continued to blush. She waved at someone walking out of the door who waved good-bye to her. The crowd that had originally filled the room earlier that night, was now down to a handful.

"But you're my wife. It's perfectly acceptable for me to flirt with my wife, isn't it?" Pastor Landris rubbed his well-trimmed goatee. He looked down at his black patent leather Prada boots before looking back up at her.

"There's also a time and a place for everything."

"'To every thing there is a season, and a time to every purpose under the heaven . . .'"

"Yes, Mr. Walking Bible, and there's 'a time to love.' In a church facility, in front of people, immediately after a lovely banquet given by members and friends of the church, is neither the time nor the place," Johnnie Mae said as she began to sashay away in her beautiful Prussian-blue, beaded evening gown. She needed to hug a few more people and thank them for their contribution to such an unforgettable evening.

"I suppose this means we have a date for later tonight, then?" he yelled at her, a little louder than he'd intended. Quickly, he looked around to see if anyone had overheard him. His eyes were immediately met by those of a woman who had recently become a member of their congregation.

"Good evening, Pastor Landris."

"Sister Morrell."

"Oh, please—I've asked you several times to call me Faith. Sister Morrell just sounds so stiff and formal." She smiled.

"As you prefer—Faith."

"I just wanted to personally congratulate you and Mrs. Landris on your wedding anniversary." She pointed to the banner on the back wall that read: *September 8, 2001 to 2004—Only The Beginning of Something Beautiful.* "Three years is a long time to be with one person."

"Not really. Not when the ultimate joy will be celebrating our golden anniversary."

"Then I probably should say that three years would be a long time for me. But I suppose had I been as fortunate as Johnnie Mae to have married someone as wonderful as you—"

"Excuse me, but I believe you have it all wrong."

A puzzled smile came across her face. "I'm sorry. I have it all wrong?"

"Yes. You see, Johnnie Mae is not the fortunate one here at all—I am," he said with pride. "I am so blessed to have found such a woman to share my life—three years with her has been more like three minutes. 'Whoso findeth a wife findeth a good thing, and obtaineth favor of the Lord.' As far as I'm concerned, our happiness together now is merely a small hint of what is yet to come."

Faith's face quickly fell. "Oh," she said, a little disappointed, then recovering her pleasant demeanor. "That is so sweet!" Pure honey seemed to drip from her lips. "You two are blessed! So blessed. Congratulations again."

"Well, Sister Mor . . . I mean, Faith. Thank you. I'll be sure and tell Mrs. Landris."

"Please do. I was hoping to catch up with her before she left." She pretended to be earnestly searching, glancing at the few people still chatting in small groups. "I'm sorry we missed each other, but I must be heading home now. My sister, Hope, wasn't feeling well when I left, and I don't want her waiting up too late."

"Your sister is under the weather? I wondered why she hadn't come to the banquet. Hope worked so tirelessly, helping to put this together."

"Oh, it's nothing too serious. She was having some difficulty breathing earlier today. Probably just another one of the panic attacks that she's been known to have from time to time. Charity is keeping an eye on her until I get back."

"Please tell Hope we'll be praying for her speedy recovery. And that she was sorely missed tonight."

Faith maintained her smile. "Of course. I'll be sure and tell her. See you tomorrow at services."

Pastor Landris watched as she left. There was something about Faith and her identical twin sister Hope that really bothered him. He felt sure they loved each other, but something was going on between them. He just couldn't put his finger on what it was.

Pastor Landris and Johnnie Mae arrived home. It had been an enjoyable but long evening. Johnnie Mae had gone upstairs to step out of her evening gown—she loved Prussian blue and hoped to find a daytime dress in that color. Everyone had been so wonderful at the banquet tonight, the congregation having given them a lovely third wedding anniversary celebration. It had indeed been a glorious night, but she was exhausted. Tomorrow was Sunday and the start of yet another long day.

As she briefly closed her eyes, she couldn't help but reflect on all that had happened over the past few years that had brought them to this place . . .

From *If Memory Serves*

*Hope deferred maketh the heart sick, but
when the desire cometh, it is a tree of life.*
—Proverbs 13:12

Landris had come home earlier than was normal
for him. In fact, he'd been caught off guard by
just how blinding the June sun could be if you happened to be facing west between four and five
o'clock in the afternoon. As soon as he walked in
the house, Johnnie Mae asked him to get Memory's
luggage out of the car and take it to the bedroom
her mother generally used. Johnnie Mae, Memory,
and Johnnie Mae's daughter, Princess Rose, were
all laughing and talking in the den next to the
kitchen when Landris came and joined them.

After Johnnie Mae felt certain Landris had Memory's full attention, she excused herself and hurried upstairs to her bedroom to call Sarah.

"Don't be giving me hypotheticals. Bring my
child home to me," Sarah said after Johnnie Mae
explained the situation as she perceived it. "Catch
a plane first thing in the morning, or if you must

drive up, then drive. Just bring my child home to me."

"Okay, Sarah. But I need to know how much you want me to tell her about who you really are," Johnnie Mae said.

Going by the name Elaine Robertson, Memory didn't have a clue Johnnie Mae suspected whom she really was. Then again, Memory didn't know that most of what she believed to be true regarding her own life was, in fact, not the whole truth. If she was truly the Memory Patterson they were seeking, the world as Memory knew it was about to quickly go from flat to round. Johnnie Mae wasn't sure she should be the one telling Memory any of this or whether this was truly the best place for it to be done.

"Tell her whatever you need to tell her to convince her to come. Everything, if you have to," Sarah said.

Johnnie Mae hung up the phone and made her way back downstairs. She walked into the den just as Landris was telling Memory one of his favorite jokes.

"There was a feud between the pastor and the choir director of this church," Landris said, smiling just a tad. "Now, the first hint of trouble seems to have come when the pastor preached on 'Dedicating Yourselves to Service' and the choir director decided the choir should sing 'I Shall Not Be Moved.' Of course, the pastor believed the song had merely been a coincidence, so he put it behind him and didn't think any more about it. The next Sunday, the pastor preached on 'Giving.' After that sermon, the choir members squirmed as the choir director led them into the hymn 'Jesus Paid It All.' By this time, the good pastor was starting to get a bit upset." Landris chuckled a little.

"Sunday morning service attendance was beginning to grow as the tension increased between the pastor and the choir director," Landris continued. "One of the largest crowds the church ever had showed up the next week to hear the sermon, which just happened to be 'The Sin of Gossiping.' True to form, the choir director selected 'I Love to Tell the Story.' Well, it was on—there was no turning back. The next Sunday, the pastor told the congregation that unless something changed, he was considering resigning. The congregation collectively gasped when the choir director led the choir into 'Why Not Tonight?' " Landris struggled to maintain a serious face. He continued.

"Well, of course no one was surprised when the pastor resigned a week later. He explained to the congregation that Jesus had led him there, and Jesus was leading him away. The choir looked at the choir director, who just couldn't resist. Jumping to his feet, he joyfully led the congregation into the hymn 'What a Friend We Have in Jesus.' "

Memory started laughing and couldn't stop. "I've never heard that before," she said, trying to compose herself. "You're really funny. I didn't know preachers were allowed to have a sense of humor."

"Oh, you didn't?" Landris asked. "Well, the Bible says, 'A merry heart doeth good like a medicine.' " Landris looked at Johnnie Mae, who stood by the couch, beaming.

"Pastor Landris can be quite the funnyman when he wants to be," Johnnie Mae said. "He's not stuffy like some preachers can tend to be."

"So I see," Memory said. She looked from Johnnie Mae to Pastor Landris and instantly picked up on an unspoken communication between them. "Miss Princess Rose," Memory began, "you're in school, huh?"

Princess Rose stood up and began to hop on one foot. "Yes, ma'am," she said, then hopped on the other foot. "Today was our last day."

"What grade are you in?"

Johnnie Mae touched Princess Rose to make her stand still. Princess Rose stopped hopping and began to twist her upper body from side to side, causing her two long pigtails to swing the way she loved for them to do. "I'll be in the *first* grade, Miss Elaine," she said, emphasizing the word "first," "when school starts back."

"Oh, you will?" Memory said, glancing at Johnnie Mae with a smile, then back over to Princess Rose. "How old does that make you? Five? Six?"

Princess Rose held up one hand, showing all five fingers, and the index finger of her other hand.

"Talk, Princess Rose. You know how to talk," Johnnie Mae said, looking sternly but lovingly at her daughter.

"Six and a half," Princess Rose said.

"Then why aren't you going to the second grade when school starts?" Memory asked.

"Her birthday comes late. She was born in December," Johnnie Mae said, answering the question for her daughter. "I considered putting her in private school for a few years so she could be in her right-age grade, but I decided against it."

"Well, I bet you're really, really smart," Memory said, looking at Princess Rose.

Princess Rose started to nod, then stopped when she looked at her mother. "Yes, ma'am. I *really, really* am," she said with a contagious giggle. "*Everybody* says so!"

They all laughed.

"M . . . Ms. Elaine," Johnnie Mae said, having almost slipped and called her Memory, "would you mind if I borrow Pastor Landris for just a few minutes?"

"Of course not," Memory said, immediately taking a swallow of her iced tea.

"I'm sure you're past ready for supper," Johnnie Mae said.

"Oh, no, I'm fine for now. That snack you gave me earlier really did the trick."

"We'll only be a few minutes," Johnnie Mae said with a smile. "I promise." Landris stood up and they went upstairs to their bedroom.

"Okay. What's up?" Landris asked as soon as Johnnie Mae closed the door.

"I spoke with Sarah."

"And—"

"And . . . she wants me to bring Memory to Asheville, North Carolina, tomorrow morning."

He shook his head. "I don't know about that, Johnnie Mae. You're pregnant. I don't think you need to even be considering anything like that." Landris stared firmly into her brown eyes. "Just put her on a plane. It'll be faster that way, anyway."

"Landris, you know how important this is to

Sarah. I'm pretty sure that's Memory downstairs. What if she decides to run away again?"

"That's, of course, *if* the woman downstairs really is her. Has she admitted to you that she is, in fact, Memory?"

Johnnie Mae glanced at the floor for a brief second, then back up. "Well, no."

"Then you really can't be certain she's Memory. And you just may have gotten Sarah's hopes up for nothing."

Johnnie Mae looked lovingly into her husband's hazel-brown eyes as she spoke softly. "I know it's her, Landris. I can feel it. So can you. I plan on talking with her and finding out once and for all, though."

"When?"

"As soon as I go back downstairs. I wanted to talk with you first." Johnnie Mae walked toward the door. "I didn't want to do anything before talking with you about it. If my suspicions are correct, then Sarah's long-lost daughter is downstairs in our den at this very moment. Sarah's been searching everywhere for her. You know this. I can't take the chance of losing her before the two of them can meet. And if that means I have to drive her to Asheville, North Carolina, myself, then that's exactly what I'm prepared to do."

Landris came over and pulled Johnnie Mae into his arms. "Now, you know I'm not going to let you go up to Asheville by yourself. You know that. But first things first. You need to be certain the woman downstairs is really Memory Patterson. So tell me. How are you planning on accomplishing that little feat?"

"Now, that much I'm not so sure about yet. She was telling me things at the church earlier today. I don't know whether I should see if she'll tell me on her own who she is, and then I tell her what I know, or whether I should just tell her what I know, and we move on from there. I just don't know."

"And precisely how much are you planning on telling her?"

Johnnie Mae grabbed the door handle. "Landris, I truly don't know. Just pray for me while I do this, okay? Honestly, I haven't a clue what my plans are from here on out. All I know is that something has to be done. And now is the time. I'm just trusting God."

"Do you want me there while you talk to her?"

Johnnie Mae released the door handle, tilted her head, and smiled before rising up on the tips of her toes, caressing his face with both hands, then giving him a quick peck on his lips. "No. But if you could keep Princess Rose occupied for me, that would be such a tremendous help. Princess Rose appears to be somewhat smitten with 'Ms. Elaine,' and I don't want any interruptions when she and I begin our talk."

"Are you sure?" Landris asked. "We both know this is some heavy stuff here."

"I'm sure. It's going to be okay," Johnnie Mae said as she smiled at him.

It was Landris this time who planted a soft kiss on her lips. "Well, whatever you need"—he planted yet another kiss on her lips—"you know I'm here for you."

She nodded, opened the door, and they walked back downstairs hand in hand.

"Princess Rose, how about you and I go to the game room and watch a little TV on the widescreen," Landris said as soon as he and Johnnie Mae entered the room. "Or maybe we can play a game. If memory serves, I believe you and I are due for an air-hockey rematch." Straightway, he noticed how Johnnie Mae's eyes widened right after the word "memory" came out of his mouth. He touched her hand to put her back at ease.

"I'm just going to beat you again, Daddy Landris," Princess Rose said, getting up off the couch and skipping toward him. "I don't know when you're going to ever learn."

"Yeah, well, we'll just have to see about that then, missy, now won't we?" Landris said with a sly grin. Princess Rose grabbed his hand and started pulling him toward the hallway that led to the downstairs game room.

After the room was quiet, Johnnie Mae went and sat down across from where Memory was sitting at the end section of the U-shaped sectional sofa.

"I suppose you want to finish what you and I were talking about at the church," Memory said, releasing a deep sigh. "I did say some things that could cause you to be a bit leery of me right now. Especially considering you've so graciously opened up your home to me—a perfect stranger, in actuality."

Johnnie Mae was still unsure of which direction she should take. Should she let Memory tell her the rest of what she had begun at the church and see whether or not she would tell her the whole truth? Or should she admit to Memory up front what she suspected and tell her the things she knew?

Namely that Memory Elaine Patterson, the daughter of Mamie and Willie B. Patterson, was neither Mamie nor Willie B.'s child, but in fact, the daughter of one prominent and extremely wealthy Sarah Elaine Fleming. Johnnie Mae prayed silently.

Vanessa Davis Griggs
introduces a new series with
Practicing What You Preach

Available now wherever books are sold.

And the hand of the Lord was there upon me; and he said unto me, Arise, go forth into the plain, and I will there talk with thee.
—Ezekiel 3:22

The sunlight seemed to pour through my bedroom window even more than usual. I pulled my blanket completely over my head as soon as I realized the brightness was affecting my sleep. I didn't want to get up today. I just didn't. I was tired. Not physically tired (although working a full-time job while putting together an elaborate wedding is draining), but tired on the inside. Tired of people expecting things from me, tired of people asking if I can do things for them, automatically assuming I'll do it. T-i-r-e-d, tired! I sneaked a quick peek at the clock. Twenty more minutes until the alarm was set to go off. *Quick! Go back to sleep. Before there are people to please.*

I don't usually consider myself a people pleaser. In fact, I would describe myself as strong and independent. But lately, I've been taking on more and more. I don't know, maybe all of this can be traced back to my upbringing—the people-pleasing part, that is. It's what my mother prides herself on, although she likes to call it being a peacemaker . . . a unifier . . . a real leader. My mother, Ernestine, is the one everybody goes to when somebody needs something: time, help, money (especially money), and everything in between. She's the one who takes care of the family—immediate, extended, and those who merely call themselves family. She forever places herself last on the list, which normally means there's nothing left when her turn finally rolls around. And at fifty-two that's what's slowly taking a toll on her. It's not the high blood pressure and cholesterol her doctor has her taking pills for daily. Putting everybody else's needs and wants above her own is what's dragging her down.

Well, I've decided at age twenty-eight that my mother's fate will not be mine, no matter how much people claim I'm just like her. I want a lot out of life, and I don't intend to put my goals on the back burner. I just need to figure out how to say no to things I don't want to do and stick with it after I say it.

Those two letters—*n* and *o*—when knitted together form a definitive answer. But for some reason I've not been able to make them work for me effectively. Sure, I may start with the *n* but it will invariably come out as, "Now?" or "N . . . oh, you *really* want me to?" Or worse: "No problem."

Two days ago my friend Nae-nae called and gave me a chance to test just how far I'd come with this "saying no" business.

"Peaches, I have something I *have* to do that I absolutely can't change," Nae-nae began, calling me by the nickname reserved and used only by a few family members and my closest of friends. "Can you take my mother to the grocery store for me tomorrow?"

"No," I said firmly, fighting off my normal knee-jerk reaction to add something else to it in the form of some type of acceptable excuse.

"No?" she said as though I had no right to ever say that. "What do you mean, *no?*"

"I have some things I need to do myself," I said as I began to slip back into my usual role of not wanting anyone to be upset with me because I'd dared not please them.

She laughed. "Oh! Is that all? Well, you can just take her after you finish what you have to do. It's not like she has to be at the grocery store at a certain time or anything, although you know she is slightly disabled and shouldn't be out too late at night. Come on, Peaches, you know I don't have anyone else to help me out. I've always been able to count on you. Please don't start being like everybody else and let me down now. Pleeeaaase?" she whined.

"Okay, fine. I'll take her," I said even quicker than I suspected I would. She thanked me and hurried off the phone. I had caved in yet again.

What I should have said was, "Well, if your mother doesn't have to be there at a certain time then you can take her after you finish what *you* have to do." That's what I should have said. But no, that wasn't what I said at all. I'd merely given in once more.

It's so funny how later on you can always think of stuff you *should have* said. So my new goal is to learn how to say what I mean and stick with it no

matter what. I just have a hard time telling someone I can't do something when honestly I know
that physically I can. Just one more lovely trait I
can attribute to my fine upbringing.

My mother never believed in telling lies, not
even the little white ones folks basically say it's
okay to tell. You know like, "No, you don't look fat
in that." Or "Cute outfit." What about, "Oh, no; I
really *do* like your hair. I was only staring so hard at
you because it's so . . . *different.*"

Not my mama. It was "Girl, now you know
you're too old to be trying to wear something like
that." Or "Somebody lied to you. Go back and try
again." Or what about, "That looks good, it just
doesn't look good on *you.*" Still, she will do anything for you.

I started planning special events as a hobby
about two years ago, but lately it appears this could
someday become my real bread and butter if I continue to pursue it seriously. Everybody says I'm
great at putting things together. That's what I was
doing yesterday after work—taking care of some
pressing business for an upcoming wedding. A
wedding, incidentally, that's huge and could really
put my name on the go-to-for-event-planning map.

I pushed myself to do what I had to do after
work, then managed to take Nae-nae's mother to
the store. It took her two whole hours to shop.
Two hours I really didn't have to spare. She insisted on doing it herself. Seriously, she could have
given me the list she'd already written out anyway,
and I would have been done in fifteen minutes.
Tops. Instead, she ended up riding in the mobile
cart the store provided. She'd stand up, get an

item, put it in the basket, sit down, then ride some-times just to the next group of items, only to begin the slow and tedious cycle all over again.

I don't know, maybe I really am as hopeless a case as Cass said. Cass is my ex-boyfriend. His real name is Cassius, named after his father who was named after Cassius Clay the boxer before he changed his name to Muhammad Ali. If you ask me, I'd say Cass thought his name was short for Casanova. But truthfully, he was the one who got me started on this self-evaluating journey I've been on lately. Cass flat out said I was too easy and a real pushover. Well, he should know, since he treated me like a disposable pen, then pushed me over and threw me away when he felt my ink was all but used up.

And to think he had the nerve to break up with me and make out like everything was all my fault. He claimed I was too self-centered for him. *Give me a break!* So I was supposed to believe that I was too easy, a pushover, while at the same time believe I was self-centered. *All righty then.* Looking back, the best thing Cass ever did for me was to move his narcissist-self on. Now, you want to talk about somebody being stuck on himself, then that is Cass, the guy I dated last for a whole year, to a T. After Cass, I started listening to my pastor and decided to pray that God would send the right man into my life, because I sure wasn't doing all that hot on my own.

This was all too much to be thinking about this early in the morning, especially with very little time before the alarm was going to sound. But I still found a way to doze off again. I hit the snooze button three times before finally dragging myself out of the bed. Standing in front of the window, I took in the stillness of the day's beginnings, then hurried to dress, made my way to work, and got to my desk with two minutes to spare.

Marcus Peeples was walking out of Dr. Brewer's office when I arrived. He often comes into the OB/GYN's office where I work. Definitely not the most handsome guy I've ever seen (especially with the glasses he wears), Marcus is around 5'11" and sort of lanky, particularly compared to me.

Some label my body type as thick, which means curvy in all the right places. My mother said we're just big-boned people. "Absolutely nothing to be ashamed of," Mama always said. It's never bothered me. After all, Marilyn Monroe was a size fourteen, same as me.

Marcus seemed like an all right guy. He was usually trying to push (what I assumed) his pharmaceutical products on my boss, who must be too nice to tell him to buzz off. But lately, every time he has come in here with his fancy briefcase in hand, he has tried to strike up more and more conversation with me.

Two months ago, he asked if I was married or dating anyone. Having just broken up with Cass a few weeks earlier, my answer pretty much conveyed that not only was I *not* dating anyone, but that I wasn't *interested* in dating anyone anytime soon. He promptly dropped that line of questioning for a few weeks. Then it happened. Today, in fact.

When Marcus walked out of Dr. Brewer's office, he stepped over to my desk and without his customary hi or how are you said, "How about you and I go out on a date."

I flashed him a quick fake, polite smile, and replied, "Thanks, but no thanks." *Who says I can't say no and mean it?*

He nodded as he smiled back at me. "Oh, I see. You must only be interested in the kind of guys who like to break your heart, then leave you to put the pieces back together," Marcus said.

For someone who reminded me at best of a reformed nerd, at worst of someone almost anyone could take down in a fight, that statement took me totally by surprise.

"No. I'm just not interested in *you*," I said, pointing my finger at him on cue with the word *you*, not caring whether my words hurt his feelings. I was on a roll today: two *no's* in a row.

Instead of scurrying away the way I expected he would do, he set his briefcase down on my desk. "And how do you know that?"

My eyes immediately went to the briefcase, then back to him. "A woman knows these things," I said, rolling my chair back away from him just a tad. He'd gotten a little too close for my comfort.

"Just as I suspected. You're one of those women who will never give a good man a chance. That way, you can have your beliefs validated about all the men who have hurt you and feel justified without those beliefs ever being challenged."

What did he do that for? I was just about to say something smart like "Is that right, Dr. Phil?" when he suddenly took off his glasses. It's amazing how glasses can change a person's looks entirely. Right before my eyes, in just that instant, Marcus Peeples was transformed from Clark Kent into Superman— I kid you not. I noticed for the first time his hair, cut low and sort of wavy, most likely with the help of a wave cap. I took note of how perfect his hairstyle fit his caramel-colored face. His goatee, which I hadn't paid attention to, was perfect for his triangular jaw. But it was those long, thick, black eyelashes framing those gorgeous, twinkling brown eyes that now had me completely fixated and, quite frankly, at a loss for words. *Dr. Phil who?*

I scooted my chair back a little bit more, smiled, then shook my head to emphasize that his assessment of me and my situation was totally wrong as I tried to right my ship. He'd gotten me a little off course.

He placed his hand on his briefcase. "One date," Marcus said. "Come on. What do you have to lose?" He flashed me a big smile. Near-perfect white teeth, and I declare one of them appeared to have twinkled.

I maintained my coolness, breathing evenly as I began to speak. "One, huh?"

He held up his index finger. "One. And you can choose the time and the place. If you find we have nothing in common or that you don't like me, then no harm, no foul. So, what do you say?"

I had to snap out of this, and quick. I had to take back control. "Okay," I said slowly, not wanting to answer too quickly. "How about tonight?"

"Tonight?" He sounded as though *that* had caught him completely off guard. I sensed I was definitely interfering with some already laid plans.

Good! Last-minute dates usually get the ones who aren't really serious every single time. "I'm sorry. Is that a problem for you?" I projected a look of true concern and sincerity. "Do you already have something planned for tonight? Because if you do . . ."

"I did, but for you, I'll change it. Tonight works for me. So where would you like to go?"

I couldn't help but grin. "How about Bible study, my church? And we need to be there by seven o'clock." I crossed my arms. Body language experts would likely say I was putting up a barrier between us. I'd classify it as expressing my confidence as I had officially regained control.

He began to chuckle. "Oh," he sang the word, "so, you're one of *those* kind of women, huh?"

"Those kind? Is church a problem for you?" I could tell despite his smile and chuckle that I'd unnerved him slightly. *Double good!*

He continued to grin. "No problem. I said you could choose the place, I want you to see that I'm a man of my word." He took out his business card and handed it to me.

"I'm sure Dr. Brewer already has your card on file," I said.

"He does, but this card is for you." He took out his BlackBerry. "Now, if I could get your home address?" He looked at me and saw what I imagine had to be a defensive expression on my face. "Miss Melissa Anderson, I need your home address so I can pick you up tonight. That's what real men do." A boyish grin broke across his face again.

I looked at his card before glancing back at him. He put his glasses on and he was instantly transformed back into the harmless Clark Kent. The information on his card was personable enough. He had his home address and both a home and a cell phone number listed. A home number given—not foolproof by any means but a positive sign—was generally a good indication that he wasn't some married man trying to find a way to sneak around on his wife. I don't play that other-woman stuff. Got burned once accidentally. I vowed never again if I could help it.

Still, I weighed whether or not I should give him my home address at this point. After all, there are plenty of crazies running around in this world. On the other hand, I did *sort of* know him, so he wasn't a *total* stranger. He'd been in here at least ten times that I know of—sometimes when patients were here, most times before office hours began. He seemed a decent enough guy.

I rattled off my home address as he keyed it into his BlackBerry.

All right now, Mr. Marcus Peeples. Let's just see how much you like Bible study at Followers of Jesus Faith Worship Center as a first date. I already sensed, based on the way he had reacted when I mentioned the word "church" that this was going to be fun.